John M. Inferrera

LOIS-ANN YAMANAKA has written a book of poetry, three prior works of fiction, and a young-adult novel. She has won a Lannan Literary Award and an American Book Award. She lives in Honolulu.

By the same author

Saturday Night at the Pahala Theatre
Blu's Hanging
Heads by Harry
Name Me Nobody
Father of the Four Passages
Behold the Many

WILD

MEAT

AND

THE

BULLY

BURGERS

WILD
MEAT
AND
THE
BULLY
BURGERS

LOIS-ANN YAMANAKA

PICADOR
FARRAR, STRAUS AND GIROUX
NEW YORK

www.picadorusa.com

Picador® is a registered trademark and is used by Farrar, Straus and Giroux under license from Pan Books Limited.

For information on Picador Reading Group Guides, as well as ordering, please contact Picador.
Phone: 646-307-5629
Fax: 212-253-9627
E-mail: readinggroupguides@picadorusa.com

Grateful acknowledgment is made to the following publications in which some of the stories first appeared: *American Eyes: New Asian-American Short Stories for Young Adults,* ed. Lori M. Carlson, Edge Books/Henry Holt: "Obituary." *Bamboo Ridge: A Hawaii Writers' Quarterly:* "Alexander Fu Sheng Kicks Bruce Lee's Ass, Sonny Chiba and Toshiro Mifune Too," "Blah Blah Blah," "Dominate and Recessid Jeans," "Oompah Loompah," and "Pin the Fan on the Hand." *Chicago Review:* "Sunnyside Up."

Library of Congress Cataloging-in-Publication Data

Yamanaka, Lois-Ann.
Wild meat and the bully burgers / Lois-Ann Yamanaka.
p. cm.
ISBN 0-312-42464-7
EAN 978-0-312-42464-0
1. Japanese American families—Hawaii—Fiction.   2. Japanese Americans—Hawaii—Fiction.   3. Family—Hawaii—Fiction.   I. Title.
PS3575.A434W55   1996   813'.54—dc20   95-14121
CIP

First published in the United States by Farrar, Straus and Giroux

D 10 9 8 7

CONTENTS

One

Happy Endings   3

Obituary   10

I Wanna Marry a Haole So I Can Have a Haole Last Name   23

Ordinary Days   35

    ☾

Crazy Like a Dream   47

Oompah Loompah   59

Rhapsody   64

    ☾

Dominate and Recessid Jeans   71

Sunnyside Up   76

Calhoon Never Lies   82

Wild Meat and the Bully Burgers   90

Two

What Love Is   99

Lessons   106

Bolohead Malibu Barbie and Marsh Pen Malibu Ken 114
A Fishbowl and Some Dimes 118
Bitter Taste Sweet 126

☾

Rags 136
God Is Love When She Prays My Name 143

☾

Alexander Fu Sheng Kicks Bruce Lee's Ass, Sonny Chiba and Toshiro Mifune Too 159
No Ninjas, Farmers, or Wannabes in This Family 165
Dead Animals Spoil the Scenery 170
My Nanny and Billy the Kid 178
The Crossing 187

Three

Hilo County Fair 207
Blah Blah Blah 214
Lovey's Homemade Singer Sewing Class Patchwork Denim Hiphuggers 221
Water Black and Bright 231

☾

The Last Dance Is Always a Slow Dance 242
Pin the Fan on the Hand 254
Wrong Words 260
The Burning 278

☾

─────────

ONE

─────────

HAPPY ENDINGS

Shirley Temple movies made me cry on Sunday mornings, cry, made me want to miss Sunday School. Wish it were just one hour later so I could see Shirley as Heidi say, "Grandpapa, Grandpapa, I love you, I love you," as her words echoed in the Swiss mountains in that Shirley Temple voice of hers.

Jerry said that him and me shouldn't watch Shirley Temple together. We'd hold back the tears. He said everybody needed a good cry for no reason once in a while. Better to watch by yourself when Shirley said, "Father, oh, Father, I found you, I found you. I knew you were alive. Oh, Daddy, I love you."

Shirley Temple sob-talked the best, and I used to wish I was just like her, with perfect blond ringlets and pink cheeks and pout lips, bright eyes and a happy ending every Sunday and crying 'cause of being happy, I mean real happy, so someone watching can cry too.

But I hardly got to those endings. I was out the door and on my bike to Sunday School when Shirley was on her way to the hospital with her black bust-up lace shawl. So Jerry and me made up the endings at church in the morning service on the

3

Sunday Bulletin, line by line, Jerry as Shirley all the time, and me as the lost daddy or newfound mother.

All of the lines until the end of the service, and by the benediction one of us was crying, we were so good, and Reverend Smith would muss up our hair thinking his sermon went straight to our hearts.

It was a happy ending every Sunday that Jerry and me wrote.

But one day I want to write my very own happy ending. It would be just Jerry and me. In my movie, the sad part right before the crying in the end is that Jerry and me are lost in New York City.

We're standing at the Port Authority when Shirley comes holding hands with my mother and Jerry's mother through a crowd of people who are actors. My mother hugs me and Jerry's mother hugs him.

Grandma is there and Father and my sister. My mother says, "I found you, I found you. You don't ever have to go to Sunday School again." Jerry's mother gives him loads of Icee points, the superdeluxe model Easy Bake Oven, and "Millie the Model" comics.

Shirley watches and cries.

Jerry holds all his goods and regrets ever saying that we weren't good enough to have the kind of love that he wrote about in last Sunday's Bulletin. That's what got me crying. We weren't good enough for the kind of love that Shirley had every Sunday, the kind of love that makes the bottom lip quiver and mothers rush through crowds to hug you at the end of the movie.

That's my own happy ending.

Every Monday on *The Checkers and Pogo Show*, they play Merry UnBirthday. And this is how the song goes:

> *A very Merry UnBirthday to you (doot-doot), to you,*
> *a very Merry UnBirthday to you (clap-clap), to you.*
> *It's great to think of someone*
> *and I guess that you will do—*
> *a very Merry UnBirthday to you!*

Then the studio lights dim and a spotlight shines all around. All the kids try to look angelic so that the spotlight shines on them. They all smile with their front teeth missing and dimples deep into their cheeks, dipping their heads side to side with the music. I saw my cousin Roscoe with his crew cut and a red-striped shirt. He was trying to look innocent too.

Then the spotlight finds the Merry UnBirthday child. Of course, it's the cutest one in the studio. The little girl with plenty ribbons in her hair or the boy with an Indians' baseball cap or Boy Scout uniform. The little boy chosen jumps up and down and acts stupid and out of control. He claps for himself.

Pogo Poge puts a silly birthday hat on the boy. The paper kind they get in birthdays on TV with the rubber band under the chin. Then Mr. Checkers tells Pogo Poge to get the giant mayonnaise jar full of pennies and the Merry UnBirthday boy gets to grab as much as he can, all that his hand can stretch, a hand full of pennies.

Sometimes Pogo Poge feels in a good mood and he fights with Mr. Checkers to let the Merry UnBirthday boy take another handful. "Awww, c'mon, Mr. Checkers," begs Pogo Poge in a baby-man voice, "just one more handful, pwwease, just one, pwwease, pwwease, pwwetty pwwwease, Mr. Checkers, huh? C'mon, boys and girls." Then the kids in the studio audience start whining and begging too.

Mr. Checkers makes a big harrumph and growls, "Ho-kay, g'won. Take another handful." What does Mr. Checkers care? I figure only fifty cents more. Once Jerry and me tried. We took the biggest handful of pennies from a regular mayonnaise jar and counted them up. Fifty-seven cents. Big deal. All that begging and whining and acting like a big baby for fifty-seven cents more.

What's the sense of practicing to grab all that money? No way will we ever be on *The Checkers and Pogo Show*. Never. Only the rich Honolulu kids. We would never be there anyway. Never.

But we watch *The Checkers and Pogo Show* every day after school. Our favorite cartoon, "Princess Knight," is about a girl princess pretending to be a boy knight. We also like Professor Fun, a grown man in a white shirt with black tie with a graduation cap on his head. He does magic tricks for the children in the studio and makes balloon animals.

Not like the balloon animals my Uncle Steven makes at birthday parties with balls and botos and the dingding balloon hats he makes us kids wear. Professor Fun makes toy poodles, monkeys, and big hearts.

And we love Pogo Poge and the second Mr. Checkers. The first Mr. Checkers was skinny with black hair and he looked like he hated being there with Pogo Poge. Like a skinny, grouchy science teacher.

The second Mr. Checkers is fat with white hair and glasses too small for his fat face. He hardly fits in the tree house they live in.

What I would give to be there sitting on those wooden bleachers in the studio of Channel 9 with all those rich Honolulu boys and girls.

I could ride the Sky Slide at the Gibson's parking lot. Take my piece of carpet all the way to the top of the most giant Sky Slide and ride down with hands high above my head over and over again.

Then I could go to Gibson's toy department, the most giant and best toy department in the world according to Checkers and Pogo, and buy toys for a low price. Not like the toys at Ben Franklin five-and-ten or Wigwam, all overpriced and dusty.

I bet I could find that Donny Osmond doll with glittery purple socks and a microphone, and a brown-hair Ken doll boyfriend for Francie, and maybe a Twiggy doll too.

Maybe I *could* be the Merry UnBirthday girl.

This year for my real birthday, I get all the usual presents:

Buster Brown panties from my grandma on Molokaʻi.

Bikini bottoms to wear under my dresses from Aunty Bing.

School skirts with elastic waistband from my mother.

A thesaurus from Uncle Ed, Aunt Helen, and Ernest.

Ten bucks from Uncle Steven if I wear the black boto balloon hat all night.

And a butterfly-sleeved smock from Jerry's mother.

But Jerry gives me the best present of all. To me, he's the best present giver I know. He says you should always give a person something they wouldn't get for themself.

I get a princess birthday hat with a chiffon tassel.

I get a kimchee bottle full of pennies.

I get a Donny Osmond 45 of "Go Away Little Girl."

Purple socks.

And handmade tickets that say:

ADMIT ONE: CHECKERS AND POGO SHOW

GIFT CERTIFICATE: $500.00 GIBSON TOY DEPT.

SKY SLIDE: INFINITY RIDES

Infinity means forever. Happy B-day, Lovey. Happiness is Jerome.

c

At the end of the show, nobody in the studio at Channel 9 knows about the handfuls of fifty-seven pennies Jerry and me hold on Monday afternoons, hold then count into piles of ten on the carpet. It isn't even my unbirthday and I know how good it feels to stretch my hand over the cool of the pennies. That fifty-seven times a hundred might be enough to get us both on Aloha Airlines from Hilo to Honolulu.

c

At the top of the slide at school, Jerry says, "Happy endings all the time, Lovey: Multiply by twenty and hold your hands up high and you going feel infinity before your feet touch the sand at the bottom."

And it happens, feeling like infinity, if my eyes are closed, closed tight like a fistful of pennies.

OBITUARY

English class, we got Mr. Harvey. Jerome looks at me and puts his middle finger on the desk to our worst teacher, because Mr. Harvey says for the fiftieth time this year:

"No one will want to give you a job. You sound uneducated. You will be looked down upon. You're speaking a low-class form of good Standard English. Continue, and you'll go nowhere in life. Listen, students, I'm telling you the truth like no one else will. Because they don't know how to say it to you. I do. Speak Standard English. DO NOT speak pidgin. You will only be hurting yourselves."

I tell Jerry, "No make f-you finger to Mr. Harvey. We gotta try talk the way he say. No more dis and dat and wuz and cuz 'cause we only hurting ourselfs."

I don't tell anyone, not even Jerry, how ashamed I am of pidgin English. Ashamed of my mother and father, the food we eat, chicken luau with can spinach and tripe stew. The place we live, down the house lots in the Hicks Homes that all look alike except for the angle of the house from the street. The car we drive, my father's brown Land Rover without the back window. The clothes we wear, sometimes we have to wear the same pants in the same week and the same shoes until it breaks. Don't have no choice.

Ashamed of my aunties and uncles at baby luaus, yaku-doshis, and mochi pounding parties. "Eh, bradda Larry, bring me one nada Primo, brah. One cold one fo' real kine. I rey-day, I rey-day, no woray, brah. Uncap that sucka and come home to Uncle Stevie." I love my Uncle Steven, though, and the Cracker Jacks he brings for me every time he visits my mother. One for me and one for my sister, Calhoon. But I'm so shame.

Ashame too of all my cousins, the way they talk and act dumb, like how they like Kikaida Man and "Ho, brah, you seen Kikaida Man kick Rainbow Man's ass in front Hon Sport at the Hilo Shopping Center? Ho, brah, and I betchu Godzilla kick King Kong's ass too. Betchu ten dollas, brah, two fur balls kicking ass in downtown Metropolis, nah, downtown Hilo, brah."

And my grandma. Her whole house smells like mothballs, not just in the closets but in every drawer too. And her pots look a million years old with dents all over. Grandma must know every recipe with mustard cabbage in it. She can quote from the Bible for everything you do in a day. Walks everywhere she goes downtown Kaunakakai, sucks fish eyes and eats the parsley from our plates at Midnight Inn.

And nobody looks or talks like a haole. Or eats like a haole. Nobody says nothing the way Mr. Harvey tells us to practice talking in class.

Sometimes I secretly wish to be haole. That my name could be Betty Smith or Annie Anderson or Debbie Cole, wife of Dennis Cole who lives at 2222 Maple Street with a white station wagon with wood panel on the side, a dog named Spot, a cat named Kitty, and I wear white gloves. Dennis wears a hat to work. There's a coatrack as soon as you open the front door and we all wear our shoes inside the house.

"Now let's all practice our Standard English," Mr. Harvey says. *"You will all stand up and tell me your name, and what you would like to be when you grow up. Please use complete sentences."* Mr. Harvey taps Melvin Spencer on his shoulders. Melvin stands up slowly and pulls a Portagee torture of wedged pants and BVDs out of his ass.

"Ma name is Mal-vin Spenca." Melvin has a very Portagee accent. Before he begins his next sentence, he does nervous things like move his ankles side to side so that his heels slide out of his slippers. He looks at the ceiling and rolls his eyes. "I am, I mean, I wanna. I like. No, try wait. I going be. No, try wait. I will work on my Gramma Spenca's pig farm when I grow up cuz she said I can drive the slop truck. Tank you."

No one laughs at Melvin. Otherwise he'll catch you on the way home from school and shove your head in the slop drum. Melvin sits down. He blinks his eyes hard a couple of times, then rubs his face with two hands.

Jerry stands up very, very slowly and holds on to the edge of his desk. "My name is Jerome." His voice, weak and shivering, his fingers white. "I in. Okay, wait. I stay in. No, try wait. Okay, try wait. I stay. I stay real nervous." His face changes and he acts as if he has to use the bathroom. He looks out the window to the eucalyptus trees beyond the schoolyard.

Jerry continues, "I am going be one concert piano-ist when I get big. Tank you."

I'm next. Panic hits me like a rock dropped in a hollow oil drum.

Mr. Harvey walks up to my desk, his face red and puffy like a pink marshmallow or a bust-up boxer. He has red hair and always wears white double-knit pants with pastel-colored golf shirts. He walks like Walter Matthau. Mr. Harvey taps my desk with his red pen.

The muscles in my face start twitching and pulling uncontrollably. My eyes begin darting back and forth. And my lips, my lips—

"I'm waiting," Mr. Harvey says.

Jerry looks at me. He smiles weakly, his face twitching and pulling too. He looks at Mr. Harvey, then looks at me as if to say, "Just get it over with."

"Cut the crap," Mr. Harvey spits. *"Stop playing these goddamn plantation games. Now c'mon. We've got our outlines to finish today."* Mr. Harvey's ears get red, his whole face like fire with his red hair and red face.

"My name Lovey. When I grow up pretty soon, I going be what I like be and nobody better say nothing about it or I kill um."

"OH REALLY," he says. *"Not the way you talk. You see, that was terrible. All of you were terrible and we will have to practice and practice our Standard English until we are perfect little Americans. And I'll tell you something, you can all keep your heads on your desks for the rest of the year for all I care. You see, you need me more than I need you. And do you know what the worst part is, class? We're not only going to have to work on your usage, but your pronunciations and inflections too. Jee-zus Christ! For the life of me, it'll take us a goddamn lifetime."*

"See," Jerry whispers, "now you the one made Mr. Harvey all mad with us. We all going get it from him, stupid."

I want to tell Jerry about being a concert pianist. Yeah, right. Good luck. How will he ever do it? Might as well drive the slop truck if you cannot talk straight or sound good and all the haoles talk circles around you. Might as well blend in like all the locals do.

Mr. Harvey walks past my desk. *"C'mon, Lovey. Start your outline. You too, Jerome."* Sometimes I think that Mr. Harvey doesn't mean to be mean to us. He really wants us to be Americans, like my kotonk cousins from Santa Ana, he'd probably think they talked real straight.

But I can't talk the way he wants me to. I cannot make it sound his way, unless I'm playing pretend-talk-haole. I can make my words straight, that's pretty easy if I concentrate real hard. But the sound, the sound from my mouth, if I let it rip right out the lips, my words will always come out like home.

C

In our homeroom is Pillis. But Pillis is not her name. Her name is Phyllis. She's the one who pronounces it Pillis. Pillis Pilmoca the Pilipina.

She doesn't look like the midgets I saw on *The Wizard of Oz.* To me, she looks like a regular-looking person except in small portions. Her legs dangle off her chair.

Sometimes I wonder what size clothes Pillis buys. She has this nice sweater with pearl buttons and a chain with hearts across the neckline. Pillis wears it like a cape. If I wear a girl's size 12, I figure she must be a girl's size 6. So small. Sometimes I wish I could have a sweater with a chain like hers.

I hate math, especially fractions. I cannot reduce them, and today I cannot reduce $8/14$. And no one in the dumbest math class helps me.

Us dumb ones from Mr. Harvey's class go with Miss Mona Saiki for math. And we all like Miss Saiki, except that when math time comes, all the dum-dums have to stand up to leave, while all the smart ones stare and snicker.

If Jerry were in this class, he'd give me the answers real fast. Jerry or Melvin. But I'm in this class with other dum-dums and they laugh at me instead like I'm *very* stupid, stupider than them for not knowing how to reduce a stupid fraction.

"You real stoopid for one fricken Jap," says Thomas Lorenzo. "But you ack real smut when you stay wit' all the odda Japs, eh, girl?"

"Yeah," says Wilma Kahale. "I thought all Japs sappose for be smut. But you cannot even reduce one stupid fraction, eh, you, Jap Crap. Stupid, thass why, you Rice Eye, good-for-nuttin' Pearl Harba bomba."

I feel so small. I want to die. I want to die, it feels like a small little fist inside, twisting.

"What," says Wilma. "What you looking at, hah, Jap? Watch how you make them Jap eyes at me. Like me buss' yo face?"

"Yeah, Wilma. Beef um recess time," Thomas Lorenzo whispers to her.

Die before recess. I put my knees on my chair and draw my body into the desk. I put my head down. I see Pillis from the corner of my eye, thinking very hard.

She puts the eraser part of her pencil in her nose and twirls it around slowly as she thinks. She scratches her head with her short wrinkled finger and writes her answer quickly on her paper. Then she puts the eraser up her nostril again.

"Jap. Jap Crap. Rice Eye. Stupid shit. I catch you recess time, you wait."

They keep talking, so I yell very suddenly, "Ooooh, Pillis, digging your nose with your eraser. Ooooh, Pillis, eraser digger." Thomas, Wilma, and the whole class look at Pillis, so stunned that she leaves the pencil eraser stuck in her nose. Her eyes open wide and buglike.

"Midget digging for small nuggets?"

"Ho, Pillis, stretching your mina-chure nostrils?"

"Midget eraser digging for gold?"

I see Pillis get small, smaller than a girl's size 6, smaller and smaller until she looks like a white-sweatered ball. She shoulder-shakes at her desk and sniffles to Miss Saiki, "I hate them. They make me like die." All of Pillis' pencils and erasers fall to the ground.

Miss Saiki waits. No one helps Pillis. Everyone continues laughing and calling her Eraser Digger. Miss Saiki says, "You are all so appalling. You are dis-gusting." She comes over quickly to Pillis and places her hand on Pillis' back, rubs gently. "Don't say things like that, Phyllis. Everything's gonna be o-kay." Then Miss Mona Saiki tells the rest of us, "Back to work. Now."

Pillis doesn't look at me. She doesn't look at anyone. She smooths her wet binder paper with both tiny hands.

Jerry likes Pillis. So do I, actually. Her big gummy laugh and her short legs that try to kick us when we tease her. She waves to us when the school bus drops her off outside their cane field and her tiny body getting tinier and tinier up the dirt road. She walks eight-tenths of a mile to her house next to the sugar mill.

I don't know what to say. Jerry would know. But I don't tell him.

That night, I struggle with my math problems on the linoleum table. My mother asks if I need my father's help. I tell her no, I'm just reducing fractions. The light above the table slides across the binder paper.

I think about Pillis. I put my pencil eraser up my nose. What a wonderful feeling, especially when you twirl it and you have to think. I do this to the other nostril too.

My mother tells me to knock it off. To get a Kleenex instead. I wonder if Thomas Lorenzo and Wilma Kahale are at home trying Pillis' eraser digger too.

I don't know what I'll say to Pillis tomorrow. I don't know if she will ever wave at me from outside the school bus again. But I know now how she feels. It is something I have always known.

(

Here lies Jerry all cold and skinny. He was a good son. He tried very hard to learn how to swim.

C–.

Here lies Lovey dead as a doorknob. She hated math and shot a mongoose.

D–/F.

We had to do this twice already. Every time we study a newspaper unit, we end up making a newspaper in class. The smartest girl be the editor-in-chief, the most creative one be the features editor, the boy best in dodgeball be the sports editor. Lori Shigemura be the "Dear Lori" column so she can read all the problems, try solve them, and then tell the whole world who "I Honestly Love You, Junior Ah Chong" or "Stone in Love with Raymond" really is.

And this newspaper is not even typewritten. And the rest of us beat reporters write articles about "The New Turtle in Rm. 5." Or "Fifth Grade Dances to the Age of Aquarius."

Then you know it, we gotta write our own obituary. Like I even care. Dead is dead. Can't see or feel or care. I seen dead. Dead rabbits. Dead dogs. Dead goats. Dead sheep. Dead chickens. Dead fish. You name it, my father shown it to me.

I saw my Aunty Kawa dead. They made her wear peach lipstick and a nice satin peach dress. Like somebody should've told them she wore red lipstick every day and a plaid button-down shirt with denim knickers.

And all of her family, they kissed her dead face, even my mother—but when my mother lifted the veil for me, I couldn't do it. Her face looked like stone.

Jerry says it's fun to write our own obituary. Like witnessing our own funeral. He wants to see all the people he hates and who hate him attend his funeral to cry. Of course, he wants me to play songs like "Seasons in the Sun," "Wishing You Were Here," "You've Got a Friend," and "I Haven't Got Time for the Pain" so that the people cry more.

Me, I don't want to go deaf or blind before I die of old age, but if I had to choose, I'd rather be deaf and learn sign language than blind and have to buy a Seeing Eye dog.

Please God forbid that I go crazy before I die.

And God forbid that I die by drowning and have that frantic, leg-kicking feeling I had when Jerry's big brother, Larry, held my ankles down in Mizuno Pond or suffocate with a pillow or garbage bag over my face with my claustrophobia.

I think about dying every night. Sometimes I want to die at strange moments in the day. Sometimes every day. My mother says it's all those books I read about concentration camps. The arsenic in the heart that I tell her about and the gas chambers with fingernail markings on the walls and ceilings.

Once I thought about suicide. Maybe twice or three times. Once when Clayton Young, who had the longest bangs with side comb for a skinny second saxophone player, said I smelled like his sister's rags to the whole woodwinds section. Twice when Jamielyn Trevino, the butchie in ceramics, pulled the chair out from under me, then whipped a wad of clay across the room which splat flat to my forehead. Three times when I heard my uncle say to my aunty in the kitchen that "Cal and Lovey, yeah, maybe my sista Verva right when she brag that they cute and well behave, but they stupid, stupid, stupid." I was sitting in his garage. He thought I'd walked home. I wanted to dedicate my death to them with a suicide note that said, "Lovey, yeah, maybe cute, but stupid, stupid, stupid."

Grandma said to me a long time ago that the Bible says suicide is a sin. Those who do it burn in the eternal flames of hell forever and will never see Jesus' sweet face. Grandma says when I die of natural causes, I'll be with Jesus, and she tries to describe the warm light and eternal peace, but it sounds like a long, hot nap to me.

Sometimes when my grandma leaves for Moloka'i, I feel like a funeral. It's a big hollow ache inside of me. Even if we did have to eat fish-head soup for two nights, then mustard cabbage and pork soup the night before she left.

I lie very still at night and wonder when I'll see her again and why days go by so fast when she's here.

This year, Mr. Harvey says, *"What would you do if your parents died in a train crash?"*

Jerry says, "Ain't no trains in Hawai'i." But he puts his head down to think.

Mr. Harvey makes us close our eyes and tells us about the changing landscape, the awful crash, the blood, the body parts, the glass cuts, and the screaming, all while we see it in our minds.

This is what I *want* to write:

If my parents died in a train crash, God forbid, knock three times, I'll probably live with my grandma on Moloka'i, who makes me take Flintstones vitamins every morning and eat S & S saimin with chopped green onions, scrambled eggs, and sliced Spam for lunch.

At five o'clock Aunty Bing will drive the Malibu to the drugstore where Grandma works. Grandma will have a whole box of chocolate wafer candy in gold paper for me.

One weekend, we'll go to Vacation Bible School. I make miniature gospels with matchbooks and construction paper. We write a Bible newspaper based on the stories by the apostles like we were there to interview them and call it *The New Testament Tribune*. I write a headline called "Jesus Born in Bethlehem Manger."

I'll advertise in the classified ads. "Wanted: A New Bible. Not the King James Version." And maybe Grandma will put one on my bed for me. Then we'll carve Ivory soaps into crosses or Virgin Marys.

At night, Grandma will cut watermelons and Aunty Bing and me sit on the porch and eat watermelon and sunflower seeds and spit the seeds and shells on the driveway.

All of this I'll do over and over again until Pal, Grandma's poi dog, comes home from the gully after two heats with her new litters of puppies.

This is what I actually write:

If my parents die in a train crash. I dunno what I am going do. D–/F.

Jerry writes:

If my parents die in a train crash. Then stops. I see him thinking. I know he's about to take this too seriously, and when he does, he might cry.

"I dunno what I might do if my parents dies. Who going buy all the food and bath soap and where I going eat at night?"

Mr. Harvey listens to our whispering and lets us go.

"What if I all by myself, Lovey," he says, "can I live with you?"

"You and me can live with my grandma on Moloka'i," I tell him, "and pick pineapples for Del Monte and go to church on Sundays with Grandma and clean the communion glasses and eat the leftover communion crackers. You and me," I tell him.

I don't want him to cry. He starts to write his obituary. All the things I told him we would do.

C

Here lies Lovey.

When she died, she didn't know how or why. She did not attend her own funeral like she planned. What do angels look like, so she'll know when she gets there? And Grandma, if you get there first, don't yell "Lovey, Lovey," because I might be deaf, or wave your arms, because I might be blind.

Lovey is dead. Come close when you take me home. I know you by the smell of a brand-new Bible and green onions on your fingers. I know you by the feel of gold paper.

I WANNA MARRY A HAOLE SO I CAN HAVE A HAOLE LAST NAME

The Perfect Haole House: There is a Dixie bathroom cup dispenser *with cups* that have blue and pink flowers around the bottom in the perfect house and you don't have to write your name on the bottom of the cup and save it. When done, throw it away in the little pink trash can. At Christmas, the mother puts cups with holly around the bottom in the dispenser.

I see a wicker hamper, not a plastic laundry basket, and a knitted poodle covering the next roll of toilet paper, rose-shaped soap in matching porcelain dishes, and rose-colored towels. A rosy shower curtain and a rose rug around the toilet and on the toilet seat that is plush, not flat. At Christmas, the knitted poodle becomes a knitted Santa Claus.

The father sprays Lysol all over the bathroom when he finishes making BM with the latest issue of *Sports Illustrated*. No burning cowboy matches to kill the smell in the perfect bathroom in the perfect house.

There are bunk beds with wooden ladders and pink ruffles and white eyelet bedspreads over beds that are made every day the way haoles do with the pillow tucked under, not a vinyl punee covered with a sheet and a folded futon or a grandma-made quilt out of old dress material crumpled at the bottom of the bed.

In the kitchen, there are blue glasses—no Dino Flintstone cups—and matching dishes with roses on them and Tupperware that's still shiny. When you want a soda, the mother pours real Coca-Cola and 7-Up, not RC or Diamond Head Lemonlime. And automatic ice cubes that drop out of a clean freezer.

At Christmastime, the mother and daughters wear matching flannel nightgowns with lace. Nobody wears Father's old T-shirts or Mother's old shortie muumuus. The mother takes out the Christmas mugs and makes real hot chocolate with whipped cream and cinnamon, not Nestlé's Quik in a cold cup of milk.

I see Pez candy holders that Santa put in the stockings with the sisters' names on top *with Pez inside.* On the coffee table, magazines like *National Geographic* and *Life* spread out like a fan, all the time like that, not just when guests come over to the perfect house.

Mother wipes the clear-plastic covers on the furniture every day and the material underneath looks crispy. The perfect house doesn't have an old pea-green bedspread over a sofa with foam padding crumbling like sand into the creases of the cushion. The father doesn't stuff the *TV Guide* into the crack of the La-Z-Boy.

A Zenith TV, a Magnavox hi-fi console, alphabetized record albums beginning with Abba, a mustard-colored shag rug, a bar with padded barstools, clean throw pillows, living-room drapes without holes, no paper plates, bendable straws with *every* drink including water. Hot-dog buns for hot dogs. And plain white bread all the time.

There is a Cougar or Torino or Duster in the garage, a playroom called a den with vinyl beanbag chairs in all colors, and an upright piano. At Christmastime, the mother lights candles on the piano that she actually bought to burn and they sing "Silent Night," at least three verses in three-part harmony, while Little Sis plays the piano and Mother puts her arm around Big Sis and Father puts his arm around Mother. Father sings while puffing on a pipe, as the cat curls up on the throw rug in this perfect house where no one swears or blows bubbles into the chocolate milk through a saved straw from the Dairy Queen or eats Spam cut extra thick and glazed with guava jelly and mustard for dinner.

Where no one encourages Mother at Christmas to dance to "Cockeye Mayor from Kaunakakai" as Aunt Helen plays the ukulele and everyone laughs and claps and throws money as the dog begins to bark and Uncle Ed yells, "We go caroling!" And they all hold each other and sing "Manuela Boy, My Dear Boy" down the driveway as Aunt Helen strums her ukulele as I watch at the picture window thinking about angels and the Lennon Sisters singing hymns.

C

Yes, hi. My name is Betty Cooper.

Yes, hi. My name is Billy Jo Cole.

Yes, hi. My name is Bobby Gentry and I look just like Liz Taylor.

"Yeah, right. Your name is Betty Correa and you live on Ki-noole Street," Jerome says. "No, no, no. Billy Jo Takahara and your family owns pigs up Uka side and your father work for the Board of Water Supply. Okay, wait. Bobbylyn Chang. Future Narcissus Queen, gotta go Barbizon Modeling School for learn how to walk. I promise, Lovey. You piss me off. I ain't ever coming to your house again. I hate play pretend-talk-haole, I mean it. No act. I so irritated, I like buss your chops, bobo your face, and I swear, I ever hear one more haole name like Lovey Beth Farnsworth or Lovey Lynn Beckenhauser, I promise, I going home and I ain't ever coming back."

C

The Beckenhausers: They lived across the street from the Church of the Holy Cross. A white house with green trim and blackened torn screens on the back side of the house.

Vicky Beckenhauser and me climbed through the back window to play in her room with the Ouija board so her mother wouldn't see me coming or going. Sometimes we played "Princess Knight" and Vicky let me be the horse, O-po.

Haoles have a certain smell. A sweet powdery smell, not like Johnson's baby powder, but like powdery flowers. Vicky had that smell.

Vicky's Aunt Theresa made her homemade rag dolls that had the same yarn hair color as Vicky and her sister Suzanne. Dark, rust yarn hair and clothes like Vicky and Suzanne.

Once, while playing Ouija board in Vicky's closet, her mother bursts in and says, "What the hell's goin' on?" She looks at me sharp. "Who's this, Vicky?"

"Mama, my friend Lovey. Can she stay for some supper?"

Vicky's mother with the greasy hair and cigarette between her red, chipped nails says, "Sure. Go warsh up and call your mama."

Me and Vicky washing our hands with a dirty bar of soap. I'm so scared, I don't even remember what we had to eat. But seeing Vicky and her mother, Suzanne, and Mr. Beckenhauser, who drinks Primo beer and stares straight at me across the table, I feel lucky to be with haoles for dinner.

Vicky takes the butter dish and slaps a huge wad all over her hot Minute Rice that falls like bullets off of her fork, not like the rice we eat at home.

The butter dish gets passed from one person to the next, each one rubbing lots of butter on their rice. And when the butter comes to me, I want to be a Beckenhauser so bad, I rub butter all over my rice and swallow each bite like a mouthful of Crisco.

☾

My number in Lori Shigemura's Slam Book is 7.

    7. BABY-OF-THE-FUTURE: A boy, then a girl

                              Hapa

                              With Japanese middle name

    7. BOY: Christopher Torao Cole

    7. GIRL: Summer or Heather Reiko Cole

7. HUSBAND-OF-THE-FUTURE: Dennis Cole,
         Jaclyn Smith's
         ex-hubby, or
         Michael Cole,
         Mod Squad

❢

Japanee girls all want haole last names like Smith or Cole. Tall blond haoles with hairy legs and bushy underarms. Blue or hazel eyes and with a real haole accent, or better yet they grew up here and their grandparents were missionaries, so they can talk local if they want—but don't.

❢

The Allens: Andrew Allen lived in the expensive house on the beach cliffs. From the outside, it looked like *Gone with the Wind* with palm trees, a golf-course lawn, bougainvillea archways, and an Oriental bridge over a river by the house.

My mother sewed puakenikeni and pakalana leis with palapalai fern and ribbons for Mrs. Allen's Big Island Women's Golf Club and sold them to her for cheap.

We'd drive up in the Land Rover and Mrs. Allen would take real long to come out of her house. When she finally came out, she'd be bouncy in her tennis whites with an elastic white headband on her blond hair.

Mrs. Allen would lift up the wet paper towel over the leis in the soda boxes, carefully peer at each lei, and say, "Well, Verva.

You'd think for the price you charge for these, you'd at least leave the bruised flowers out."

Andrew Allen, "Andy," on the porch swing out on the lanai—he'd laugh at Calhoon and me. Say at school in his perfect English, "Hey, Lei Seller. Hey, Bruise. Hey, Lei-lani and her stupid sister."

My mother would say to Mrs. Allen, "Take an extra puakenikeni for yourself and a pakalana for Mitzi Hall. Sorry about the bruises." Mother said this in perfect English that sounded pretend-talk-haole.

Cal and me in the backseat of our car get a dollar each for coming along and Mother cursing and spitting all the way down the Allens' steep driveway.

C

Mokes like haole girls with strawberry-blond hair. They come to our school from places like Kenosha, Wisconsin, talking real straight, and next thing you know, haole girl with moke-y boyfriend.

C

Ginger Geiger. Daughter of Mrs. Gloria Geiger, new Sunday School Youth Choir director. Mrs. Geiger forced us to memorize "This Is My Father's World," the Twenty-third Psalm, all four verses of "Just As I Am," and "M Is for the Million Things She Gave Me." We were also forced to attend Saturday rehearsal.

Jerome quit. Bradley Kinoshita quit. Adele Ige went back to

college. This left Cal, me, the Kimura twins, who I swear only moved their lips to the memorized verses, and Ginger Geiger.

Ginger Geiger when she first came to Youth Choir:

Goody barrettes and two ponytail braids, plaid cotton blouse buttoned to the lace collar, high-water bell-bottoms, white socks with lace, and Buster Browns.

Ginger Geiger after Baron Ahuna, Kenneth Spencer, and Levi Nalani, JV and varsity volleyball players, started driving into the parking lot of our church at Saturday rehearsals calling, "Eh, Ginga Grant, where you stay?" Ginger Geiger after all of that:

Red lipstick and kissing potion glossy lips, long hair down with plumeria behind her ear, hiphuggers, halter top, and Dr. Scholl's exercise sandals.

Ginger looked like Maureen McCormick.

C

We watched *The Greatest Story Ever Told* on the Geigers' console TV. Mrs. Geiger and Ginger taught Cal, me, and the Kimura twins how to make popcorn balls with Karo corn syrup. Ginger let me wear one of her baby-blue baby dolls to sleep when I showed up with my mother's old muumuu for nightgown. She told us about wintertime in Kenosha, Wisconsin, and black ice. We prayed before and after the movie. She nicknamed me Jenny 'cause her best friend in Kenosha was Jenny Williams. Ginger said, "Hey, Jenny, you and me, let's go to the mall after Youth Choir next Saturday, okay? You, me, and Cal, how 'bout it?" Mrs. Geiger smiled on and nodded gently.

The next Saturday, after Youth Choir, Ginger, me, and Cal

walked to Poi Kakugawa Store to catch the sampan bus down-town, when all of a sudden, Levi Nalani pulled up in his blue Mustang.

"Eh, Ginga Grant," he said. "We go for one cruise down Banyan Drive. Just you and the boiz."

Ginger leaning into the window right over Kenneth Spencer's face. Climbing in the backseat with Baron Ahuna. Laughing. All of this without once looking back at Cal and me sitting on the sidewalk of Poi Kakugawa Store.

She never said much to me and my sister after that Saturday at Youth Choir but always walked with us to the store, Mrs. Geiger smiling and nodding as we left the parking lot of the church.

One time, I heard her tell Levi Nalani that since she was Gin-ger Grant, that made me Lovey Howell and my sister, Gilligan. She never looked at the Kimura twins except to roll her eyes or blow a gum bubble at them. Never had the scared haole look or braided ponytails. Kept her eyes on the street outside the church.

C

My father says, "Out there in that great big world, and believe me, when I was in the navy, I seen the world two times over and all the people in the world two times over too, and, Lovey, I telling you, got one in a hundred haoles, just one, worth being call your friend.

"Look at me. I got any haole friends? Just one. Wilcox. But the bugga half Chinese, so no really count to me. One in a hun-dred, just one. And if I was you, I wouldn't even bother to look."

Lori Shigemura's Slam Book: #7

7. HOME-OF-THE-FUTURE: Akron, Ohio, or Boise, Idaho

7. WEDDING COLORS: Salmon, champagne, and eggshell white

Scott Yamasaki

    Dennis Kawano

    Ricky Morioka

    Vincent Takeyama

They walk alike, talk alike, sit alike. They hate fags, hate girls taller than five feet, hate silliness or laughing too much. They play basketball, but don't go out for the school team, or do go out, and get cut.

And the girls always gotta say, "Oh, Scott looks like the Japanese Charles Bronson or Vincent looks like the Japanese Neil Diamond." With the haoles, you say, "Oh, Andy *looks* like Jan-Michael Vincent," and that's that—'cause he really does.

    Winston Wang

    Carleton See

    Kent Wong

    Tareyton Tong

All the Chinese boys have names straight from the cigarette machine. I don't know why a mother would want her son named after nicotine. And they have such large gums. Lots of nice plates and elephant statues in their house.

C

Blond hair. Good. Betty Cooper and Marcia Brady. Barbie and Twiggy. Peggy Lipton and Elizabeth Montgomery. Debbie Reynolds, Doris Day, and all the Gidgets except for Sally Field and look what happened to her. Forced to be a flying nun in Puerto Rico. Want to fall in love with Alejandro Rey, but cannot.

Black hair. Evil. Veronica Lodge. Alexandra Cabot. Serena, Samantha Stevens' cousin, Big Ethel, Nancy Kwan, and all the evil stepmothers in Walt Disney movies. Miss Mims from *Thoroughly Modern Millie*.

Just better to be haole. Live in Riverdale. Be Vicky or Jenny. Talk straight to the mainland Japanee cousins who say things like "Gee, you talk *funny*. Do they talk like that at your school? How come you pronounce words so *inarticulately*? My mother says that the relatives who grew up in Hawaii have *difficulty expressing themselves verbally*. Gee, Lovey, does *everybody here* speak so *strangely*?"

Better to have straight blond hair and long Miss America legs and lots of boobs like Ginger Geiger, 'cause, to me, no sense in sending Miss Hawai'i to Atlantic City unless she's haole 'cause she never makes the finals, only Miss Congeniality. She got lots of Aloha Spirit that's why.

I want a great name. Beckenhauser. Allen. Geiger. Smith. Brown. Cooper. Have a father with a great nickname like

Richard—Dick. Robert—Bob. James—Jim. A mother with a great nickname like Debra—Debbie. Cynthia—Cindy. Susan—Sue.

Live in a house with Dixie cup dispensers, bunk beds with ruffled sheets, bendable straws, rose-shaped soap, Lysol, and Pez.

And eat potatoes and biscuits. Minute Rice with lots of butter. Baby-doll nighties and popcorn balls. Boyfriends in Mustangs. Porch swings and bougainvillea archways.

I wanna be Lovey Beth Cole. Mrs. Michael Cole. Wanna marry you, Dennis. Be a Cole. Be a haole. A Japanee with a haole last name.

ORDINARY DAYS

Mother smokes Parliaments. We're not to point at the cigarette machine and say, "That the kine Mommy smokes," if Grandma is around. I like when Mother and me sit on the porch to pick fleas off of Melba and Spam, the two black poi dogs we found in the ditch by Grandma's house.

It's another Sunday. Mother with her Parliaments hanging off her lip, watch the ash grow long, grow, crackle, then fall. Watch the smoke rise, and Mother squinting her eye like a real Wrangler Jane.

She puts an empty can with turpentine between us. We pick the fleas and kill them in the turpentine. We don't have to squeeze them until they snap between our thumbnails. We lose a lot of fleas that end up jumping on our arms and clothes.

Mother and me on the porch picking fleas and we don't say very much unless one of us finds a blood tick, fat and gray, whose body indents when you press your fingernail into its back.

Mother and me. Mother, who rips the fat blood tick out of Melba's ear. Melba, who cries on the porch every Sunday, who makes Spam howl like a wolf, knowing his turn comes next.

Mother smoking Parliaments while picking fleas and me watching the smoke rise.

〔

The next day after school, waiting for the sampan bus to take me home, count the beauty spots on my arms.

Connect them with pen lines.

Try to make a pattern.

I ask my mother when I get home how come I have so many beauty spots. How come my little sister Calhoon has none. Only me, everywhere on my face, on my arms, my hands, my legs, and Mother says, "Everywhere there's one beauty spot, you going be lovely when you grow up."

I believe her.

〔

I like best to pinch blackheads off her back before she takes a bath on Friday nights. Sit with Mother and watch *The Partridge Family,* then *The Brady Bunch* on Channel 4. Mother says, "I use to use two cowboy matches to squeeze the blackheads off of your grandma's back. Still do. Cannot stand the sight of that white worm come wiggling out the blackhead hole."

That's the best part to me. Squeeze just a little harder and poop, out jumps the blackhead cork like a smashed tube of Colgate, squirting white oil that I carefully cut off with my thumbnail, careful to keep it in its spiral splendor so that I can show it off on Mother's forearm. So that she can say, "Whoa, that's a beauty."

Then I point out all the splotchy red islands on her back, connect all the islands with fingernail-scratch bridges until Mother says thanks and gives me my big word for the week. *Nocturnal.* "Means a night animal. Gimme some example."

"Barn owl."

"Uh-huh."

"Bat."

"Uh-huh."

My word last week was *marsupial.*

"Means a animal with a pouch. Example."

"Koala bear. Kangaroo."

Then Mother soaks for a half hour in bath-oil beads melting in the bathtub every Friday night.

☾

Sometimes on Saturdays I get paid ten cents if I see a pure-white cow on the hillside of the Kapapala Ranch on the long rides to the macadamia nut farm near South Point. I pretend like I see five white cows so I can get fifty cents, and Father never checks, because he's driving.

Mother is busy singing war songs with Calhoon. We approach Volcano and Mother sings,

> "K-K-K-Katy, beautiful Katy,
> you're the only g-g-g-girl that I adore.

When the m-moon shines on the c-cow shet,
I'll be waiting at the k-k-k-kitchen door."

And Father always corrects her. "Cow *shed. Shed,* not shet."
Mother laughs and says, "Cow shet, right, everybody?"

Sometimes we sing the doxology from church very loud but
beautifully. The way you sing when you're not shame. When the
youngest deacon and his haole wife aren't in the pew in front of
you turning their side eyes to your loud but beautiful voice.

Praise God, from whom all blessings flow.
Praise Him, all creatures here below.
Praise Him above, ye heavenly host.
Praise Father, Son, and Holy Ghost.
A-men.

It's the A-men we like so we can harmonize. Then Father
starts on Christmas songs, then church songs like "Rock of
Ages Cleft for Me."

I pretend to find more white cows. Before you know it, we're
near the Volcano Store, and Father slaps two quarters into my hand.

C

Whoever told Father about making extra money picking
macadamia nuts must be nuts himself. Must be mean and must
enjoy bending over all day picking up unhusked macadamia nuts
until your fingers get all raw from the rocks under the trees. For
eight measly dollars a burlap bag.

Burlap bags are huge. And bottomless. We make eight dollars for a whole day's work. That's all Calhoon and me together can pick.

Father plans these wage-earning weekends for us to contribute to the Family Money Pot. The last Family Money Pot was spent on a portable heater from Sears for the kitchen in the winter. All those weekends of odd jobs or sitting in the garage full of junk for the weekly garage sale for the dinky heater.

After running the new heater for a few months, Father gets ambitious. Then he convinces Mother to go along with his new wage-earning weekend idea. A Magnavox console stereo with wonderful carved wood engravings of elephants like it came right from Taiwan. Like the ones you see the Raggedy Ann and Andy couples win on *Let's Make a Deal*. The Family Money Pot will pay for this new stereo system.

The macadamia nut picking comes easy when we first get there. I stand up and bend over easily for each unhusked nut that I drop into the bag. Picking nuts standing up and bending over. Easy when you first get there.

Then I take a water break.

It may have been my biggest mistake of the day.

I begin to wonder if this is all worth it. I pour the water from the washed-out Malolo syrup jug into a Styrofoam cup, and when Father says, "Write your name on the side of the cup, eh. Conserve money. No waste, eh. And hurry up. No let us do all the work," I know I want to listen to the radio for the rest of the day.

I start to pick nuts sitting down. Gather the nuts around me, then squat-walk to the next arm's radius of nuts and pick like that until the next water break.

"Machines cannot pick the nuts," Father says. "Too rocky, the ground, and gotta pick the nuts off the ground, not off the tree. C'mon, snap it up. Hup, hup, hup." He's trying to be inspirational.

Finally after lunch, I lie down on the rocks to pick the nuts for Calhoon's and my bag. I put all the nuts in the scoop of my T-shirt, then roll to the burlap bag to empty my shirt.

Mac-nut fields may look grassy from the roadside, like plush grass under a huge shady tree, but mac nuts got thorns on them and the leaves too. And the ground is rocky.

I look to the right side of my face for nuts. I see roaches right next to my eyes, but I'm so tired, I don't even care. I stare up at the sky and watch the clouds pass, then disappear between the thorny leaves.

Cardinals race into the treetops, and I roll my body to the next place under the tree to pick nuts lying down.

I listen to the radio. To Wild Billy B. All the dedications of songs. The staticky station whose radio waves get messed up from Mauna Kea and Mauna Loa being in the way.

"No let Lovey play one damn record on the new Magnavox," Mother says. "Look at her, Hubert. Lying there picking nuts while the rest of us buss our asses. I mean, dammit, Lovey, look at Cal."

So I turn toward my sister. Her face so tired and her hands so red, but I don't say anything. Neither does Calhoon, who's playing the noble good child versus the lazy sister with no ambition.

"Go wait in the car. *Now.* And don't you ever put your Mark Lindsay records on our turntable, I swear it," Mother screams at me.

I put down the tailgate to the Land Rover. I make Father's sweat towel into a rolled-up pillow. I pour a tall Styrofoam cup full of water. Take small sips. Spit at roaches below. Hang my arms over the edge of the tailgate. Feel the blood rush down my arms and my head. Hear Mother muttering about me to Father. Watch the clouds move. Wonder about the evenness of a blue sky. How it happens like that even on the most ordinary days.

C

Mother says I gave her white hair. That no matter how many times she perms at AnToinette's Beauty Shoppe, she can never fully curl those white hairs. The ones that are thick as fishing line.

I don't see too many of them, but I get ten cents for every one I pluck out with the tweezers. Mother says I have to pull it out completely or I get nothing. After each time I pluck, Mother takes the tweezers from my hand and examines the waxy bulb at the end of the strand. Lays the hair down, waxy bulbs one way, on her dark blue pillowcase.

She says I gave her white hair from the moment I was born; she saw stars first and sprouted white hair. White hair that won't perm. White hair that comes with raising girls in a small town like Hilo, she says. "Two of you got nothing to do," she says, "but hang around the soda fountain or the gym picking scabs and eating them. And all those crummy boys making cracks about you two and you two too dense to even cross your legs. *Dammit.* Thass why I get white hairs. And I dunno why I gotta pay you to pluck out the white hairs that you wen' give me in the first place."

I don't say nothing or else she'll start up all over again.

"White hairs," she says, "two girls, *dammit,* and I ain't going through giving birth just for get one boy for Hubert, I tell you." Mother soaking her feet in Palmolive like Madge says and Calhoon rubbing the pumice stone on her heels to smooth them down.

Sunday afternoons, Mother smoking Parliaments on the porch of our house, grumbling about white hairs, and me picking fleas off our dogs.

c

I kill five ants in a row. I let one talk to another one, then I kill them both mid-sentence. I let one crawl on my finger to become a pet. Watch him go around my finger twice. Cross the bridge of my finger to the other hand. Then lower him into a drop of rain. I watch him swim and try to breathe. Then I kill him.

I watch the door to AnToinette's Beauty Shoppe. Mother's whole head is wrapped up in white curlers. AnToinette puts her under the big dome of the hair dryer. Mother gives me the eye, the "be good, dammit, before you get it in the car later" eye.

I pull a strand of hair from my head. I examine the waxy bulb at the end. Roll the bulb between my fingers. Stroke the strand of hair. I split the split end slowly and watch one side kink. I try to unkink the curl. Throw it into the wind and watch it spiral down. Neat. I floss my teeth with the other side and it breaks in between my teeth. I can't pull it out.

I pick up rocks and juggle three of them. Put one between the fingers of one hand. Then the other. I squeeze my fingers together. Relax. Squeeze. Relax. And I throw the rocks at the road all at once.

I look for olivines. I find seven big ones and three small ones. I line them up. Get a rock and try to crush them. They all fly off except for one. This one I try to flick at a passing ant. Miss.

Stare at an object like the stop sign. Close my right eye. Then my left eye. Back and forth. Open, shut, and see the sign shift back and forth like a moving object.

I watch the cars pass. A blue Dodge Dart. Like Hiram's. A brown Duster. Dexter's. A Valiant. Uncle Its's. A green Datsun. Like Henry DeJesus'.

I pick fuzz balls off my shirt.

I bite my fingernails and crunch each nail until nail bits on the tip of my tongue rub on the inside of my lip. Roll the nail bits all over the inside of my mouth.

Mother's in the chair. AnToinette shakes the plastic cape hard. Now she teases my mother's hair. Mother gives me the eye again in the reflection of the mirror.

Ordinary stink eye.

I watch old ladies go by.

I listen to old Filipino men talk story and I stare longer than I would if my mother were next to me. 'Cause she'd say, "No stare. Whassamatta, you got eye problems?"

Squint my eyes to see the porno movie posters across the street outside the theater without seeming like I'm looking.

I cross my legs.

I uncross my legs.

I kill another ant. And another.

My mother walks out of AnToinette's Beauty Shoppe. The

gold bell hits the door. A cool rush of beauty-shop smells comes out the door.

A beehive sits high on Mother's head. She'll look grand like this for the rest of the day. And tomorrow, like her old self. She'll tease and try to make a beehive again but will end up with crazy-man hair and get angry at the first person who comes near her bathroom. She smiles at AnToinette and puts her hand to the back of the beehive and pushes it up gently.

Mother grabs me off the ground and dusts my ass hard. "Gunfunnit, Lovey," she says. "Next time, you stay home. You so goddamn impatient. I ain't taking you no place. All I wanted was to go to the beauty shop. Whassamatta with you, huh? I seen you making fun of the Filipino men."

"But I wasn't," I tell her.

"Then what you was staring at across the street? I seen you staring at something."

It's porno movie posters or Filipino men. Think. I can't win.

Mother arm-drags me to the car. My feet dangle-walk. Once we're in the car, I get two more good slaps because she says what will AnToinette think of me.

Tomorrow, it'll be an ordinary day. Mother will look like her old self.

Tonight she sits me on the back steps of the house for being a rude person to old men downtown. How cruel it was of me. And she saw it all. "Can you believe this kid? How dare she make fun of people. Who the hell she think she is? Pain in the goddamn ass."

I'm to sit on the back steps until it's time to sleep. No dinner and no bath. Tough luck, hungry and stink.

I watch the mosquito-punk smoke coil into the air, thick at the bottom, then real thin and gray near the top, where I blow it gently.

I watch geckos eat termites on the screen.

Mosquitoes flapping dead on the concrete landing.

Kill them with my big toe.

I count all the stars that I can.

I stare at the biggest, most reddest one that my father once told me was Mars and I close my right eye.

Then my left eye. Back and forth.

Open, shut. And the whole sky moves.

CRAZY LIKE A DREAM

The old ladies stand behind the chain-link fence. Sometimes they walk along the fence, run their fingers over the rusty links. Back and forth. Back and forth. All of them in faded blue or pink flower prints. All of them with white nylon knee-highs and orthopedic shoes. Staring eyes and brown wrinkled faces.

Calhoon and me play on Aunt Helen's porch on Saturdays when my mother sews leis or cashiers at the Lei Stand for extra money. We watch the old ladies. Today, Aunty buys for us wax candies with sweet juice inside soda-bottle-shaped wax. Calhoon and me bite off the tips and spit them out on the lawn to watch them melt in the hot sun. Cal's chewing her wax flat. Slowly making false-teeth imprints and sucking it to make sure every bit of juice is gone.

"Why they gotta walk like that all day?" Cal asks Aunt Helen, who's watering her African violets on the porch. "Sheez, they look so tired and hot, back and forth, back and forth."

"They crazy," she says. "How many times I gotta tell you that? They all nuts. Thass the crazy house for crazy ladies. They gotta wear diapers to sleep. You lucky that one over there, the one in the blue dress, she don't lift her dress to the cars. Before, she do that, you know. Ho, before, nighttime, I hear all them crazy old ladies crying and screaming like babies. Nah, like ghosts. And I hear slapping sounds like somebody getting lickens."

Today, the old lady in the blue dress walks all the way to one end of the lot and all the way back to the other over and over. She's Japanese.

Nobody visits her. All the days Cal and me sat on the porch, nobody came. Not one. With obake anthuriums for an old grandma to put in a tall vase or aku bones for shoyu-sugar that an old grandma can suck down to fish head and skeleton, grandma-sucking with smacking lips, all of the pointed aku bones. Then slurping up the fish-oily, shoyu-sugary hot rice. Or bananas and papayas from the yard for an old lady's breakfast. Nothing.

And it's hot today. So hot that we're here on the porch sweating and wondering why our Aunt Helen made us Campbell's vegetable soup for lunch. But the crazy lady walks back and forth.

Cal says, "She must be one real mento hospital case, I tell you. Look, Lovey, she scratching her ass and her hair all not combed like a real buta kau-kau lady ready for feed her pigs."

But I wonder, as Cal says this, what crazy really feels like. Crazy can't be like sad, because the old ladies never cry during the day. They're soundless. Crazy must feel like old and ready to die.

Like the way I stay up now at night and listen to the TV in the faraway living room and watch the light seep in the crack in the wall thinking that I gotta sleep before everything shuts down in the house, before I have to lie here in the dark all alone and think about where I will go when I die and what dead feels like. How I drive myself crazy wondering what it feels like to die. Is it like suffocating? Or drowning until all the air sucks out of you?

Then the lights go out. I hear my mother's pink house slippers walk down the hallway. And I feel all tight inside because I didn't fall asleep before she turned off the TV and now I have to lie here and think about dying, dying and where will I go, and how will it feel, and why people had to die. This is the feeling of me being crazy.

That's why I feel better when Calhoon says, "Crazy must be like dreaming, not dying." She could be right. She *really* could be right. "Maybe just like rocking your own self to sleep, what you think, Lovey?"

I decide that crazy is not like dying. Crazy is like your inside wanting to leave but not knowing how, so revving the body engine along a chain-link fence every day, getting ready for that flight as a mist or a shadow.

All those old ladies walking along that fence, not even looking at each other as they pass. Just walking arm over arm along the chain link.

C

Calhoon and me play Candyland on the porch. Then we're playing a game of Battleship when Cal all of a sudden runs across Aunt Helen's yard and presses her face to the fence. "Lovey, Lovey! She fell. Lovey!"

Aunt Helen yells from the window, "Don't you two leave the yard, you hear me, Calhoon? Lovey? Gunfunnit. Stay in the yard. You two hear me? I going put both of you in that crazy house.

Get over here. Come back here. Okay, right there, you asking for it. I shoving you in that house. Lovey! Calhoon!"

Cal and me run to Aunt Helen's gate. The old ladies across the street scream and cry. One stomps her feet, but not one of them goes near the old lady that fell to check and see if she's alive or breathing.

"Help her, you crazy old futs," I scream at the ladies. Another old lady shakes the fence. And the old grandma, all brown-skinned and wrinkled from so many days in the sun, lies rumpled on the ground.

Somebody runs out from the house. Pretty soon, an ambulance comes and police too. And old ladies being held back as the chain-link gate opens. Old ladies pulling at their white hair and screaming and crying.

"You two stop staring like that," says Aunt Helen. "Like me put you in that house for staring? Here, rake the lychee leaves and pretend like you cleaning yard." Calhoon and me rest ourselves on the rake handles and watch a body being carried away and the silent spinning of the ambulance lights as it pulls onto the road so slowly that I hear gravel under the tires.

It's later on that night when Calhoon and me are almost asleep on our bed that she says, "Crazy *is* like *dreaming*. I seen um in the lady's eyes. Then when you die, all the crazy gone, like your whole life was one dream. Lovey, what you think dying feel like?"

How did she know that I made myself crazy night after night about dying? In her head right next to mine on our bed, was she watching the light through the crack in the wall and thinking about it too?

I think about the crumpled blue-dressed body on the gravel road. A body that wanted to leave anyway. A body so sad and ready to die. All revved up for that flight and finally, on a very hot day, like mist through the chain links.

C

My other neighbor Katy and me sit on her porch across the street from my house. It's really Katy's mother's house with the big jacaranda tree in the front yard and a white wicker swing like the plantation lunas have on their lanais.

I put Katy's big, swollen legs on an old apple crate. She says, "Eh, Lovey, try press my legs. So swollen going have one white dot where you wen' press your finger. Try."

I do and the white dot on one of her swollen red legs stays for a second, then fades back to brown. I make four dots with all fingers at once and Katy laughs. We drink Kool-Aid with lots of ice cubes.

Katy says she likes the name Charlene if she has a girl and Charles if she has a boy. Named after her ji-chan who was a kendo sensei at a dojo near the pancake house by the airport.

I give her my suggestions since lately I've been Katy's main visitor. "Autumn, Summer, or Heather for a girl." Katy winces. "What, what?" I tell her. Then she says nothing, so I continue. "Christopher, Michael, or Dennis for a boy." Katy turns her eyebrows down.

Katy says, "When the baby comes, I let you bathe him and change his diaper like that. But no name him—you too haolified with your names, Lovey. Who you think you? Sometimes you act too haole-ish to me. You crazy—you like be haole or what?" I don't say anything. Katy goes on. "I know I got one boy in here. But I gotta name um."

Katy calls me crazy all the time. But I don't care, 'cause I *know* what crazy is. What I really want to ask Katy is if she would let her baby call me Aunty Lovey. It's a secret wish of mine. Like some of my classmates at school, they're aunties already and they say neat things like "Oh, this my niece. She just turn one."

Another secret wish I have is being pregnant. I play at home when Katy cannot see me. How I like to sit down with one hand pressed to my back and the other hand bracing myself onto the chair. And walking around the house while holding the small of my back and huffing and puffing with a pillow or volleyball under my shirt. Sometimes I get lost inside myself when I play pregnant.

Lost in how I want a baby to sleep next to my face at night, so I put my pillow there and talk to it soft, "Mommy's here. Mommy's here." How I want to take my baby to the May Day pageant at school and have everybody fight to carry him.

"When the baby comes out of my, I mean your stomach," I tell Katy, "will you tell him to call me Aunty, please, Katy?" I figure I'd just ask, what the hell.

"Your stomach?" Katy screams. "You crazy or what?" Then Katy laughs. "Lovey, babies no come out of your stomach. That what your madda tell you? Lovey, babies come out of your fufu."

My fufu? How? No, Katy, *you* crazy. You lie to me. Omigod. It's not possible. Babies are pulled out of your stomach. That's why my mother's stomach is so full of shiny stretch marks, because I grew in her stomach. No, Katy. How come my mother never said nothing when I pulled the pillow outta my stomach? My fufu? No. No way.

Katy laughs. Not a har-de-har-har laugh but a heh-heh-heh. I stare off the porch and into the leaves of the jacaranda. Sunlight seeps through. Jacaranda has a sweet odor that only those who love jacaranda can take in deep breaths.

That's why I love Katy's house in late summer. And when the wind blows Kona, it comes to my room at night where I lay on my bed and think about Katy and her huge round stomach that I saw move. Katy said that was his leg pushing out. The baby inside who would come out of Katy's fufu.

I cannot imagine this.

In the morning, I hear Aunt Helen's voice down the hallway. Mother fries eggplant in hot oil for her and Aunt Helen to eat for breakfast. Aunt Helen makes a mayonnaise-and-shoyu sauce and clicks the rice button on.

I walk into the kitchen. "Howzit, Lovey," says Aunt Helen.

"Ho, go down that hallway and comb your messy hair," says my mother. "And brush your stink mouth while you at it." Aunt Helen laughs. I stand there for a while until my mother says, "Lovey, you heard me?"

"Ma," I say, "Katy told me that babies come from your fufu. Thass true or I crazy, Ma?" Mother and Aunt Helen stop for a moment and stare at each other across the hot frying pan full of eggplant.

"Owee, the oil splashing, Verva." They both stare at each other and make funny smirks. Then they talk to each other like I'm not even there.

"Ho, Helen, when I gave birth to Lovey, Hubert drop me off at that Hoʻolehua Hospital and I swear from ten in the morning for the next twelve hours they put me on one cold iron table all by myself with the meanest nurse you eva met. And I was seeing stars by the time Lovey was coming. I wen' lose it big time, nuts out, yelling to the max. I mean, I seen stars from my head to my toes, I felt all that, and this one had such one big head, nine-pounder, you know, she got stuck. So finally they put iron forceps in and pull her out. That's how come she get the scar by her eye. Come here, Lovey. Show Aunty your scar."

I walk over to Aunt Helen and lift my face so she can see my scar. "Oh no," Aunt Helen gasps.

"And all that time, Helen, they strap me down. And I was screaming like one crazy lady, 'No no no strap me down,' but they grab my wrist and put the straps on."

"Just like me, Verva, when Ernest was born, they put me in this room with bright lights and me, every time one labor pain came, I dig my fingernails into the wall, then I scratch the wall like one dog, you know, Verva. You think you wen' lose it? I tell you, if you go Hilo Hospital, maternity ward might still yet have my fingernail diggings in the wall."

They both laugh a different laugh.

That afternoon, I go to Katy's house. We sit on the white swing. Katy's big. Big and tired. Her forehead shiny with sweat on her red face. It looks sore to be this pregnant. And swollen feet.

We're talking about the new deacon at the church, who has a harelip, and what a harelip is and why did they make him song leader 'cause he can't pronounce some words like *gwace* and *we-pent,* when all of a sudden water comes outta Katy. A trail of water dripping on the porch, in to the living-room carpet, and down to the bathroom.

Katy's little silky terrier named Libby smells the water and cries and runs around in circles crying. "Her bag broken," screams Katy's mother. "Eh, Lovey, call Jeffrey."

And this is the last I see of Katy. Her mother carrying a small pink suitcase into Jeffrey's Ford truck and Katy turning around to wave goodbye to me. Katy's mother crying and sobbing in the driveway and honking and blowing her nose. Katy didn't look sore at all. But her mother did.

By the third day I'm thinking maybe Katy didn't make it. Maybe it was so sore, that baby needing forceps to come outta Katy's fufu, that she died of the pain.

Like Katy's little dog, Libby. When Libby gave birth, she ran around the house screaming crazy too. Then she hid in the dark closet. Katy showed me how to rub her belly to help her stop crying.

I remember Libby didn't know that the baby came outta her, so she screamed, then ran to the other side of the room with her baby still stuck in the black sac and she breathed hard.

I remember. The scared look especially. I feel sorry for Katy. Every day I wait for Jeffrey's white Ford truck to pull into her driveway.

My mother says when Katy comes home I'm not to visit her for a month. A month? She says, "You full of germs and filth and nobody suppose to visit the baby except relatives for the first month anyhow. You think Katy going have time for you any-more? She one mother now. So catch the hint and leave her alone."

I start thinking, well, maybe I don't want a baby after all. Katy not home yet and all that sore fufu pain everybody keeps talking about. I stop playing pregnant. I don't sleep with the pre-tend pillow baby anymore.

I just wait on my bike in our driveway every afternoon.

And the day when the white Ford truck comes home, I run over. Katy still looks like she has a baby inside her. Her hair is all oily and her face looks gray. Her lips are dry. Katy looks differ-ent. Her eyes are the most faraway. But she smiles at me. "Was crazy, Lovey, giving birth," she says.

"But crazy like dreaming, Katy," I tell her. "I wen' think long time on this one—no can be, Katy, that giving birth is crazy 'cause my madda said—"

"Hah, Lovey?" Katy says. "Whateva." She closes her eyes and breathes in deep. Maybe my mother was right. Maybe I needed to wait a month.

"A boy," she says to me. "I name him Charles."

She lifts the blue blanket off of the face, very pink and puffy. Right then, all the crazy's gone as Katy and me stare into each other's eyes for a moment. I know he is my secret nephew. I feel it all in my eyes that already adore him and when his head shifts, like in slow motion, I touch his soft, spongy forehead.

Charles with his mother's dark black hair, lots of hair. Large rich man's ears. A cry full of air which says he's hungry. And Katy walks slowly into her mother's house.

Katy gets really good at being a mother. She changes a diaper without poking Charles not once and sponge-bathes him without wetting his black belly-button stump not once and makes the bottles and washes the bottles and rocks him and sings to him.

I sit with Katy though my mother tells me not to, that I should let Katy sleep when the baby sleeps, that I should sit my bony ass at home and listen to her before Katy has to tell me off and hurt my feelings and I come home crying.

And when Charlie wakes up, I blow bubbles for him on the porch. Bubbles that lift into the high branches of the jacaranda tree that turn marble colors that swirl and spin pinks and blues and violets. Bubbles that drip down my arm and onto the porch and Charlie watches them with baby eyes that have a hard time focusing.

Charlie with his mother's dark eyes and dark skin with purple knees and elbows. Charlie with pink see-through ears in the morning sunlight. My new neighbor, Charles Heima.

And when the time is right, when Katy and me are sitting on the porch and the jacaranda is in full bloom and Charlie is fed and full, I ask Katy did she really lose it?

And her answer is "Yes. But I forget already. That's how God makes it be. See that scar on your eye? You remember how sore it was? No. 'Cause that's how it is—God no let you rememba no pain or else we all be nuts. And the ones that no can forget and let go, they the ones go crazy for real. But we forget. Thass why we keep doing stuff to ourself over and over."

It was a summer morning that Katy brought home my new neighbor. My new neighbor who I hear crying at night. My new neighbor who is dark and handsome, who wears blue all the time, who makes aunties and uncles and cousins stop over every day now to see him, the baby that I secretly call my nephew, who came outta Katy's fufu but is secretly mine, the baby who will call me Aunty because I'll teach him to say it, the baby that I visit every day, the one who I call my Charlie Bubbles.

OOMPAH LOOMPAH

I want curly, fine baby hair. I want Mary Magdalene wavy hair. I want to look like an angel.

But I have a Toni perm now. I don't look like Toni on the perm box. I don't look like anyone I know. I don't smell like Toni or smile like Toni. I don't smile at all anymore.

My mother sits me on the dining-room chair. She uses a clothespin to keep an old towel around my neck. Calhoon sits on a stool and watches as I pass the perm tissues with little airholes to my mother.

My mother uses her teeth to pry open the flimsy pink plastic perm rods and combs thin layers of hair with her rat-tail comb. She tightly winds my hair into each rod. Then she wets the comb in a guava-jelly jar. She does this until I look like a plastic pink-headed hair-curler model.

Calhoon snips off the top of the perming solution bottle. My mother mumble-reads the next steps off the box. Mumble-readers scare me. In the first grade, if someone mumble-read, they ended up on the reading slow boat for making a mistake and could only get back on the fast boat by reading correctly for the next round.

The perm solution burns my head and my mother tells me to keep the solution out of my eyes with the corner of the dirty-white towel. I'm probably wiping my eyes with the dog towel.

The smell burns, a stinging smell worse than Mr. Clean right under the nostril, worse than Clorox or boiling tripe. A smell like no other that burns the hairs right out of the nose.

My mother says, "When I pau, you gonna look just like Farrah Fawcett, or if you like change your look, Angie Dickinson, or if you put ringlets, just like Shirley Temple." The perm bottle hisses empty, and squeeze, squeeze, my mother gets out every last drop.

Cal and me wait in front of the TV. "Ho wow," says Cal, "like Farrah Fawcett. You can be one Charlie's Angel." An angel, I think, and thirty minutes pass slow.

My mother takes each rod off slowly and removes the sopping-wet tissue paper. The smell's even stronger now. She drops the flimsy plastic rods into a soda box. And with each rod, I watch Calhoon's face change shape. Her eyebrows wrinkle together. *Oh no.* Then they lift up high into her forehead. *Oh no.* Then her mouth turns into a tight doughnut. *Oh no!*

"Knock it off, gunfunnit you, Cal," says Mother.

"Gimme a mirror, Cal," I say.

"Put that damn mirror down," says Mother. "Lovey, you better listen to me good—the hair is curly like this because we neva rinse off the solution yet." She grabs the box and mumble-reads again.

I feel my heart drop to my belly button. My mother is *mumble-reading*.

When we go to the washtub outside, I see myself in the car window. "Oh my God. I have an Afro."

"Hey, what did I say? Knock it off, Lovey. We not even pau yet."

When we finish, I have an Afro. Not like Shirley Temple but tighter. Like Get Christie Love. Frizzy and borinki.

When my mother tries to make me into Farrah Fawcett, I have stiff, very fuzzed-out, rectangle hair standing straight up in the air. *I'm no angel*.

Even the old church ladies don't know what to say about this hair that I have. "How . . . the . . . how nice, your hair, Lovey. Your—mother—did um herself, or what?" How do they know?

"Yeah," I say mildly. "She did a Toni perm on me." I want them to know so they don't buy the dusty old box off of the drugstore shelf.

I don't want to go to school. I mean, why should I? I can hear all the "stick your finger in a socket?" jokes in my head already. This hair that I can't even cut off, it's so close to my head.

Calhoon thinks it's so funny how I begged to be first to perm my hair. How there's another box of Toni perm in my mother's bathroom. How she thinks I look so stupid. It's Calhoon who says, "I cannot figure who you remind me of, Lovey." And she acts like she's thinking about this for the first time when she already had the answer. Then she fake-screams, "I know! *Oompah Loompah*."

It's true. I look like an Oompah Loompah from the movie

Willy Wonka and the Chocolate Factory. Like the fat midget Oompah Loompahs with their green faces and purple hair like mine. This becomes my tease name. "Move, I cannot see the TV, Oompah Loompah. Eh, Oompah Loompah, bring me one strawberry Nehi. Ma, Lovey acting like one sassy Oompah Loompah."

Everyone laughs now, including my mother, who made me into a home permanent wave monster. My father shakes his head but I see him laughing too.

I refuse to go to school.

Oompah Loompah has become one of our household sayings that means anything so goofy that it has no word for it. Worse than ugly.

Grandma's black orthopedic shoes.
Oompah Loompah.

Calhoon's banana-seat bike with faded basket.
Oompah Loompah.

My best friend Jerome's Speedos.
Oompah Loompah.

Father's faded olive Bermudas,
his yellow Hang Loose Hawaii T-shirt
and black rubber boots
that he wears downtown.
Oompah Loompah.

The borinki hair Midge and Skipper.
Oompah Loompah.

Bobby Sherman's new baby and wife, Sheila.
Oompah Loompah.

The Andy Williams record albums.
Oompah Loompah.

Grandma just came over for the week. She asks if Mother can perm her hair. I tell her, "No, Grandma. Oompah Loompah." She looks at me confused.

"Eh, knock it off, Lovey," says my mother. "Gramma need one perm *bad*. She looking like the buta kau-kau lady. Cal, go get the Toni box from Mommy's bathroom." Calhoon runs down the hallway. I hear her laughing.

Mother starts to mumble-read all over again.

RHAPSODY

When I close my eyes, I can still hear the music, Jerry playing scales and the soft *tock, tock, tock* of the metronome. Jerry says I'm lucky because he'll teach me what he learns for free. That he'll be a good teacher as long as he stays one lesson ahead of me.

My mother refuses to send me to piano lessons. She says Miss Marjorie Loo, the piano teacher, is a meanspirited, cranky-ass, old maid, elementary school music teacher with nothing better to do in her retirement but rag on little kids. And she overcharges. "Three dollars an hour. Jee-zus Christ! Think your father going fork over that kine money? Think twice," my mother says. And I'll regret taking lessons from her when I feel the sting of her baton on my knuckles. But I've never heard Jerry being hit.

I would be a good piano player, I think. Play my favorite songs, like "Rustic Dance," "On a Paris Boulevard," and my all-time favorite, "Cavalleria Rusticana." When Jerry plays, it sounds like a sad song through the closed door.

Jerry brings Miss Loo a single rose each week with the bottom wrapped in a wet paper towel, then tinfoil, and then Saran Wrap. She says, "Yellow. For Jealousy." Or she says, "Pink. For

Friendship." Or if Jerry brings a red one, she says, "Red. Ger-rard, red means *LOVE*." She doesn't even know that Jerry's real name is Jerome. Not Ger-rard.

Then she says, "Come. Come, Ger-rard. I have something for you upstairs in my kitchen." Jerry motions for me to sit and I wait in the basement. I put my head back on the faded rattan chair cushion and read old *People* magazines.

Jerry says she gives him strawberry Nehi and homemade sugar-and-shoyu-soaked squares of arare. Today, he brings a handful of the sweet rice crackers down for me before Miss Loo takes him inside for his lesson. The door closes. *F scale*. It has a B flat. "One hand. Now both hands. Treble clef. Good. Bass clef. Yes, Ger-rard. Again, please."

I've heard the music through the closed door. I eat my arare slowly. I suck each tiny square until all the sugary shoyu sauce melts off of each tiny rice cracker. Then I let the rice cracker melt too. One by one.

Once Jerry asked Miss Loo if I could sit with them on the other piano bench while she gave him his lesson. She said in a very sassy way, "No N-O. Ab-so-lute-ly NOT!"

If I carry the rose to piano lessons, she pretends not to see it. Then Jerry takes it from me. "Oh, Ger-rard! White. For Inno-cence. Come. Come, I have something for you upstairs in my kitchen."

Today when Jerry plays "Cavalleria Rusticana," I listen. I lis-ten to each note he plays of a song I'll never learn to read. I imag-ine his long fingers over the white keys, the black keys, and me, my fingers on the blue rattan furniture, faded and thread white.

And each note closer and closer to the crescendo, I feel inside me through the closed door, listen and feel. The music in my eyes so light, so clear, each sound Jerry plays.

And when the song ends, I hear Miss Loo say, "Won-der-ful, Ger-rard. Sim-ply won-der-ful." She claps lightly for him and I think of her fingers taking the roses Jerry brings for her.

I say *Yellow*. For Jealousy. For piano lessons.

I say *Pink*. For Friendship. A handful of rice crackers.

I say *White*. For Innocence. A hand that will not take a rose from mine.

I say *Red*. For Love. For Jerry. He will teach my hands to play my favorite song. When we go home, he will place my fingers on the keys. And my hands will play "Cavalleria Rusticana."

C

I should have played the flute. Like all the good Japanee girls. Or maybe I should have played the sax. All golden curves and deep. But only good boys played the sax. The drums, all the lesbians. The trombone, the chubby. The tuba, the tall or fat. I should have played the trumpet. I wanted to hear melody all the time. I did not understand.

You let an instrument pick you.

That's what it was about band. The sounds of the voices from each instrument. I couldn't hear my clarinet rise above the others.

I carried the black clarinet case home every day. Wet the reed and placed it just right in the mouthpiece and tightened the screws. I heard my true voice. My fingers over the holes, I heard the silver pads close softly. A deep voice. Like invisible waves.

And my mother outside picking up the stiff wash or watering the plants, the plunk of a heavy laundry basket on the washer or the squeak of the water pipe turning off—I heard her stop to hear my voice.

I took all the band-geek comments to hear my music rise. Even in the band, they never liked me. They all looked alike and acted alike. The boys all clean with glasses. The girls, straight hair with Goody barrettes, plaid shirts, and double-knit long pants. Everybody wore Keds. I took it all.

When my reed showed *one* streak of green mildew, I skipped lunch to buy a new one. One little chip and I turned over my quarter to Mr. Hokama. He looked like Jack Soo.

Our first song in Beginning Band was "Begin the Beguine." My voice disappeared from the first note. Up into the roof of the smelly band room. Down into the pool of spit by my feet. Out into the smelly spit rag I dragged through each piece of clarinet at the end of the class.

Then I heard my true voice.

But from someone else's lips.

That day, Mr. Hokama sent Lori Shigemura, First Clarinet/First Seat, to the high school campus with a pass for Crystal Kawasaki, Concert Band, Jazz Band, Elite Band, and House Band, First Clarinet/First Seat, to come to our band class. The room was still.

So still that we heard the squeak of cork as Crystal twisted together the pieces of her clarinet.

The second song in Beginning Band was "Rhapsody in Blue." Clarinet solo, piano solo in an opening duet. Crystal Kawasaki and Mr. Hokama to demonstrate for the class.

When Crystal played her first note, she shut her eyes. And the sound, the sound so clear and the trill so spine-chilling, I closed my eyes and listened to her voice rise high and reach, hold, then drop low and deeper into vibrato.

And when Crystal finished, she rested her clarinet across her lap and looked at me as if she knew that I wanted that solo.

Couldn't wait for the sheet music. For me to practice at home. I watched as Mr. Hokama stepped out from behind the piano bench, stepped up onto the conductor's platform, held the sheet music to "Rhapsody in Blue" like gold paper, looked at all the clarinet players, at the whole band as he handed it to Lori Shigemura. Big juju ass, chocho lips Lori full of wind and smug-faced like it was hers from the moment she walked Crystal's pass across campus.

I understood the blue in "Rhapsody in Blue." I knew what rhapsody meant. I felt the color blue, *the sky through the band-room window, Punaluʻu near the reef where the water turned aqua. The sound of piano music through a closed door.*

All Mr. Hokama had to show me was the color of *my* voice in the music *I* played. Was Mr. Hokama too busy selling fund-raiser M&M's or uniforms or reeds in his office? Too busy teaching all of our fingers and mouths to play?

☾

You let an instrument pick you.

It was long, black and silver. With a voice that haunted.

☾

68

At the end of the day, my mother's fingers smell like smoke. She puts the laundry basket down and turns off the water pipe. We sit on the porch and she watches and listens to me play my clarinet. She lights another cigarette. The smoke curls in front of her eyes. When she nods her head slowly, the smoke disappears.

I wanted to hear myself play the melody. All the time. I understood the color blue. I quit the band before I learned the next song.

DOMINATE AND RECESSID
JEANS

This is what I have seen: The smoky sac with a puffy-eyed bunny inside plop onto the bed of hair my rabbit, Lani, pulled from her chest. Then Lani eating away the sac so a blunt-nosed, no ears, pink-and-black baby can breathe.

This is what I have also seen: Hokulani, Lani's daughter, in her first hutch, bite the sac, but bite the baby too, who wiggles wildly, but Hokulani keeps biting anyway, eating the baby, who dies covered with fur from her mother's chest.

This is what I have heard: On a night darker than ink, the high shrill cry of the babies, babies being stepped on by their mother on a night too black for even rabbit eyes. And I pull closer to Calhoon, who holds her blanket under her chin in deep sleep.

C

My father gave all of the rabbits to me. For me to feed pellets and water. For me to clean the cages. For me to dry and mulch the rabbit shit for fertilizer. For me to mate and breed, then sell to the pet store or put in the classified ads. For me to make lots of money to buy a bicycle with a white seat full of flowers and a white basket in front with matching plastic flowers. He promised to special-order this bike from the Sears catalogue.

And I learned from my father, who teaches me everything I know about dominate and recessid jeans. How pea flowers that are red and white make red flowers. Or white flowers. Sometimes pink. I consider this when I breed my Dutch bunnies.

Lani is black and white. Hokulani is brown and white. Clyde is black and white. It's important to make a chart of each mating to see who dominates. My babies are pure white, black and white, brown and white, buff and white, and the best, the best of all, a rare gray and white.

The gray and whites, I don't sell. I give them to only special people who love bunnies as much as I do. One to Uncle Ed's son, Ernest. One to Jerry's cousin Ingrid, who toilet-trained her gray and white to use kitty litter. And the rest, I'll build cages for them to keep and breed.

I bring them into the house to feed them snacks like lettuce or cucumber peelings, carrot peelings or celery tops. To their mothers, I feed the ti-leaf center shoots or milkweeds, pink thistles, milky sap, and all. But my babies, my beautiful babies, I bring them in the house so they get tame and don't buck or scratch when carried.

Calhoon starts a nervous twitch. She wiggles her nose and lips into a ball and moves it in a circular motion. My mother says stop bringing the bunnies into the house. Calhoon imitates the bunnies, her new twitch, a very bad habit. People will think she's retarded. I tell my mother it's because of some recessid jeans in our family history. On whose side is there a retard? She tells me to shut my stupid mouth.

Now Calhoon and me play with the bunnies on the grassy hill next to the cages. And when we see 'io circling, brown hawk wings and yellow talons overhead, we gather up our babies and hide under the lychee tree.

Cal just learned to ride her bike without her training wheels. I see her at the top of the hill and I hold my gray and white close to my face. I see her bolt down the hill. "No. NO! Brake! My rabbit cages!" I see her hit the cage and fly over the totan roofs and rabbit shit sprays out in all directions like a million flies.

This is what I hear: It's a Sunday morning. My father feeds my rabbits. "Hello, Lani. Hello, Hokulani. Hello, Clyde." He doesn't know I'm watching and listening. I copy him by talking to the rabbits when I feed them in the same gentle voice.

This is what I have seen: My father puts Clyde into Lani's cage for the breeding. He tells me that Clyde will mate Lani and now I'll have plenty new babies. Maybe a gray and white that I can put in the new cage. "Now go into the house already," he says. I walk around the garage once and go back to the cages. My father pulls the long green hose toward his anthuriums on the other side of the yard.

I see Clyde on Lani's back. Her eyes pull out of her head. His claws dig into her side. Her ears pull back and her head too as Clyde moves up and down. Clyde dominates. Lani recessids. When he's through, Lani runs to the corner of her cage very scared. She breathes hard in and out with flaring nostrils. Clyde sits there and rubs his face with his paws. *Never, never let someone dominate.*

I do not see or hear: wild dogs late that dark night steal into my yard and kill all of my rabbits. In the morning, bodies are splayed all over the yard, stretched-out rabbit bodies, broken necks and blood.

Hokulani, her eyelids translucent blue and thin, over her purple blind-looking eyes. Clyde, his mouth open. *I didn't hear them cry.* And babies all over the yard covered with purple, fat, black flies, the sound of buzzing. Lani, her fur bloodied and wet. The totan roofs are scattered and the wire cages torn open. "Can you imagine," my father says, "dog teeth tore open those wire cages."

No, I cannot imagine it.

My father says not to worry. That he'll buy for me Netherland Dwarfs, which are better rabbits than Dutch bunnies. I can start my business over again and make it better. Calhoon says she'll kill those dogs with my father's 12 gauge.

My father takes us inside. He says he'll show home movies tonight to make me feel better since I love to watch them over and over so much.

And even though the screen he bought from Kino's Second Hand Furniture Store broke, the screen that made us glitter on its diamond sandpaper surface, we can watch on the refrigerator door. He'll even buy us buttered Jiffy Pop for Cal and me to cook over the gas stove.

Tonight my father sets up his 8-millimeter camera projector. The little reels scatter on the countertop. They're dated with pieces of masking tape. This is what I see:

Calhoon doing cartwheels on the grassy hill. Her friend Yvette Benevidez doing the splits. Jerry cartwheels to the camera and does cockeyes very close to the camera. The shot cuts off. I remember my father chasing Jerry for getting silly and hitting him on the head with the camera.

When the movie continues, I'm standing over Lani's cage. I lift the rusty totan roof. Count four bunnies there. I feed them milkweeds and honohono grass.

Then I hold a gray and white. Calhoon comes running over. I see her saying, "Gimme it, gimme it," reaching her arms up to me. But I don't give it to her. She walks toward the camera, points at me, saying, though we can't hear her, *Daddy, look at Lovey.*

Look at Lovey.

This is what I hear:

The end of a film. The last shot of me holding the gray and white to my face. The white dots like white bunnies running across me, and the sad, sad sound of celluloid hitting the end reel again and again.

SUNNYSIDE UP

Twelve tiny bantam eggs all at once, all sunnyside up, until the brown lace on the edges crackles around yellow, yellow yolks. Yellower than store eggs, which Father says is because bantam eggs are fresh from the coop.

My father cooks a pot of hot rice. We put all twelve sunnyside-up eggs facedown on the hot rice. Father slurps up the egg white that hangs from his fork. I cook up more bantam eggs for my mother, who likes her yolks broken, Calhoon, who likes hers over easy, and myself. I like mine sunnyside up just like Father.

The sunlight is pink on these mornings.

Last Sunday, Father took us to Jimmy Lee's to pick out new chickens. He wants Araucanas, which lay blue-and-green eggs. Then we can have Easter eggs for breakfast every Sunday.

Araucana chickens are bigger than bantams, like regular chickens without fancy feathers on their legs. And a little uglier. But the blue-and-green eggs—I imagine them speckled in a tuft of grass, ready for finding. The Araucanas live near but not with the bantams in our yard.

Father had injected each chicken with pox vaccine. Mosquitoes had stung the red-rubbery part of their chicken faces, making them all bumpy with chicken pox. The real kind.

Father held each chicken and injected each rooster and hen with the medicine he bought from the Garden Exchange Feed Store. And he gently told them what he was doing as he poked their faces.

I saw a bantam rooster fly into the air once and spur my father on his eyelid. Blood dripped into my father's eyelashes.

The rooster that knifed him got a second chance, until the other day, when it spurred him in the ankle. Father was trying to shoo the rooster and his hens out of the garage. The cut bloodied his heel.

The rooster got this: Father, taking his wallet out of his back pocket, slowly walks up to the rooster. And WHAM! Right on the head. The rooster is stunned, so Father grabs him, ties up his legs, then hangs him upside down from the clothesline, nice leg feathers and all.

The morning turns to noon and it gets hot. The chicken tongue hangs a little out of the beak. Then it turns to night. The chicken hangs until he dies. Even in the end, Father doesn't want his chicken to die. He looks funny with the tiny Band-Aid soaked with Mercurochrome over his eye. And he walks with a slight limp for a couple of days.

Every day after breakfast my father gives his papaya rind and lots of papaya seeds to the chickens. Every day by noon the entire rind is gone. Father says one of the Araucana roosters must be pulling it off into the bushes somewhere.

This goes on for days. Calhoon finds the rinds first. Rinds, chicken bones, and pork-chop bones stuck in a hole under the aluminum shed from the Sears catalogue.

On a humid day, Father sees a huge rat, the size of a kitten, drag the rind, seeds and all, to the hole under the shed. So we set trap after trap after trap. Nothing. Nothing kills this rat, who Father says must love chicken eggs too.

Uncle Ed tells my father, "Eh, Hubert, the fuckin' rat like papaya so much, bradda, why no poison that sucka?" So simple.

I watch my father pour grass poison all over the papaya rind and some chicken bones. I smell the poison strong and pure. Father places the rind and bones under the puakenikeni tree. He keeps all the chickens in their coops. Later in the morning, the rind and bones are gone. Father and me never see the rat again.

The other night while watching *Combat* with Vic Morrow, we hear the coops being hit like wire pulling and loud chicken squawking. I grab the Eveready and run outside with Father. We see two white dogs, one huge and one medium, running from the coops. "Gunfunnit," my father yells, "goddamn Portagee dogs. No can even chain um up nighttime, shit."

This goes on for several nights. We hear loud noises, run out there, and throw a couple rocks. The dogs run off again.

Uncle Ed suggests that we get a cage from the ASPCA and "trap those fuckas, then call the dogcatcha up and he gas those suckas by Saturday. Then you teach that damn Portagee one lesson to chain up his fuckin' dogs nighttime, Hubert." My father agrees.

We set up the cage that night. We put goat meat and some broken Araucana and bantam eggs inside the cage. And we wait. The chickens cluck low and soft inside the coops. The manure smells like sour scratch. And my father chicken-clucks to his bantams and Araucanas. He seems to say, "Nothing going harm you. Nothing."

In the morning, I wear my black rubber boots to the coops in the back. "I got something! I got um!" Father yells. When I get to the cage, it's a huge tomcat.

"You mean it was a cat, Daddy?" I say.

"No. No way. Was two dogs. The two white dogs from that Portagee's yard. Gunfunnit. He neva do nuttin' to my chickens. Let um go." The cat runs straight-tailed into the honohono.

Today, Father gathers smooth stones to slingshot the dogs to death. He goes by the lychee tree and practices. He aims for the fruit and when the big red ones fall, I gather them and peel their bumpy outsides and let the juices drip down my lip. I spit the seed Clint Eastwood style like in *High Plains Drifter*. Father practices all morning.

The dogs return at eight. Father creeps up to the anthurium patch. Then closer to the kumquat tree, then SMACK! Right in the white dog's ribs. The huge one screams and they both run off. Father dances in the backyard like an elf.

The next night, both dogs return.

My father gets his pitchfork and puts a hapu'u log near the aluminum shed. "The hapu'u is those dogs," he tells me. "Watch this." Father raises the pitchfork above his head and hurls it at the hapu'u log. WHOOMP! Threads of hapu'u fly off into the grass. "Then you the backup man, okay? You stone that sucka. Here. Practice. Okay, wait." He runs to get his pitchfork.

"Okay, ready?" WHOOMP! "Stone um, stone um! Throw the rock, Lovey, you the backup man." I hurl the rock, hard as I can.

We do this again and again. His pitchfork throwing gets very accurate. Always in the head.

At night, the puakenikeni bloom. The white dogs come. Father readies his pitchfork. I hold my stones. Father steadies. He gets within range. Close. Closer. He throws.

I drop the stones to my feet.

The pitchfork breaks flesh. And a human sound of something screaming. A frenzy of legs jerking and pulling, dragging a body, and chickens squawking, hitting their bodies against the wire coops. The big white dog, brown shepherd eyes, and the concrete of the chicken yard covered with thick, purple blood. I swear, I see tears falling. I swear it.

And the sound of the pitchfork handle hitting the dog's skull. It's a small, sharp cry in the end. We never see the other white dog again.

C

The sky is pink.

Father has gathered the chicks of one of his bantam broods into a cardboard box. When the hen wants to leave, Father lifts the chicken mesh off of the box and puts a lightbulb over the box to keep the chicks warm.

One has a crooked beak. She cannot get the mash quickly enough as the others peck away wildly. He feeds her from the palm of his hand. She gets her own papaya rind and seeds. Father carries her everywhere and strokes the dark black feathers on her back. She has no name.

He lets the one with the crooked beak roost at night in the

stuffed pheasant he bought at a garage sale. "It must be comforting," he says. She greets him at the back step every morning because she belongs to no rooster strutting his hens around the yard.

The sky is pink on the morning when I watch her settle down and lay her first egg. I wash this one very carefully in the washtub outside. I carry the egg, warm in my hands, into the kitchen.

Her first egg, the one with no name, Father fries up in the big black frying pan with lots of hot Wesson oil. He fries it until the brown lace forms a crackly halo around the yellowest yolk you have ever seen. And Father eats this on hot, hot rice.

C A L H O O N   N E V E R   L I E S

Calhoon never lies. She has seen the pueo, white owl face, by the old Buddhist temple perched on the fraying electric wire. She has seen the francolin in the early morning near the cow pasture. Calhoon has watched the slow circle of the 'io above her as she flapped her arms calling him to take her in his long talons. And she never lies.

Calhoon has seen the California quail bob his feathered horn in the tall grass past the first cane field. And the Chinese ringnecked pheasant near the eucalyptus grove. "But one day," she says, "one day, you and me going see the Japanese blue pheasant."

Father loads up the Land Rover with the guns. His 12 gauge and a .410 for Calhoon and me. He says we'll hunt the wild turkey in the ohia forest past the Buddhist temple. He brings a water cooler and a breakfast of Spam sandwiches. My father never cooks the Spam.

Father says the last time he hunted the wild turkey was with bow and arrow. I remember how he roasted the tom. I remember him stuffing it with wild rice and bacon. The first bite was pure leather. I ripped it with my teeth like a savage on TV. And swallowed the wild taste of it.

I remember Father saying, "The only way for kill one wild turkey is to get um up the ass. Get in close enough and downwind so that you get um right up his ass." I plan to get my torn with a .410 today like Father says.

When we see the manure still steaming under the low branches of an ohia, Father motions for us to lower ourselves. We walk slow and soft. I want to cock my gun. Calhoon says no because she's in front of me. I think about the turkeys. I want one bad to mount and eat but I can't imagine dying such a death.

When we get to the rise, Father says, "Too late. All the damn turkeys went up the higher ridges already. Since we here, we might as well scope for wild goat instead." He tells us to have our breakfast while he scouts the area.

Calhoon and me sit on a lava hill. I tell her, "I wish I could shoot a trophy of a bird or even a bigger animal. Maybe a tanned hide for my bedspread, tail, ears, and all, and a blue feather lei like Daddy has. And I gotta be the one to kill the bird or the animal."

"You crazy," Calhoon says. "Why you like be so damn rough and tough for, Lovey? You like be like Daddy, thass why."

"Not. You dunno nothing," I tell her.

"Oh yeah? First you like be like Daddy. And then you like be haole. And then you like be like Jerry. And Katy. And now you like be one rough and tough hunter like Daddy. Why you no can just be you, hah? Why you like be something you ain't?"

I don't answer her. She's small. With a pigeon face. She gives the gun to me and eats her Spam sandwich. The wind is cool here. Up the slopes of Mauna Loa, the forests look purple. I see Father's neon-orange hunting hat poking up and down in the distance. Calhoon suddenly sits upright. "There," she says, "there by the kukui tree! A Japanese blue."

I think she's kidding me. But Calhoon never lies. "Lower yourself." I hit the ground. After I hit it, I remember it's lava and not the movies. From here, time seems to be in slow motion.

We crawl toward the kukui tree. The pheasant bobs his head. I watch him. Stop. Then Calhoon stops. I remember his deep blue chest, his face red, bright red, eyes orange, and two feather horns on his head. A neck whiter than teeth.

Aim. "No, Lovey. No!" she says to me. The bird turns and readies to fly. "No!" I hit her on the shoulder with the butt of the gun like in the movies, like in slow motion.

Calhoon rolls on the ground. She starts to cry but doesn't, because I shoot right over her body. She covers her head when she hears me fire once, then twice.

I would think a bird would cry when shot. I hear wings flapping but no other sound, dust scrambling in the sunlight of this morning.

I hurry to the bird. Calhoon watches as it shakes in the dirt. See it take a final shiver. "You killed um, Lovey. You killed um. I told you not to." She picks up my blue pheasant by the legs, then turns. "Look at um, Lovey. No more no toe claws on this pheasant. Omigod, Lovey, how come no more not one toe claw on this bird? I told you not for shoot this bird. Going come for get you, Lovey. I tried for tell you."

I take the blue pheasant to the edge of the gully and with all my might I fling it by the legs so far and so hard that I don't hear it fall. "Couldn't mount it anyway 'cause I blew off the head," I tell Calhoon, like I don't care. "And couldn't make a feather lei 'cause I blasted him in the chest."

"Omigod, Lovey," Calhoon says, "you heard um fall? Shoulda wen' fall on some branch or bushes down there. Going come for get you, Lovey. I telling you now."

I remember what I told you now when I started this. Calhoon never lies.

C

There was a stretch of eucalyptus on the old Kona road. Father, Mother, Cal, and me would drive this winding old road in Father's Land Rover. There was no moon when the shadow followed the car from the beginning of the grove till the end of the grove.

Mother snores though she'd never admit it. And me, I sleep because Father puts the backseat down and makes a nice bed for Cal and me.

Calhoon sees it. And Father too. Always this way, just the two of them. The shadow, huge and black, that flies alongside the car, black wings and light for eyes.

C

There is a lady in the sugarcane in my back yard. A lady with long white hair, a flowing dress, and no lower body. Father sees her while watering the anthuriums late in the evening, watching him.

A lady who rests in the corners of my house in the room way down at the end of the hall. Calhoon never sleeps in the end room. "Ever since she was one baby," Mother says, "she point to the corners of the room and tell, 'The lady, the lady.' "

Calhoon saw her once when she was in the end room listening to Stanley Robello fight with his new Japanee girlfriend next door. "I turn off the light and sneak to the window like we always do," Calhoon says, "and see Stanley's shadow hit the girl's shadow. The girl, she cover her face, and Stanley screaming, 'You fucka, you fucka, you fucka.'

"Something make my eyes look down below the window, and when I do, there's the lady, her long white hair pin in a bun. She staring up at me with white face and red, red lips."

This is the lady who pushes at Cal's bed and pulls her futon. Sometimes the lady pulls Father's futon and he yells, "Okay, okay, I coming. It's babachan calling me," he says, "to put obake anthurium on her grave."

Father takes photographs of red cardinals. The bird babachan became when she died. And Cal and me are never to shoot red cardinals that eat the papayas outside anymore. Babachan, the red cardinal, came to the funeral and then to the burial and ate the persimmons Father left on the grave.

My friend Blue says his mother, when she died, was a ring-necked turtledove who sat on the fence by his house. Came every day with his father, the bigger turtledove and his tutu, the smaller one.

The lady in our house sleeps back to back with Calhoon.

"I not scared," she says.

I am.

C

There was a night we sat on the roof of our house and watched the Fourth of July fireworks down at Coconut Island near the bay front. This was the night Calhoon slept in the room at the end of the hall.

It was 2 a.m. She says, "When the lady wake me up nowadays, my eyes just open by themself like I stay wide awake. So I look at the door, Lovey, and I see like one cloud, but this cloud, I can see right through, you know, and hang there long time, so I rub both eyes. Then something suck um up into the ceiling like one up-wards drain and the whole cloud spin out of our house.

"She used to be one bird. One big white bird with long talons that can pry your eyes open but not sore." I tell her to go back to sleep and we both dream about a white-faced bird on the tele-phone wire across our front yard.

Now remember that Calhoon never lies.

I put a cross in my room. I tell Mother to make her shut up. Stop telling all these strange stories. I tell Father, who says she's telling the truth. Grandma calls and decides to pray. Our neigh-bor Katy comes over with Charlie Bubbles and her husband, Jef-frey, and they pop fireworks Chinese style for good luck and to scare the lady away. Even if it's not New Year's.

Katy says she'll bring Charlie over for the night and sleep with me in the living room if I want, when Jeffrey goes down to King's Landing to camp on Saturday. Nobody's home at her house anyways since her mother and father went to Las Vegas.

And even if Charlie still gets up three times a night, I tell Katy okay and she comes over with a laundry basket full of bottles, diapers, clothes, and blankets. We camp out, me, Katy, and Cal-hoon, on the living-room floor.

I don't see it or hear it.

Katy says Calhoon is right. At about 2 a.m., "Charlie get up, so Cal wen' get me the bottle from you guys' refridge. So he suck couple times like he always do and Calhoon, she take the bottle out slow kine and put um down next to her. I promise, I neva did see this kine before, but something was sucking Charlie's bottle. Eh, was going in and out, the nipple, and had for-real sucking sounds. So Calhoon, she pick up the bottle and give um to me, so I put um down by me this time. And one more time, something stay sucking the bottle, so me, I get all nuts, right? I wen' fly that bottle against you guys' back door.

"You snore just like your madda, Lovey."

☾

Father takes photographs of red cardinals. A lot of them and he orders the wooden carving of red cardinals from the Walter Drake catalogue. He makes a few watercolor paintings of a red cardinal on a papaya tree, a red cardinal eating persimmons on the grave. Father enlarges some of the photos and frames them. He tapes some to the wall. All over my room.

When the lady wakes me up, I see her in the cross above my bed, the cross that I put on the wall to protect me, the lady hanging in the cloud of smoke that I can see through. I know it's her though I cannot see a face, a shadow, or light for eyes.

I look at Calhoon and her eyes open by themselves. Wide-open eyes that know to look at the cross on the wall. Eyes that look, stare, don't blink, and know. She looks at me slowly. "You shouldn't have kill the Japanese blue, Lovey. I told you. I told you not to. You shoulda just been you, not somebody you ain't." Calhoon presses her back to mine. "Now you get one lady too. She came for get you just like I said. But yours no more claws, remember, Lovey? The bird you wen' shoot, neva have claws. Maybe your lady no pry your eyes open in the middle of the night. No going be sore, Lovey. No scared."

Maybe she always leave my eyes alone.

WILD MEAT AND THE
BULLY BURGERS

Sheep stew smells up the whole house. Like the mornings when my father starts boiling tripe. But sheep stew stinks worse. Even if rubbed in salt, garlic, and grated ginger, then soaked in lemon juice, he cannot kill the smell of the meat, like wet wool boiling. And the wildness of it.

Father and Calhoon watch the pot after he plops in the can of Campbell's tomato soup, waiting for it to come to a boil. Then they eat a huge saimin-bowlful of sheep stew with hot rice. I skip lunch and dinner.

Same with sheep burgers. I help my father grind the sheep meat with the meat cranker, which squeezes out fat fingers of ground sheep. Round, long coils of meat and gristle into the glass Pyrex bowl. Father will cook sheep burgers tonight, and if we're lucky, he'll mix it with store-bought ground beef.

Calhoon takes a long piece of goat jerky in her pants pocket when we go out to feed the chickens tonight. I watch her tear a piece with her hind teeth. Father dries the meat in his aku-drying box with a screen to keep out the flies. He tells Calhoon not to eat it raw since goats have worms. But she doesn't listen. She sucks the stringy strands of goat meat until all the juice is gone. Right out of the drying box.

And smoke pig. Father cooks this well in lots of oil with pepper and shoyu to kill all the germs. He cannot kill the wild taste, but Uncle Ed and Gabriel Moniz sit with him in the garage, drink beers, and eat the smoke pig.

I hear Mr. Moniz tell my father about deer hunting on Moloka'i. That he shot a doe and when he got there, "she was crying, Hubert, I no joke you, brah, crying like one goddamn baby. Nah, like one goddamn wahine, so I had to put her outta her misery. Me, I no can stand for see things suffa, know what I mean, eh? So I tole my bradda Stanley, 'Eh, brah, I gotta put her outta her misery.' So I went up to her head right between the eyes, brah, and wen' shoot um and you know what, Hubert, all the fuckin' brains wen' shoot out and stuck on my glasses, and all blood and brains all over my face except where had my glasses, brah."

Everyone laughs. And drinks beer. And eats smoke pig.

The venison from Mr. Moniz tastes good, though. It's the only wild meat that I enjoy. My father grates ginger and puts in green onion with shoyu and mirin. And lots of roasted sesame seeds. He soaks it overnight, and the next day I help him weave the thin strips of meat onto bamboo sticks and we hibachi it.

Once my father cooked turtle meat and said it was steak. It tasted like fishy chicken. He never tells us when he changes the meat. I can only tell by a faint smell in the kitchen. Yesterday's fishy-chicken smell turned out to be frog legs. And rabbit also tasted like chicken, though he never tells us.

Today my father brings home a black-and-white calf. Father,

Gabriel Moniz, and Uncle Ed put together their money to buy this calf for meat. The black-and-white calf, with round brown eyes and crying so loud that Calhoon and me see his fat black tongue. Cal and me pet him. He cries all day and all night for two days.

Calhoon names him Bully, and Father says, "Don't name him. Don't you dare call him that. We going eat um and how you going eat if you name him?" But every day now, Calhoon and me go to play with Bully. Cal with her goat jerky and me with my handful of milkweeds.

"Gimme it, gimme it," says Calhoon as she shoves the jerky into her mouth. She pets Bully first, who begins jumping up and down, up and down with his big black hoofs, and stomps Cal on her toes. She screams, grits her teeth, and punches the rusted car we have Bully tied to. Her toenail turns black in a few days.

Pretty soon, my father starts clearing the honohono grass on the other side of the lychee tree for Bully to eat. Lots of honohono that he cuts with his cane knife. And me, I give him the whole ti leaf. What I like most is the sound of Bully eating and the way a cow smiles. I also like his smell.

Father tells us that Gabriel Moniz will be taking Bully to the pasture behind his house since it's larger with lots of honohono and California grass. Some guava and waiwi on the side and lots of ti leaf. I tell Cal that they'll kill Bully soon. They want to make Bully nice and fat and want us to forget him. She says she'll never forget Bully and runs outside. I see her cut some of Bully's tail hair. She comes inside and wraps thread from the sewing chest around the hair. She puts it in her pocket.

It takes Mr. Moniz, Uncle Ed, Katy's husband Jeffrey, stupid

Ernest, Larry, and my father to tie Bully's four legs together and lift him into Uncle Ed's Ford truck. Lots of swearing from everyone. And Bully crying, not like a baby, but like a grown man.

Cal hits the toes of her rubber boots in the dirt harder and harder. All the men shake hands and pat each other hard on the back. *We can't help him.* And they drive away.

My father never lets Calhoon and me see Bully again. Not even to visit or say hi with some milkweeds or ti leaves. "How you going eat the delicious steaks and veal cutlets I going cook for you? I told you no name him." Father keeps saying this over and over to us.

On Friday night, I hear this story. Father, Uncle Ed, and Gabriel Moniz are drinking beer in the garage. Gabriel tells the story.

"So this damn Hubert, he bring his .22 Mag my house and tell me, 'Here, Gabriel, you go shoot Bully.'

"Nah, nah, I stay telling him, you do um, gunfunnit, Hubert. I no like kill the cow.

" 'Nah, go, Gabriel,' this bugga telling me, 'I no can kill Bully, I mean, the cow—was my house too long.'

"What you mean too long? I tell him.

" 'Here, you shoot um. C'mon,' he tell. 'Thass half yo' cow.' Then this Hubert, he keep pushing the gun at me, so I take um. Then I ask this bugga how I going kill um and he tell me, 'I dunno, Gabriel. Just do um, gunfunnit. No ask me questions. I dunno. Go shoot um right between the eyes. Shit, just kill um. I no care.'

"So me, I walk toward the cow, get grass hanging out his mouth still yet, and next thing I turn around, Hubert, he stay running behind the house. Gunfunnit this bugga, whassamatta you, Hubert, I stay yelling. I betchu wen' cova your ears and close your eyes, eh, you bas-ted you. Me, I neva like shoot um but I wen' close my eyes and blass um right between the eyes."

Calhoon closes the window. She falls on our bed and pulls out the Bully hair from under her pillow. She sweeps it over her lips.

C

Father made hamburger for us tonight. With real hamburger buns and OreIda crinkle-cut fries baking in the oven. And a plate of tomatoes, lettuce, and Maui onions sliced real thin. A bowlful of pitless olives. And the mayo, relish, ketchup, and mustard all on the table.

Father stands over the frying pan with hot oil jumping up and onto the stovetop. He folds a paper towel and puts it on a plate. With the spatula he presses the burger patties down as if to make them well done, then places them on the plate. The oil spreads out brownish red on the paper towel.

There is a faint smell in the kitchen.

Calhoon fixes up her hamburger all the way Big Mac. Me, I don't fancy mine up too much. I put lots of olives on my plate. Father watches this and says cheerfully, "C'mon, Lovey, eat up." Father even says we can have dinner on the coffee table and watch TV.

The first bite tastes strange. Not sheep or goat. To me like honohono grass. To Cal like guavas and waiwi. She puts her hamburger down. "This is a Bully burger, isn't it, Daddy?" She swallows hard. My father looks at her for a long time, then puts his hamburger down too. I see Father's first bite—a large lump that slides slow and fat down his throat.

Tonight, nobody eats. Nobody cleans the kitchen. The faint smell in there stays. Father will boil some saimin later on and fry two eggs and Vienna sausage. He'll put it in big saimin bowls for Calhoon and me and give us strawberry Nehi. We don't have to drink our milk tonight. We eat later on without speaking in front of the TV. Father, Calhoon, and me.

☾

———

TWO

———

WHAT LOVE IS

He's a boy who acts like a girl.

I'm a girl with not *one* girl friend.

He has no boy friends.

People say we make a strange pair. We *match*. Some say we should get married someday. They don't know what Jerry and me got going.

Some girls at school tease us: "When's the wedding? Lovey be the groom and Jerry be the bride. They should be May Day King and Queen, but they going fight for be queen, get it, *queen*?"

The Japanee girls snicker at Jerry and me when they pass by us. Or they say, "Cute *couple,* yeah them. She no mo' friends, that's why. Look her clothes. Look her bag. All dead the rabbit fur. *Omigod.* And, Jerry, you *IT,* you *shim,* we go trade stickas and erasas for all your *pink* foldas."

Lori Shigemura, a popular Japanee girl, likes Jerry.

She always says, "Eh, Lovey, what you said about my *friend,* Jerry? Watch what you say 'cause what you figga, he your *only* friend. No eva, eva let her forget that." Then back to me: "You *lucky* he even *let* you hang around with him. Right, Jerry?" And Jerry sometimes says, "Nah," to back me up small kind.

I got no friends. Nobody. I only got Jerry.

"You cannot let men know how much you need um. Otherwise they step all ova your face, spit on you, and leave you bleeding, fo' all they care." My Aunty Bing, nine years older than me. "Hate to bust yo' bubbles but best you know."

But Jerry's all I got.

I used to be friends with Natalie Lynn Deems in the second grade. She was the only haole in our class. They lived in the house across from school with a twisted aluminum front door with ripped screen and two German shepherd dogs that slept on Natalie Lynn's bed. Then she moved without last-day cupcakes for the whole class like when Patricia Aoki left our school. I was seven years old.

I still had Jerry even if he was into scrounging Icee points for a six-inch fan for his Kool-Aid stand.

This year like last year, I get all the boys in my low math class. They grab the sunflower seeds outta Jerry's bag and I try to kick them in the balls.

"Yeah, you stupid macho ducks on Pop Warner teams," I tell them, "short legs, long body, middle-comb-hair Japs. When you grow up, I betchu make mustache too. Leave my friend alone."

Lunchtime Jerry always makes home lunch so we don't have to eat in the caf. He makes a sub sandwich every day. Lots of mayo, fried egg with takuan and furikake. We take turns taking a bite, the bigger the better, and we fight when the other person takes too big a bite. And we laugh and laugh at each other's seaweed teeth, no matter if everybody looks when we bust out rolling and punching each other's arms.

In the fifth grade, Jerry used to go with this girl from Japan. That *Thing* was his girlfriend. They traded stickers and erasers.

Never mind that Jerry knew that she had the biggest sticker collection this side of Tokyo before he *went* with her. Never mind that she gave Jerry so many Little Twin Star pencils, tablets, pencil cases, and erasers that he filled a whole shoebox. Never mind that she could read Japanese and tell Jerry what all the trashy articles said about Kenji Sawada so he could catch his thrills. Never mind that she was ugly, moon-face, and stuck-up. Never mind that he made himself a slut for stickers.

I wasn't jealous.

It's not about that with Jerry and me.

She wrote Jerry some letters, which I read. And she gave him all the pinup pictures of Japan singing stars like Saijo Hideki and Go Hiromi and Agnes Chan. Junko gave Jerry every single 45, pinup, wallet-size, and album of Kenji Sawada, also known as *Julie*. I liked *Julie* too.

I wanted him back. Back as my best friend.

This past summer, Jerry wanted me to go with Jenks. Jenks got the biggest one and he kind of loves me. But that ain't love. Not to me anyway.

Sometimes I watch the seventh- and eighth-grade couples by the lockers on the upper campus at lunchtime. The boy on the railing and the girl between his legs.

And how they walk each other to class when the bell rings. And that long kiss goodbye. Jerry's older brother, Larry, says that's love and Jerry and me don't know shit.

Nobody knows what to call what me and Jerry got 'cause nobody's done it before. All the girls pretending to hate the boys. All the boys pretending to hate the girls. But you see it on their folders and on their desks and on the side of each finger, they write the name of the one they love.

C

A list of all the things they call us:

Queers or queens.

Boyfriend and girlfriend.

Fag and lez or fag and hag.

"Not even true, stupid morons, dunno shit from flies. Come here and say that to my face so I can kill you," I yell back, "you short Jap, fat lips, Okinawan peanut."

I'll tell you what love is. Jerry and me in the Kress store. We bought matching T-shirts to wear to school. Says "Keep On Truckin' Mighty Viks." I bought french fries from the fountain, and Jerry bought a large strawberry Icee from the candy store across the street, for the Icee and the Icee points. I made the ketchup sauce with some mustard and pepper. Then we found a booth in the farthest corner 'cause sometimes the waitress forgets to clean the table. We steal the change. Then we mix the french fries left on the plates with the fresh ones we just bought. Some old haole lady with twinkie hair didn't finish her lunch.

After we eat, we walk to the fabric section and run our hands over every piece of material. When we grow up, we want forest-green velvet or velour furniture.

We walk to the bus stop wearing each other's rubber slippers.

C

Jerry and me love David Cassidy. *Tiger Beat* magazine and Donny O. in glittery purple socks, a mouth full of teeth. And Bobby Sherman. Easy come, easy go after he makes a girl named Sheila pregnant. They aren't even married, so we stop liking him. *Tiger Beat* runs the picture of Bobby and Sheila in the hospital bed with the new baby.

Jerry and me lie on his bed and we flip through the pages to see who we love. And we cut the pinups and paste them on the wall. And B. J. Thomas singing "Raindrops keep fallin' on ma head," the record I crack when Jerry's big brother, Larry, smashes me against the closet the other day. Jerry and me take a couple of his Hot Wheels and smash them on the sidewalk when Larry goes to baseball practice.

Jerry and me take his mother's permanent laundry pen and autograph pinups in *Tiger Beat*. I go *To Jerome, Alwayz, Maureen McCormick.* Or *Jere, Luv Ya, Cher.* I make the C real big and loopy. Jerry takes the boys. *Lovey, Love You, Baby, Jay O.* or *Lovey, Never Can Say Goodbye, Jermaine J.* I make mine the best, though. I say things like *Dearest Jerry, To my most adorable fan. Livingly and Lovingly, Susan Dey/Laurie Partridge.*

When we practice our Donny and Marie act, Jerry's brother and his friends groan and swear, "Aw, fuck this shit, man. Beat it. Fuck, get these two clowns outta here." Jerry's mother forces them to listen to us sing, makes them turn off the TV, and pisses them off, as I sing, "I'm a little bit o' country," and Jerry belts, "And I-ma little bit-a rock 'n' roll."

Jerry and me laugh and run to his room and laugh some more

and lie down together and dangle our feet together and eat homemade punch-syrup pops made in the Tupperware pops maker that Jerry's mother bought from Aunt Helen. We look at *Tiger Beat*. We figuring who Donny Osmond or David Cassidy would like better. Jerry or me.

Jerry is very thin and tall. I'm kind of short and fat. Whenever my mother puts me on a diet, Jerry gives me the last bite of whatever he was eating. Like a Dilly Bar or Mr. Misty.

Today, Jerry says that he thinks that David C. would rather have someone skinny. I say, "So what you trying for say, Jerry? So what if you skinny? Who cares? David C. probably want one girl, not one boy. And one girl but so what? David C. probably wants one haole girl anyway, not two Japs like us. And for sure not one *boy*, a *guy*, get it, Jere, you're one *boy* and David don't want you."

Jerry says nothing. So I go on. "If I was haole, twenty, skinny, and blond, I might be the perfect girl. And I get more chance 'cause I one girl."

Then Jerry says, if he were a girl, haole, twenty, and blond that he'd be perfect.

We put David's poster on the wall today. We both enter the "Come to Hollywood and Be David's Dream Date." See a taping of *The Partridge Family*. Second prize, all the Partridge Family record albums and a phonograph. Third prize, an official Partridge Family tambourine. We really want third prize.

I don't think I'll ever *meet* a movie star. Jerry says one day he'll *be* a movie star.

I say, "Yeah, right, fat chance. No Japs on TV except Mrs. Livingston and Kay-to. You'll *never* find your flat face in any magazine. Not in no movie or no TV. No Japs nowhere but here. Dream on, Nancy Kwan."

Jerry turns to the wall. I look at his back and his shiny black hair. Want to tell him something. Something about me busting his bubbles. Busting my best friend. Like someone who doesn't care.

LESSONS

---

*N*umber *One: Never eat the last anything, Spam, Portagee sausage, or fried chicken drumette, or you'll be pulverized.* We're talking peel your face off the floor, don't move till Jerry's brother Larry gets way out of sight, and say sorry as many times as you can, to which Larry'll say, "Love means you never have to say you're sorry," and you better not laugh.

(

Number Two: Don't stare at Larry. Not even from the corner of your eye or he'll say, "What the fuck you staring at, queer? No look at me, man, no look at me, 'cause I can't stand the stinkness of your eye. Eh, what I said? What I said?" And by this time you have your chin pushed into your chest, your eyes closed tight, fists clenched, and then Larry slaps your head.

(

Number Three: Never sleep on Larry's bed. Well, who would want to? It smells like ten years of unwashed blankets. But don't or he'll kick your ass to kingdom come. But somehow Larry seems to know the shape of his smelly body versus the shape of your body or ass if you sat on his bed. Then he'll accuse you of touching pictures of his girlfriend, Crystal, after which he'll hold you up against the closet by your neck and tell you never to touch Crystal, that's his job and don't you ever forget it.

C

Number Four: Never, never, never HOING Larry or risk broken bones or near-death experience.

HOING is an expression Jerry made up. He uses it in many situations like you make a very stupid mistake but want to appear innocent. Like oops.

Jerry and me ate the last hamburger patty that Larry was going to eat for breakfast. Luckily Crystal's there, so when Jerry HOINGs after Larry asks, "Who ate the last goddamn hamburger?" Larry doesn't bruise Jerry's arm.

Jerry HOINGs by putting his index finger into his cheek. He makes his eyes big like a fish and makes his lips into a tight doughnut. At the same time, he yells out, "HOING!"

HOING also happens like this. My mother doesn't want to buy us Fig Newtons at the superette. As she pushes the shopping cart away from the cookie aisle, Jerry and me do a HOING behind her back. Calhoon also started HOINGing, but this time she tells on Jerry and me, which ends up in us getting slapped on the head in the car. My mother says, "Don't you dare HOING me in public."

Jerry causes Uncle Ed's beer to spill the other Friday all over the poker table. HOING.

Calhoon falls off of her bike after running over Jerry's Pan Am bag. HOING.

The Land Rover can't start. My mother hits the wheel because now we can't get to school. HOING.

I always laugh when he does this, which makes him do it more. And everyone else gets mad. Especially Larry.

Crystal calls on the phone. Jerry drops the receiver. He says "HOING" into the phone and Larry punches his ear.

The other day, Jerry and me were listening to records on his phonograph. Jeremiah was a Boo-frog and Chirpa-chirpa-cheep-cheep. Then Jerry says, "Let's listen to Larry's 'In-A-Gadda-Da-Vida,'" which we know he doesn't want us to touch.

Jerry places the record on the phonograph and we switch it to 33⅓ speed. We hear Larry saying, "Wait, Crystal, I gotta get my jacket."

"Oh no, Jerry," and just as Larry comes into the room, Jerry whacks the phonograph and the needle slides across the record.

"That's MY Iron Butterfly record," yells Larry. Jerry's stunned but he HOINGs and looks at me, which is my signal to HOING also, which I do, and we start to laugh hysterically out of fear. "You two goddamn peckerheads. Yeah, you like HOING, shit, I give you something to HOING about," and he grabs both my and Jerry's index HOING finger.

"Owee, oweeee. Leggo, Larry, leggo."

"Go ahead, peckers, HOING some mo'."

He twists our fingers and our knees buckle under us. Twirling by the HOING finger, both of us, I try to kick Larry. Jerry tries to punch him in the balls. I see Jerry's face twisting, his eyes squeezed shut. I hear like chicken bones, the cartilage part, cracking. "Larry, Larry, sorry, sorry," I scream. "Help, help." But he doesn't let go.

Jerry's mouth falls open but no scream comes out. Larry laughs that very sinister laugh of a person who enjoys seeing others in pain.

Here comes Crystal. "Lawrence. LAWRENCE! Stop it! Please, let them go."

Larry lets us go and we drop to the ground. Both of us wriggling like brittle stars when you lift the rocks off of them in the tidal pools. "They ain't HOINGing for a long time. Wait till I tell Ma, Jerome. She gonna thank me."

It's true. My mother, my father, Jerry's mother, Jerry's father, even Uncle Ed and Aunt Helen will thank Larry. Jerry wipes a tear from his eye.

I hold my finger. It looks crooked. I wonder whose bones cracked, mine or Jerome's. He brings vanilla popsicles from the freezer. "Here, eat this fast. We need the sticks," he says. So we bite them even if we normally suck them and try to be the last to finish to make the other guy jealous.

Then we go to the bathroom, where Jerry rinses all four popsicle sticks. He straightens out my finger and puts a popsicle stick on each side. Then he wraps it with Band-Aids. My finger feels better. I do the same for him.

Jerry and me sit on the punee in the playroom but don't turn on the TV. We just sit there. This is the last time Jerry and me ever HOINGed.

C

Number Five: How to swear. We're talking every dirty word and every combination of dirty words. For example, the combination of the words *fuck, fungus,* and *ass.* Jerry and me have been called fucking fungus assholes, ass wipes, fucka fungos with asinine fungusitis of the fucking ass extinct fungasaurus, do you want this piece of fungus grown from Jerry's ass to be shoved up your fucking tightly fungus cultured asshole too?

C

Number Six: How to spit like a real man, thick tobacco juice, Jerry and me, and to say, "Dance, asshole, dance," as Larry spurts the brown liquid at our feet. Someone starts to whistle the Mexican Hat Dance faster and faster till Larry laughs and farts at the same time, making him miscue and spit the tobacco juice all over Jerry's legs, which is what he intended to do in the first place.

C

Number Seven: You gotta rule what you can when you can or to someday rule that tree house.

Larry's tree house is made from leftover lumber. The ladder

to the tree house is driftwood. The roof, aluminum and rusty totan. Boards with nails sticking up all over the ground below the tree house. Only Larry, Ernest, Dwayne, and Dwayne's brother, Jenks, have the map. Larry nails a sheep skull to the tree that he got from the taxidermist shop downtown. And a sign in red spray paint that says: KEEP OUT THIS MEAN U JERRY.

No one dares to go there anyway. On New Year's, while Jerry and me play sparklers in the front yard, Larry, Ernest, Dwayne, and Jenks catch toads in the backyard and stick Duck brand firecrackers up their asses to blow them up. Then they tie a string to the legs and a stone to the other end and fly the toads over the branches near their tree house. Now there's about twenty dry toads hanging there. They know Jerry's scared of toads.

Whenever Jerry has to burn rubbish, he runs across his backyard with the trash can and screams all the way. When Jerry lights the rubbish, we do the Toad Dance around the fire to protect us on our way back to the house and to protect against warts. Jerry had one on his finger once. Larry called him Warticus the brother of Spartacus. Next time, we'll dance to curse him for all that he's done to us. May his tree house break and his "In-A-Gadda-Da-Vida" record warp.

On Friday night, poker night for the adults inside, Larry, Ernest, Dwayne, and Jenks camp in the tree house. They take the Coleman lantern, their army sleeping bags, some mosquito punks, potato chips, and Coca-Cola. I see a *Playboy* magazine but Jerry says don't tell. It's his father's. That night, we put on a lot of Off! and go out to the tree house with Jerry's father's pen flashlight.

We hear Larry say, "I heard something. Asshole, Jerry, beat it. Goddammit, we know thass you." I see the red tip of a cigarette glow, then fade in the blackness.

"Ha-la, Larry smoking cigarettes. I going tell your mother right now. They smoking cigarettes," I say to Jerry.

I look up. The toads on the strings look like ghost fingers. And a swarm of mosquitoes, I mean like a swarm of angry bees on the cartoons, surround Jerry and me. All over my face like spiderwebs and buzzing wings. "Run for it," Jerry says. But not before Larry and Dwayne bean our heads with rotten mangoes and stones. "Tell, you fricken squealers, and we shove this rotten mangoes down your fat throats." The boys in the tree house laugh so hard, the whole mango tree shakes.

Jerry and me run so fast that I step on a toad and hear it pop. Jerry throws the pen flashlight in the air and screams. He starts to cry. White slime and wart blobs—all on my foot. I see it bubbling and growing right in front of my eyes.

My mother and Jerry's mother come to the back door. They hold their poker hands. "What the heck is going on? Gunfunnit, you two damn troublemakers," my mother yells.

"Leave Larry alone," Jerry's mother says. "What did I tell you? That's HIS tree house. You hear me? Go play in the playroom." *Twack. Twack.* Jerry gets his head slapped twice. *Twack.* Me once.

C

My Dream: to jerome. fr. lovey. No let no one read. To someday rule that tree house.

The Dream: To get in there with mop, broom, Pine-Sol, and Clorox and clean it. To remove the sheep skull and put a Home, Sweet Home sign. To remove the KEEP OUT THIS MEAN U JERRY and put a Visitors Welcome sign. To someday be its queen and Jerry its king. To plant anthuriums around the base. Cut a few branches on top of the mango tree to let sunlight in.

Jerry and me leave the playroom. We hide the Vicks, the Campho-Phenique, and the calamine lotion. I know that the swarm of mosquitoes got Larry them next, and they're being eaten alive out there, but they stay in the tree house to be macho. Our mothers, fathers, Aunt Helen, and Uncle Ed play poker in the living room. Jerry and me go to the bathroom and scrub my foot with Ajax to prevent warts.

We go outside and light the rubbish fire. Do the Toad Dance to protect us against warts, to place a curse on Larry, to protect us on our way back.

BOLOHEAD MALIBU BARBIE
AND MARSH PEN MALIBU KEN

Barbie and Ken used to live in a shoebox in my closet. They don't live there anymore. Beautiful Malibu Barbie and handsome Malibu Ken with their blond-white hair and tan faces, their bumblebee sunglasses perched on tall noses and miniature blue towels to lie on the sand.

I gave my Barbie pierce ears with the sewing pin from my mother's Singer chest. White sewing pin ball earrings looked nice on tan skin. Then Barbie's plastic ears started to turn black and blue.

Today, Jerry says to me how come my Malibu Barbie got bruises on her ear around her earrings. I tell him I don't know but I'm sick because I wrecked my perfect blond Barbie.

Jerry watches as I stand Barbie on my jewelry box. She's wearing the pink feathers robe I bought from Kress. Underneath she has on her one-piece baby-blue swimsuit. And Barbie twirls midair because at the same time I open up the jewelry box and "A Time for Us" plays. Jerry holds Ken, who waits for Barbie to take off her robe.

I tell Jerry let's Ajax the bathroom sink, then fill it with water and make pool party with the miniature iced-tea pitcher and tray. But even at our best pool parties, I never wet Barbie's hair. She and Ken sit halfway wet in the pool. You can't ever wet her hair.

You should see the Midge and Skipper whose hair we wet. All matted and frizzy now, the two most ugliest dolls alive. Not silky blond smooth like Barbie. "Lucky thing we tried it out on Midge and Skipper 'cause they mostly just sit on the side and no say nothing anyways," I tell Jerry, and he agrees, because they look damn ugly, like two Puerto Rican sisters from down the street with absolutely no relation to Malibu Barbie and Ken.

But Ken doesn't really matter, because he had a plastic head and a stupid smile to begin with. One time I put baby oil on his head before him and Barbie went to the drive-in movies in their shoebox living room turned automobile.

Somehow Jerry doesn't play Barbies right. Jerry makes Ken say dumb things to Barbie, like "Barbie, honey, what are you cookin' for dinner? I hope it's some mashed potatoes with roast beef, babe," with a real pretend-talk-haole accent, or "Barbie, sweet cakes, let's watch us *The Carol Burnett Show* in our PJs." Or "Gee whiz, Muffins, did ya see my house slippers? I left them right by the telly." It's not even a real TV, just a matchbox with a picture of Cassius Clay that Jerry pasted on.

Then he makes Ken ooof Barbie. Lie on top of Barbie and go ooof, ooof, ooof, three times usually, and then kiss a real big one, which makes me sick, because Jerry wants me to make Barbie turn upside down while he makes the smooching sound.

But I gotta let him play. He's been stealing all kinds of Barbie clothes from his cousin Ingrid. She's rich, with her own playhouse outside. I mean she has real Barbie store-bought clothes. Pants suits, bell-bottoms, matching boots, high heels, red leather jacket, and sequins wedding gown. All mine now.

Before, mine had only handmade halter tops where if you saw them you could see all the stitching. And the string would keep breaking, so Barbie's plastic boobs kept getting shown to Ken at the oddest times, if you know what I mean. That's all I had was the halter tops, sarongs, and the one-piece baby-blue swimsuit.

C

Larry was in my room when Jerry and me were watching *The Odd Couple* and I figured no big deal, right, because Jerry and me always go in Larry and Jerry's room when I go over to their house.

Then Larry comes out all happy and smiling. So I go to my room to see what he did. And what I see, I die right there. My perfect Malibu Barbie all bald with crew cut, I mean every strand of hair cut off bolohead. Only Ken had hair because his was plastic and perfect to begin with but Larry gives him marsh pen fuzz and underarm hair. And Ken only had a lump for balls before, but Larry draws in real-looking balls and a dingding with the black marsh pen.

But Barbie, she looks so prisoner-of-war with her tan face, beautiful smile, and crew cut. And worst of all, Larry draws nipples on Barbie and a chingching with fuzz, bushy underarm hair, and a goatee.

I don't even move. Larry shoves Jerry out of the way as he

laughs down the hallway, "Stupid silly muffies, *gooood* for you, your Barbies all wasted."

Jerry says nothing.

C

Later on, Jerome says sorry for Larry and tells me that this will be a day he'll never forget. Me too, I tell him. That maybe now him and me, we better be smarter than Larry. Don't let him or nobody else know how much we really love Malibu Barbie and Malibu Ken. Maybe we should act on the outside like we like brunet-head Francie or Miko the Oriental Barbie. Maybe we should act like we like Hot Wheels and Larry'll destroy those instead of what we really like, you know?

And we don't know what to do next really, except to take Ken to the bathroom to Ajax his fuzz, his balls, and underarms and hope Larry didn't use the permanent laundry marsh pen.

He did.

So Jerome and me, we put all of them in their best clothes. Barbie in her wedding gown with the veil and white heels. Ken in the maroon velvet tuxedo with the black shoes. Midge in the mod hiphuggers with tie top, boots, and leather-fringe handbag. Skipper in the cowpoke outfit with real felt hat with "Skip" on top.

Then Jerome and me, we stuff the nicely dressed bolohead Barbie, frizzy hair Skipper and Midge, and marsh pen fuzz, balls, and underarms Ken into the shoebox turned coffin, stuff them in the very back of my closet.

117

A FISHBOWL AND
SOME DIMES

The rich people in Hilo live on Reed's Island.

Across the bridge over the muddy Wailuku River.

Jerry decides that we'll trick-or-treat there this year. Every year I'm an Indian princess. I cut my father's T-shirt at the bottom and shred the sleeves. Then I paint it with leftover house paint from the shed. My mother always lets me have her flattened lipsticks and I dig my finger into the red wax and put it on my cheeks like war paint. Jerry braids my hair into two ponytails. He always says how real I look. Like the social studies book picture of squaws.

Jerry stole real leather strips from his shop teacher for the braids and real Revlon rouge and peacock-blue eye shadow for me from Woolworth's. But this year my mother took an art class. She made for me a papier-mâché mask. She used Uncle Steven's basketball as a mold.

The mask is blue with red circles around the two eyes and yellow around the mouth. She says I have to wear it with my striped turtleneck and a white sheet. She wants to enter the mask in this year's 5th Annual Hilo Shopping Center Halloween Costume Contest with me in it.

Jerry is a bear. His mother made for him a costume from head to toe with furry brown fabric from Kress store. All I can see is Jerry's face. He carries his long tail in one hand and his pillowcase for candy in the other. I tell him how cute I think he looks. Like a real bear. He already knows it.

I tell him maybe I would've stolen some black pipe cleaners from Ben Franklin five-and-ten if I knew he was going to be a bear this year. Jerry says never mind 'cause he's going to win the ten-dollar first place for sure anyways.

C

The houses on Reed's Island look like *Gone with the Wind* or like the sugar plantation owners' houses on the cliffs above the Big Island Sugar Company mill. They have big shower trees in their yards. Jerry's mother tells us to hurry because we have only half an hour before the costume contest. Mr. Biggs *allows* Jerry's mother and my mother to wait at the *bottom* of his driveway. "And please don't leave any of your trash around, ladies," he says. "Mahalo." Like he's a kamaaina or something, but he's just another rich haole.

I don't know why Jerry wants to trick-or-treat here. I mean everyone knows that all the house lots kids get dropped off by the truckload at the Reed's Island bridge 'cause they give real chocolate here and not that cheap black-and-orange candy wrapped in waxed paper.

And everybody says the next day in school if you have choco-late in your bag, "Ho, brah, went Reed's Island, eh? I seen you, brah. You was the ghost?" And all the Reed's Island kids like Tri-cia London and Kawehi Wells say things like "What were you do-ing in *our* neighborhood? Don't they give out candy in the house lots or is everybody Jehovah Witness around Halloween?"

Jerry says he likes being around rich people and so what if they know we come from the house lots. He says, "And anyway, who can see you under that basketball head mask of yours? Just no open your mouth and shift the eye holes mo' back if anybody try see who you."

Jerry and me run up the long walkway to the first house. "Trick or treat," Jerry screams. No one answers. I see a box full of premade goodie bags. I take one. "Take more," Jerry says. "We only got half hour." I slowly look around, then take another one. Jerry takes three more. He grabs his tail and runs away.

Mrs. Wells, this local lady married to a redhead haole man, stands under her yellow bug light. She makes Jerry do a trick for a treat. "Sing me a song," she says all perfect English.

Jerry sings, "Mam-mo-rees light da cornas of ma mine," loud with lots of feeling and eyeballs rolling back even.

Mrs. Wells laughs at him. "*Mammaries* light the corners of my *mine*. Now that's an interesting notion. And that's why the state was absolutely justified in sending us to those English Stan-dard Schools," she says to Jerry.

I shake my head and shrug my shoulders. "But your parents probably didn't pass the oral entrance exams. It's really clear. Too bad."

We get a whole bar of Nestlé's Crunch and Big Hunk. Not the miniature kind but the real candy store kind. Jerry says it's worth more than the trick we had to do and so what if Mrs. Wells wised off. He grabs his tail and runs full speed up and down three other big houses.

At the house next to Mr. Biggs's, Jerry and me see a very weak light by the porch. A screen door hits and hits the doorway like in a spooky movie and tree leaves rustle. Jerry says, "Let's chance it. It's the last house." He's sweating so his black nose runs down his upper lip and his pink cheeks run too. He wipes his face with the back of his furry paw.

When we get to the porch, there's a fishbowl full of dimes. They sparkle under the light. A sign says, *Happy Halloween. Please take one.* Jerry looks at me fast. I already know what he's thinking. "No, Jerry. Don't," I say. "These rich guys on Reed's Island, they act like we *real* poor or something. C'mon. Don't. Let's just go."

I can hear Tricia London say with that haole mouth of hers, "So, Lovey. How many dimes did you take from the fishbowl outside of my grandfather's house for your Trick-or-Treat for UNI-SELF can?"

"Quick, see if my madda looking. I might not win the money at the costume contest. Quick, look. Take as much as you can. This not stealing. Who tole them leave money instead of candy? Ass their problem. C'mon. As much as you can."

"No, Jerry."

"Hurry up," he tells me. "Take some more. Ten make one dollar. They so damn stinken rich here. They not going even care if we take the whole damn fishbowl." Jerry takes two handfuls, sticks his tail and pillowcase under his arms and runs down the long sidewalk. I take a handful and run too.

Jerry runs like a crazy person. All of a sudden, he trips. His pillowcase opens all over the lawn, Doublemint gum, jujubes, Big Hunk, everything. His fists full of dimes open, dimes flying in front of him.

Jerry's mother and my mother come running over. "JEROME!" *Twack!* His beautiful furry costume is torn at both knees. He's bleeding badly. A crowd gathers. And when my mother takes the basketball tomato head mask off of me, I see Tricia London. She's standing there in a purple wig, Elton John glasses, and a lime-green pants suit—must be "Crocodile Rock," or the stupidest-looking alligator I've ever seen. Then I see Kawehi Wells. She's in a sarong with a fake flower lei and giant orchid in her hair looking real *South Pacific*. "See," Tricia says, "the sign says, *Take one*. Can't you read? On top of everything else, they're stupid too. T-a-k-e o-n-e." They laugh, of course.

Jerry's mother carries him to the car. "C'mon, you," my mother says, and yanks my arm to follow. I want to pick up Jerry's pillowcase and candy. And all of the dimes. Even with Tricia and Kawehi and Troy and Traci looking, I would pick up all of the dimes for Jerry.

C

When we get to the 5th Annual Hilo Shopping Center Halloween Costume Contest, Jerry says he will not, no way, "I ain't getting outta this car with every mento kid from the damn house lots trying fo' win prize money, 'cause I no mo' chance with my rip costume any way."

"Suit yourself," says his mother.

"I bleeding," he screams, but the car door slams.

I'm given #17. I wear this number around my neck. The striped turtleneck gets hotter and hotter as all the contestants march down the ramp.

"Put on the damn goblin head," my mother says between her teeth. I put it on. It smells like newspaper and clay in the goblin head. I barely see a person in a lion's costume ahead of me but I can tell it's store-bought and probably Thomas Lorenzo's small brother, Arnold. A witch with a broomstick is behind me. Chocho lips Lori Shigemura can't hide those lips with black makeup. I also see a clown in a store-bought clown suit. Tareyton Tong with big Chinee gums and a painted-on red smile.

Then they announce the winners. "Third place, a five-dollar gift certificate from Hilo Music . . . number seven." I clutch the goblin head. It slips backward so I can't see. "Second place, a five-dollar gift certificate from Lanky's Pastries . . . number twelve!" Lori Shigemura, the witch next to me, jumps and screams. Good, it's almost over. "And the winner of this year's Halloween costume contest for ten dollars in cash . . . number seventeen!"

At first I don't realize it's me. When I do, I wonder how I could have won with the ugliest homemade, papier-mâché, tomato-head-shaped mask, a sheet, and a striped turtleneck. I see my mother clapping for me with Jerry's mother.

In my hand, the man with the microphone puts ten dollars cash. My mother helps me off the ramp and holds my hand to the car.

Jerry sits there holding his knees. I can see that he was crying. Our mothers excitedly plan next year's costumes. I thought to put the ten dollars in Jerry's hand, really I did. I thought that's what they would do in the movies or on Friday night TV. But I don't. I mean, it's ten whole bucks. "I won first place," I tell him.

"Bully for you," he says.

"You not glad for me?" I say.

"What you think, stink fink?" he says. "Go suck a duck. Get a glass and cut your ass. Whoopee-doo." Then he turns to the window.

I don't say anything all the way home. When we drop Jerry and his mother off at their house, Jerry doesn't even say bye or see you tomorrow. He runs into the back door and slams it shut.

The next day, I go to Poi Kakugawa Store and ask Mrs. Kakugawa to change my ten into all dimes. "All dimes?" she says. "I dunno if I get. Try wait. Eh, Harold. You get some rolls of dimes back there?" Harold, the store lady's grown son, brings four rolls of dimes to the front.

I put the dimes in Calhoon's old fishbowl from the shed and leave it on my dresser for a while. Then I rip open all the paper and run my fingers through the money. It's cold and makes my hands sweaty.

I could take it to Jerry's house and leave it on the porch. Then it's like the movies and he comes out while getting the morning paper for his father to read with coffee. He finds the fishbowl full of dimes and looks up like to God or something and smiles a knowing smile that I left it there all for him.

But I take some of the dimes to the candy store. I pick up a dusty package of the black-and-orange candy wrapped in waxed paper. "Why you buying this shit?" Harold asks. "Whose ten bucks you had this morning? Jee-zus Christ, you neva go trick-oa-treat oa what?"

C

In case anyone asks tomorrow in school:

No, it wasn't me in the papier-mâché mask with striped turtleneck who won first place in the stupid Halloween Costume Contest. And no, it wasn't me with pillowcase for trick-or-treat bag on Reed's Island with Jerome, who was a bear, you say, in phony fur bought from Kress store, all bloody knees and dimes and Big Hunks all over the sidewalk.

It wasn't me.

Prove it? Here, I can prove it. I'll open my bag at this point. Here is the candy, the cheap, house lots, black-and-orange candy wrapped in waxed paper. That's where I was. Good enough? That's proof.

BITTER TASTE SWEET

The Hershey's Special Dark. Semisweet chocolate morsels. It's a taste you have to learn to love. Like coffee or beer. The slippery texture of dark chocolate, not creamy or buttery. Special Dark.

"And how come it doesn't taste bitter in chocolate-chip cookies?" I ask Jerry.

" 'Cause the flavors get all mix with the brown sugar, vanilla, and flour," he says.

It gives him an idea. He makes me bite the Hershey's Milk Chocolate first, then the Special Dark. Jerry always thinks up these great ideas to make it better for me. So we lie on his bed, our feet dangling together, and we peel the chocolates, mix the flavors to maybe make me like the bitter bite of dark chocolate like him. Jerry and me eating chocolate, making plans, and telling secrets, of course.

"Man, they got a sale at Wigwam," Jerry says after a while. "I saw all the Barbie stuff for cheap. Everything goes."

We hadn't played with the Barbies since Larry cut them all bald and gave them fuzz and underarm hair. I didn't have the money to buy new ones.

"All cheap?" I ask.

"Yeah, fifty percent off everything."

"Like what?"

"Okay. Had the Barbie Camper, the Barbie Sports Car, the Pool Party Play Set, and Barbie Airlines too. We could get everybody else plus one more Barbie too. Like Midge, Francie, PJ, Skipper, two Kens, and one new Barbie, of course. And I seen one Donny Osmond doll with real hair, not plastic head like Ken. We can get two Donnys too so everybody get boyfriend. And all the clothes and accessories all less than one dollar."

"How much would all cost?" I ask him.

"I figured um out already. We need thirty dollars."

"Thirty dollars?"

"I got five from my birthday. You too, right? Right?"

"Okay," I say slowly. "Yeah, I got five from my grandma when she came last month."

"See, only twenty dollars more." Jerry looks at me anxious and waiting for an answer. He always makes the plans. All he wants me to do is nod and say yes. So I do.

We don't dangle our feet. There's no more chocolate. My mouth feels chocolate thick. Only a cold glass of water can take it away. I still don't like dark chocolate. Too bitter and too dark.

C

The sale will end soon. There's not enough money. Nobody wants their car washed and waxed, porch swept, or lawn mowed. No advance allowance, and anyway, Jerry can't tell his father he needs twenty dollars to buy Barbies.

But the thing is, we talk every day about the pool parties and camping trips and airlines with Ken as pilot and one of the Donny O.'s as passenger with PJ as his girlfriend and Barbie is jealous because she has to sit next to her little sister, Skipper, and Francie is the stewardess. And all the miniature grill stuff, hot dogs, cups, and pitchers for the lunch on the airplane or for the pool parties. High-heel shoes, hats, and mod boots.

C

Sunday night. Jerry comes over with his father, who sits with my father in the garage. Jerry pulls me down the hall and into my room. He locks the door. He slowly takes out from his pocket a Ziploc bag and a matchbook-size Zig-Zag rolling paper.

"We roll all this into twenty-five joints. This one three-finger bag," Jerry says, "maybe about twenty bucks. I stole um from Larry's shoebox by his bed. If we roll um all tonight, we can sell um all tomorrow in school for one dollar each and we get more than nuff money for everything we like."

"But, Jerry," I say, "we cannot. That's Larry's. He gonna kick our ass, Jerry, like the time you dropped the last corn beef hash patty and he shoved your head in the toilet bowl, then chased you around the house with the meat cleaver, remember? And he kick my ass too like the time I broke his B. J. Thomas record. No. I too scared, Jerome. He kill us fast. I mean kill us dead."

"The sale ends on Tuesday, Lovey. And when I went to Wigwam today, had only two Donny Osmonds left."

"Tuesday?"

"The Barbie Camper is the one with umbrella, you know, and

we gotta get new Barbies. Plus that, Larry the one busted up all the old Barbies and marsh-pen the only Ken us had too, gave um mustache and underarm hair and fuzz, dingding, balls, and nipples too. He deserve this. We sell um all by Tuesday and go straight to Wigwam after school. C'mon, Lovey. So what, you in?"

"I dunno how to roll a joint."

"Good. We practice first. I get um all figure out. Get plenny paper in this pack. We practice till we get real good, then we do the real thing."

"Practice with what?"

"With pencil-sharpener shavings. Go get your father's electric-sharpener tray."

There's loud talking outside and laughing. Gabriel Moniz comes over too. Pretty soon, out come the beers. My mother cooks up some nigagori with bacon for them to pick on. The smell of the parboiled bittermelon comes down the hall.

We roll the pencil shavings with our clumsy fingers, then lick the paper. Jerry says he saw Larry do it once in their room. "Gotta be tight inside," Jerry says, "and no twigs or seeds, just buds and leaves." We roll about seven fake joints each and Jerry gets pretty decent. "See, they getting better. Okay? Ready?"

Jerry gets the little fingernail scissors from my drawer. He cuts up the buds and leaves into twenty-five piles and puts them on a piece of folder paper. He pulls twenty-five Zig-Zags. "Okay, break um up good," he says, and we start rolling.

There's a knock at the door, and I swear, I never jumped so high in my whole life. "Lovey, Lovey," screams Calhoon. "Jerry, let me in."

"Fuck you, Cal. Go away," I scream back.

"Act normal, act normal," whispers Jerry.

"You wait, you ass pigs. I going tell Mommy right now that you said fuck, Lovey."

"Tell her sorry, tell her sorry. Quick before she tell."

"Sorry, Cal, sorry."

"Better be," she says, and she goes away forgetting that she wanted to come in. It seems like forever that we're breaking the dope apart, rolling it, rolling it, tighter, then licking the paper. Real long. Finally we put all the joints back in the Ziploc and seal it. The Zig-Zag too.

There's a funny taste in my mouth and my fingers smell sweet. Too sweet. Jerry runs down the hall to get the Lysol. He sprays the whole room. Even his fingers.

By Tuesday, we have twenty-six dollars. Jerry and me catch the sampan bus straight to Wigwam. It's raining, so the bus driver lowers the musty-smelling canvas flaps and the striped awning too.

We're so rich. I want to feel the wind. That's what this feels like, so rich, and going to buy everything in the store. There's even a list. I have it in my purse.

Jerry gets a shopping cart and we push it down the toy aisle. Big red 50% OFF signs all over and the fluorescent-orange price tags with SALE on top slashed in half with black pen.

The camper, the sports car, the pool party, the airlines. Then we pick the dolls. Have you noticed that even the same Barbies have different expressions? Really. We go through *each* Midge, Francie, PJ, Skipper, Barbie, Ken, and Donny O. to find the best ones.

And picking one outfit each is like a fashion show and you're the designer. The salesgirl has to put our dolls and stuff in a huge garbage-size bag, the pink one that says WIGWAM on top. And with the extra money, Jerry buys a Special Dark. I eat it with him, bittersweet and all, on the bus ride home.

It's not easy sneaking gigantic pink packages with boxes and dolls into his house. So we go to my house because no one gets home for another half hour. Run down the hall to my room. Break all the boxes open, hurry and shove the stuff under the bed. Rip the staples, take the little plastic bags with miniatures and shove them into my drawers.

Now the dolls too. Take them out of the boxes. "Hurry, Jerry, my mother come home soon." We take off the plastic covering over the dolls' hair and start ripping all the boxes up. We shove all the rubbish back in the Wigwam bag. Take all the new clothes and hide um in my panty drawer.

We gotta burn the bag. Jerry and me running to the back of the lot to burn all the boxes and pink packages. The smoke is dark black and the edges of cardboard blacken red in the wind, blow, and gray smoke all around. The feeling not too good inside me, hurry, burn. Burn rise smoke and eyes tear, cover my mouth and nose but neither Jerry or me step back from the smoke. We stay there until we are inside it.

C

"Gotta be them, those two fuckin' queers. Fuck, man, fuckin' assholes. Who else can be? Nobody else come in this fuckin' room. . . . Yeah, I at my house. You coming over? . . . Yeah, come over, 'cause when Jerome come home, I gonna kick his

ass. . . . Nah, they neva smoke um. What you think? They probably still get um someplace but we scare the shit outta them,
okay? . . . Nah, you think? Them two? Smoke joints? Fuckas
dunno matches from cig'rettes. Pussies from dicks. . . . Yeah,
come over and bring Jenks too."

I can't believe Jenks sits with them. Larry and Dwayne. When
we walk in the back door of Jerry's house, they all three sit on
the punee with their hands folded on their laps. They stare
straight at us. Dwayne starts.

"Fuckin' stealas."

Larry: "Stealas? Fuckin' takers and gonna die for it."

Jenks just stares. Hard, soft, hard all in a second. I didn't
know it was his too.

"That's fuckin' thirty bucks, you two assholes. Where's the
goddamn dope, Jerome?"

He's so scared and I don't feel my feet.

"Where, mothafuckas? C'mon, where?" Larry gets up. He
walks toward Jerry and hits him across his ear. "Where, goddamn pussy? You fuckin' fag, I swear, what you did with my
dope?"

Jerry's on the ground all bust up but not crying, just holding
his ear. I feel my feet backing up to the door, then Dwayne
charges up so fast that I jump and he blocks the door.

"And you, cunt," Dwayne says to me. "I bet you know." He
grabs my shirt until his face is in mine. "You betta say what you
know, you lesbian cunt, or I will shove your face up his ass."

"I, we," I stammer. "I, we," I try again. "Jerome took," and I
look at Jenks and he looks hard and soft, then hard again all in a
second. Then he looks away.

"No look at him for help, assholes. He's over with you. That was his money too wen' buy that dope, right, Jenks?" And Jenks nods.

"You fuckin' faggot. Puss. Dickless." The words come out of their mouths so easy.

The words I could never bring to my lips, ever.

I start to say, "It's 'cause you cut their hair, Larry. You cut them bald," and he says, "What, dog? Speak up. What you saying? Cut whose hair, bitch? What the FUCK are you TALKING BUBBLES for?" he screams in my face.

They hit us once more each. Jerry gets it in his eye and he falls backwards and hits his head on the wall. I get a crack across the face so hard that my lip cuts and bleeds.

"So who tells the story?"

"I told you, Jerry," I say soft. "I told you."

"Shut up," he says. "Shut up," he screams at me. "You hear me, Lovey?"

"Jerry, you. You. You fuckin'—" The words want to come out but I don't let them. "You asshole."

"Lovey, you fuckin' cunt tattletaler."

It's that *word* that I hate, the word that people who hate you always know when to use. When you're the weakest. It bites into you every time they say it. *Cunt.* But I didn't say no word to him. I didn't say it.

That's what they wanted.

It's enough to make them laugh. All except Jenks. Only when he gets the elbow to laugh does he join in.

"Funny, yeah, watch one fag and lesbian fight." They laugh until tears fall out. "Fight, c'mon, beef."

Jerome and me. We sit there and breathe in and out, in and out, hard and deep. I feel my nostrils flaring and my lips starting to quiver but I grit my teeth, say no, no, no, no, will not, will not, will not. Which is when I taste the blood in my mouth.

Feel it thick over my teeth, the sweet rusty taste of blood that I swallow and taste pure all over my mouth and throat. Warm, as it escapes out of my swollen lip and onto my shirt. I wipe my mouth with my sleeve, the blood that leaves a taste so bitter not even a cold glass of water can ever wash it away.

RAGS

Everybody knows.

Everybody can see.

The plastic pad clips.

The knotty lump of the Kotex in the plastic pad clips.

The elastic of the belt and the elastic of my panty. There's a difference, you know, unless you can match up both elastics exactly.

"Wear a thick panty today. The Buster Browns."

"Nobody can see."

"You crazy, or what?"

"Get ready for school."

"Everybody in your class going get um someday."

"And the ones that *don't* are abnormal."

"You crazy?"

"Did I leak, Calhoon? Did I leak a little? Is there blood (blood) on my seat? Can you see the lump? Can you? Can you see the plastic pad clips?"

Everyone knows.

I feel dirty.

What will I do in PE? We strip naked for shower.

Everyone will see.

I want to stay home.

"You crazy, or what?"

"You cannot stay home every month."

"This is every month, you know."

"Every twenty-eight days."

"For the rest of my life?"

Theresa Esteban leaked blood on her flowered dress and everybody saw and everybody knew. It was on her chair too and everybody knew. And Theresa didn't come to school for three days and the weekend passed, but on Monday everybody remembered and everybody teased. And somebody wrote BLOODY MARY and RAGS with red marsh pen on her desk. And everybody started saying that Theresa has fuzz and hair under her arms, because they saw it in PE. And Theresa got her rags.

"You no like go school?"

"You have to."

"You crazy."

"No wear white on menses days."

"No forget one extra pad."

"Put um in one brown package."

"But they know what one brown package in your purse is."

"Oh."

Calhoon heard my Theresa Esteban Bloody Mary story. Now when she's mad at me, she says, "Bloody Mary, Bloody Lovey, full of tomato sauce." Over and over she's singing this loud, everywhere, in the store, in the house, when even my *father* can hear.

My father, who walked into the kitchen with the bathroom trash can and said, "Oh. So you one woman now, eh?" and how he ruffled my hair before he walked out the back door. I was supposed to be his apprentice.

Learn how to lay the orange seeds off of the nose of the anthurium on the hapu'u.

"We going self-polly-nate these buggas."

Mix and pour the concrete for anthurium pots.

"For all our anthurium keikis."

Learn to cure and tan sheep hide myself.

"For the foot of your bed."

Be a hunter's apprentice.

"Oh. So you're a woman now."

Woman now.

Woman now, not an apprentice anymore.

A woman now.

Father, we had plans, didn't we? Did I do something wrong? How can I make this blood stop? How can I make my blood go away? I cannot even look at you anymore. *Oh, so you're a woman now.* Why did you say this to me? What did you mean? I'm shame of this thing. So shame that I cry and punch myself hard over there and ask God why do I have this thing.

Full of tomato sauce.

And I don't even care to hurt my sister. I'm too stunned to do anything when she sings this in the store. I don't even chase her down the aisle. I hang my head. In church while we sing hymns, "full of the grace of *tomato sauce,*" I don't even care to hit her. In the car, with my father driving, my father. *Full of tomato sauce.*

And when I look at my sister, how little she is, how she looks like a pigeon, I can't think that this blood will come out from her too, brown and spotted at first on a white panty.

"They all can see the plastic pad clips."

"Buy Kotex."

"It's softer."

"Modess stiff, even for me."

"They all can see."

"They get X-ray vision, right, Lovey?"

"Ma, they can, they can."

"You put deodorant today?"

"Your underarms smell stink."

"You wearing one bra, or what?"

"You put deodorant?"

"Everybody can see, you know."

"You wearing one bra, Lovey?"

So I count twenty-eight days. And on the twenty-eighth day, I take my menses belt out of the panty drawer. I wear a bra every day too, even if it's binding and digs into my skin. I put deodorant on every day from the Mums cream jar. I put the Kotex carefully into the plastic pad clips, making it flat, flat as I can. Every day.

For fourteen days, but I have no blood. I think maybe God took my blood away. I'll never have blood again. I can be my father's apprentice. But it comes with one pad left in the Kotex box.

"Why you wen' use um all?"

"Whassamatta with you?"

"You suppose to put one in your purse, and when come, you put um on."

"You crazy, or what?"

"Expensive, you know."

"Gunfunnit."

"Dammit."

"Whassamatta with you?"

"You crazy?"

Mommy, I'm so afraid of this blood that I can't even tell you. The words don't come to my lips about this thing. I think it'll come pouring out of me, like a river of blood, just like Theresa Esteban. And how will I run to the bathroom, pull my Kotex out of my brown package, carefully put the Kotex into the plastic pad clips nice and flat before all the blood pours out, match the elastics of the menses belt and my panty, and go back to class without EVERYBODY knowing? Mommy, I'm afraid.

"You make me so damn mad."

"This one natural thing."

"Get a grip."

"Get it straight, Lovey."

"Grow up."

"You one wo-man now."

"I am?"

"Go to the store and buy me one new box of Kotex. Now! And to teach you a damn lesson, tell Mrs. Kakugawa don't give you one package. Go."

Omigod. Omigod. Omigod.

I get on my bike with the white flower basket. Calhoon says, "I go with you, Lovey." We ride fast and furious to the store. I want to feel the wind strong in my face until it stings, until I can't hear anything anymore. Faster so it can all fly out of my head.

Cal won't even come in the store. I walk up to the blue Kotex box and put it under my arm. The coolness burns. My heart beats quick. And after my shaking fingers pay, I tell Mrs. Kakugawa and Harold, her grown son's right there too—I don't know how the words come out of a beating body and shaking face and lips—"No need package." I run out of the store and stuff the box into my white bike basket.

"Why you neva get one package, stupid Lovey?" asks Cal real loud.

"Because Ma said not to, you asshole."

"Why you yelling at me for, you Tomato Sauce?"

The world ends here.

All noise stops.

Cars stop.

Eyes turn.

Mouths open.

Old men stop talking.

People getting mail from their mailboxes stop turning their combinations.

Traci and Gina stop eating their frozen slushes to my sister's words.

"Eh, Lovey. You full of tomato sauce, eh?" And Calhoon rides off laughing. And for the life of me, I don't know how to cover the blue box in my white bike basket.

(

Theresa Esteban and me should be friends. But we're not. My hair has started to grow too, soft and fine like baby's hair and light, light brown. Theresa's is like my mother's. Dark and coarse hair, wiry and plenty.

I know Traci and Gina wait and watch me for a sign of hair every day when we change in PE. They're the height of fourth-graders.

They wait to call me Fuzz, Brillo, Policeman, Oromots, Bloody Mary, Rags, as I pull my towel tight around my chest.

God. Dear Heavenly Father. Why me? Take this blood away. Father? Father. Tell me about our plans. Tell me.

Everyone knows.

I know it.

Everyone can see it.

I am not crazy.

I am not crazy.

Somebody help me with this blood.

Somebody.

Oh.

So you're a woman now?

GOD IS LOVE WHEN SHE PRAYS MY NAME

———

My teacher loves me.

My teacher wants to braid my hair, comb it until my head yanks and static sparks in the air around my head, then twist the fat pole of hair so the split ends stand out. Snip. Here. Snip. A couple there. Snip them off with her sharp teacher scissors.

She French-braids my hair down to the very bottom strands and wraps it with a red school rubber band. She chews on rubber bands, this teacher, and when she pulls my hair tight into the braids, I hear the squeaking of the rubber bands between her teeth.

My mother asks every day, "Who braiding your hair so nice, Lovey?" And something tells me to say it's Nancy Miyamoto, who's practicing to be a beautician when she grows up. And Mother says, "Eh, tell her she do such one nice job, I let her be my beautician someday."

"You know what," my teacher tells me, "you my pretty girl. All mine. I never had a girl, you know. Just my four boys. Ho, but I wanted a girl." Then she presses the loose hairs to my head with her palm and some spit.

I never have to take the written exams for PE class.

I get an A every quarter.

I never shower in the gang shower. She lets me go into the isolation stall for girls who have their rags. Every day sometimes.

"One of these days," she says to me, "sew me a blouse with butterfly sleeves like the kind all you girls wear. The kind with lace and gauze, can? I buy you the material and the lace like that, can?"

I'm so happy to take the fabric and the lace home the day that she brings it in a brown paper package so crispy, it feels like an armful of money.

I get her lunch from the cafeteria every day. Carry it all the way up to the PE locker room with all of my books and my bag. Sit with her and watch her eat.

Sit in the front row during class so she can wink at me. Be the referee and take roll every day. Sell PE uniforms and take inventory on all the equipment. Walk her to her car before running to catch the sampan bus home and kiss her goodbye on the lips like she says.

C

My teacher asks my mother if I can spend the night at her house. My mother thinks nothing of saying yes and I'm so happy that she sends me over with a pound of frozen bacon and a dozen fresh blue-and-green Araucana eggs.

I love my teacher so much. I want to do everything. All the girls there feel the same way too. Even Jerry starts coming over.

Jerry, Nancy Miyamoto, Barbette Yanagi, Ruby Hagimura, and me. But nobody loves my teacher as much as me. And she tells me that she loves me the best of all.

That's why I fight with Barbette over who'll Ajax her bathtub and toilet. I fight with Nancy, who wants to fold all the laundry all the time. Basket after basket of baby clothes and toddler clothes and the two preschoolers playing in the dirt outside making more dirty clothes. "Frank's gonna seed the lawn any day now," she says. "Anyone wanna help when we plant the grass?" And all five of us screaming me, me, me.

Clean the toilets, get the mail, scrub the tub, wipe the fuzz out of the corners of the bathroom, vacuum the floor, sweep the kitchen, wash the dishes, wipe the counters, fold the diapers, hang more diapers, pick up the diapers from the clothesline, make the Tang and Exchange Orange Base half and half in the blue Tupperware pitcher.

"Oh, you girls are good. And, Jerome, you make a good husband for Lovey one day, I tell you. You don't even have to be told what to do, you guys so good kids. Your parents lucky to have kids like you, but I betchu they complain like nothing about you guys, eh? I betchu they don't even talk to you guys like reg-la people with feelings like that, eh? Sheez, I knew you guys had hard life. That's why I treat you special—'cause you are special to me."

Burp the baby. Change his diaper. And best of all: "Go get me his bottle from the refridge. Yeah—you can feed him, this bottle, the next bottle, every time if you like—but only 'cause I trust you."

Pretty soon, we're there every Friday night and all day Saturday.

Pretty soon, it's only Jerry and me. Because we really love the teacher the most.

C

One Friday, Jerry and me go to the Palace Theatre to see the six o'clock show of *The Exorcist* before we go to the teacher's house to spend the night. Lori Shigemura's YMCA club went already and talked in secret about it in English. And Larry and Crystal.

My mother drops us off but the theater lady says, "Rated R. Seventeen and unda accompany by adult. So so-lee—no can go in." We consider spending our movie money on cheeseburgers at the Woolworth's restaurant but end up sitting on the curb waiting for someone to take us in. Finally, we ask my next-door neighbor Katy's ex-high school boyfriend, Jay Teramoto, to take us in and he does.

The girl in the movie plays with her Ouija board. Just like us. She looks like a regular haole girl and talks kind of like a baby. OMIGOD. All that green vomit and neck crunching around 360 degrees. Those eyes and that voice. Jerry and me so scared, we don't see half the scenes after she got possessed. But we hear that voice. And that laugh.

Jerry says this to me as we wait for our ride home, sitting on the curb but too cool to hold on to each other, "If I ever see anything as ugly as that girl, I swear, Lovey, I not waiting for nobody from hell to catch me. I'm outta there."

Easier said than done.

"No, I really mean it, Lovey. Reverend Smith tole Pearly and Pearly told me that no Devil can catch you if you get the hell outta the dance. And Pearly the Reverend daughter, so she should know, right?"

"What dance?" I ask Jerry.

"The school dance, stupid. Reverend Smith said, 'Don't put y'all-selves in a place of sinners. Be in fella-ship with utha Christians and y'all find ya-selves in the company of angels.' What he mean is split, don't wait for one invitation."

"So you saying that girl shoulda run away from her basement?"

"Maybe."

I cannot get the green eyes and red hair out of my sight. I close my eyes and I see her. Open my eyes and hear her voice. It's her laugh that I keep hearing. And Jerry says, "You ever hear laughing like that, Lovey, I no care what or where you stay, you and me better run outta the dance, okay?"

C

That night, the teacher tells us about God. The Kingdom Hall of Jehovah's Witnesses says only 44,000 can live on earth after God destroys the planet. The end is near. It's so, so near.

And the streets will be covered with blood and bodies. My mother's blood will run through my fingers and rush past my legs and at the moment of her passing through me I'll feel her blood and know it's her blood in the streets. And my grandma and my father and my sister in the river rushing through my fingers. They were not part of the 44,000. Catch them if you can, but God says you won't.

I want to throw up.

"I want you be part of the 44,000. Be with me so we can see God. All of us together. I want to be with you guys *forever.*"

C

My mother thinks I'm nuts. All this talk about the Devil, green eyes, and laughing.

"What blood and how the blood going run in the streets, huh, Lovey? I swear thass the last time I letting you and Jerome go that kine movie. See what you get? Like ack big. You guys shoulda gone see *The Sting* at Mamo Theatre. What blood? What bodies? What 44,000? Thass the first time I hear that and I use to go Baptist church with your grandma every Sunday. She telling you kids all that crap, I tell you, thass the last time you going up there. Don't you tell me no more about this, Lovey, or you neva stepping foot in her house eva again."

C

Small, small, make the body small. Don't talk. Don't say nothing. Just me and Jerry.

"No tell nobody," the teacher said. "The world no understand you. Especially your parents if they of the world, which I pretty sure they are. This is a secret between us and God."

C

There were stones in her house that gave birth to stones. Stones in a pie pan on the counter. I saw them move and birth babies like the old ones in the myths at school said. Pebbles that shifted, the stones in the house that made more stones until the teacher took some of them outside and left them to birth under the lychee tree in the back.

Her baby cried at exactly 12:07 every night, nobody knew why, screaming and crying like there was no end. Until the church elders came and prayed and burned the stones that gave birth to stones. Burned the poster of Bruce Lee behind the baby's door and the Easter bunny and Kikaida Man dolls. "They represent violence. They were the means by which the evil one entered my house."

"You mean the Devil came here? When?"

Burn them in the fire of stones.

❨

My teacher's chewing on red rubber bands squeaking in the night-time and telling Jerry and me about God.

"Little men surrounded my bed. All of um about one foot high. They holding hands and chanting something that sound outta this world, man. And they're laughing at me 'cause I'm choking. A strangling ghost got me by the throat and I'm screaming and trying to get up, but the bugga holds me till I pass out. And when I wake up, my small baby been crying so long, his throat's all raw."

Wants to tell us about God.

"You love me, Jerome? You love me, Lovey? You trust what I

tell you tonight, I telling it 'cause I love you guys with all my heart? Eh, that I wouldn't tell you this if I didn't think it was for your ultamate good?

"You guys be part of the 44,000. I begging you, please. I love you. I calling the church elders be here in the morning for pray for you. Eh, God is love. I make you be in the flock of the lamb."

And what if we wake up in the middle of the night and something says we don't want to do it? "If something says to call home," the teacher says, "if something says don't do um, don't do um, remember—that's the Devil. Just like the movie you guys was telling me about. He wants you too. He wants to be inside you too. That's him the one telling you don't do um. You better remember that. He's so cunning and he wants you, but God is love, *remember?*"

At 12:07 that night, the baby cries. And Jerry's so afraid, he doesn't even scream. The teacher starts to laugh in her room. Her room has a strange green glow. I clutch Jerry hard. We hold on to each other and pull our sleeping bags into the corner of the living room.

"If we go, thass the Devil," Jerry says. "The doors going lock shut," he says, " 'cause God is love. He wants us here. They all like us here. The elders coming in the morning. Thass the Devil telling us to go, Lovey."

But I say, "No. Jerry, you said we gotta run outta the dance once we hear the laughing. That's all it takes is the laugh—listen to her. We gotta run, Jerry, 'cause nobody from hell can catch us if we get outta here."

Unlock the front door, Devil or no, slowly pull it open. Don't let her hear us. Door don't squeak, floor don't move, screen don't slam. The teacher's still laughing; it sounds like crying; *"I love you, I love you, I love you."* Wailing and laughing.

Run quick and quiet, Jerry and me, into the night that whistles coldly around our thin pajamas. Jerry and me holding hands and running, dogs barking and howling, the gravel on the road cutting into our bare feet until we can't feel our feet on the pavement.

I pull the rubber band off of my hair; unwind the French braids until my hair swirls in the night wind, running two blocks before we stop in the bushes next to an all-night launderette.

Jerry and me, huddled together, waiting for God.

C

"I warned you. I told you. How many times I gotta tell you that I know best?" my mother screams. "How long you two knuckle-heads was hiding by the launderette? Why didn't you call sooner? How the cops found you? You two nuts better start talking now. I want the whole story before I call your mommy, Jerome." Then my mother stops. She stares at me hard.

"What she mean, the Devil? She the very work of the Devil. How many time something told me, Verva, no let the kids go up that lady's house. But no, I trust. I think she one teacher—what kine harm is that? Gunfunnit.

"Look at you. Scared of your own goddamn shadow. No can sleep in your own room, the bed shaking, close the closet door— you nuts. I cannot handle this.

"Don't answer the phone! Put the phone down. Who's that? That's her, eh? What she saying? That I the Devil? You gimme that phone right now. Don't you dare hang up."

"Don't need to, Mommy. The line got cut."

☾

Mother puts me on a plane to Moloka'i the very next day. "Pack the small pink suitcase, hurry up. Get in the car, now." Drive me to the airport. See me to the gate. Wave at me, Calhoon and her, through the chain-link fence until I'm sitting on the airplane. Press my hand to the window so they cannot see me. Breathe in deep and gasping quick air.

☾

Grandma makes me sew from the moment I arrive. All kinds of clothes to pass the time away, and she buys me magazines.

I take long walks with her to the Baptist church to dust-mop the aisles and Lemon Pledge the grand piano. We sweep and mop the pulpit. Grandma makes me straighten out all of the hymnals and Pine-Sol all the pews.

We go to Sunday School, Sunday Morning Service, Evening Prayer Service, and Wednesday Bible Study, just Grandma and me, dropped off by Grandpa on the dusty road in front of the church.

I love the way my grandma sings in church. She doesn't care how loudly she sings with her vibrato voice that sounds like a shaky old angel. Grandma doesn't say very much about God. But I hear her in her prayer room at five-thirty in the morning. Sometimes I hear her saying my name.

☾

Grandma grows okra in her garden. She makes me cut it in half, sprinkle it with flour until the flour turns pasty on my fingers, and then she shows me how to fry it in oil. Grandpa likes okra browned nice and crispy. We eat this with hot rice and dried fish straight from the aku-drying box. Grandma and me make Lipton sun tea in a big gallon mayonnaise jar and we squeeze a big lemon from her yard right into the jar before we pour it over ice cubes for Grandpa to drink with his okra, fish, and rice.

She buys raw sunflower seeds for me and makes me eat warm papaya for breakfast. "Brown bread is healthy," she says every morning when she puts the plate with toast in front of me. "Brown rice too, but our half on one side of the pot and Grandpa's white rice on the other side. Take care of business and everybody happy. Let's go," is what she says every morning before we're off to do whatever she's planned for the day.

But Grandma doesn't know something and I don't want to tell her. I don't want to tell her that I don't sleep until the sun comes up. I'm so scared of the little men. I stay up all night if I don't sleep before she sleeps. I hear the teacher laughing all the time. Especially at night. There's too much pressure on me to fall asleep, because I want to be asleep before she sleeps, so I end up struggling. That's why I stay awake all night.

153

When I see the first light of the sun and hear Grandma's roosters crowing, hear her heavy house slippers in the hallway, hear Grandma flipping through the onionskin pages of her Bible, sometimes hear my name, right after "Dear Heavenly Father, protect our Lovey," my heavy eyes shut until twelve noon.

I overheard Aunty Bing ask Grandma why she lets me sleep until lunch. "What wrong with the kid? Why her eyes move like that? Whassamatta her? What she looking for? Ma, you tole Verva all this? Betta tell Verva the kid's nerves all raw."

I cannot even take my clothes off over my head. I shut my eyes and see the little men in the green glow. I hear the teacher laughing with my eyes open. And the wailing. *I love you, I love you. God is love.* This all happens when my eyes are open.

(

Grandma listens to the staticky Bible station on an old pocket transistor radio in her sewing room. I'm sleeping lightly and she's singing softly. When the strangling ghost grabs my throat that day, I scream to Grandma, *Help me, help me,* but no words come out of my open mouth. I want to wake up but can't get my eyelids open. Pull myself up, wake up, get up, but I can't.

I see Grandma sitting on her sewing bench. I see her clearly. See her biting a loose thread off of the blouse she's sewing for me.

Help me.

See her look over to me and smile.

Get up.

Then Grandma's gone. And sitting in the corner of the room is a man, a little man, with green hair like flames. Red, red eyes and laughing the teacher's laugh. *You should never have run. God is love.*

After dinner, Grandma and me are washing the dishes. Aunty Bing is mopping the kitchen. Grandma puts her warm hand on my neck and I fall to the floor. I hit my head on the Formica countertop. When I wake up, I see the ceiling and then my toes like I'm sleeping. Aunty Bing fanning me with a Japanese fan and Grandma splashing water on my face. Grandma sits me up and I tell her everything about the teacher. About God. About the Devil and the little man in the bedroom today.

Aunty Bing stops mopping and sits on the floor with us too. Then she says, "Ma, you take this kid church tomorrow 'cause this is just too much for live like this all scared. How many nights you neva sleep? Going on two months, I bet you."

I tell Grandma, "From now on, I sleep with my fist to the wall whenever I take a nap in your sewing room. The man with the red eyes come only during the day." I tell my grandma, "When I punch the wall, when I hit the wall like this, please, Grandma, please wake me up." After we plan this, I never see the little man with the red eyes in the sewing room. But I sleep with my fist to the wall. Day or night.

⟨

Grandma's watching the ten o'clock news. I hear the pages of her newspaper turning slowly. I want to sleep. I want to sleep. And this night, after so many nights of being awake, all by myself, so quiet at night that I can hear my own heartbeat, I fall asleep. I'm asleep. I know this.

Until I look at the bureau mirror. I see two tiny red dots like the dots you see when you're in the sun for too long or when you shut your eyes too tight. Way, way back in the very back of the mirror. I don't know why I watch the rest of this. I should've known to punch the wall or to turn my face away. Run out of the dance.

The red dots get closer and closer to me, bigger and bigger, green hair like flames, until his eyes are the size of my face in the mirror, his green hair licking the edges of the mirror and laughing at me. *Come, come. O lamb.* I try to scream. I try to hit the wall and this time I guess I do. When Grandma runs into the room, the lights in the mirror shatter, but she says to me, "What happen?" Like she saw nothing at all.

My grandma covered the mirror that night for me with Aunty Bing's old bedspread. The pink one with the gypsy fringes. This time she heard my fist hit the wall and then I told her maybe if I could call Jerry long-distance tomorrow and find out if he's okay. Then she says, "Let us pray." She asks God to protect me through the night. Which he does.

In the morning, Grandma walks with me to the Baptist church. Reverend Keene sits with me and Grandma in his dusty office full of stacks of paper, old Bible study quarterlies, and offering envelopes in koa bowls.

Nobody says nothing about God is love and 44,000 and blood and little men. He says, "Let us bow our heads in prayer. Be the Lord of this child's heart."

Grandma held my hand all the way home. We picked okra for dinner. She never said anything much more to me about God that summer. I still heard her pray my name. I knew who lived in my heart. It was the way she said my name to him, the way she covered the mirror with the pink bedspread every night until the day I left, the Bible she left on my bed one afternoon. It said, *To Lovey. From your Grandma.*

ALEXANDER FU SHENG KICKS BRUCE LEE'S ASS, SONNY CHIBA AND TOSHIRO MIFUNE TOO

I get seasick watching the Ra Expedition at the Palace Theatre, so I sit in the lobby, the red French-designed carpet and heavy velvet drapes with gold cords smelling old and unwashed.

I act like I'm not looking but I side-eye the theater owner's grown-up, tunta, skebe, pomade-and-rotten-teeth son who rips tickets in half.

He's the most f-ugly man I've ever seen. Crew cut and purple lips and gums with a cigarette hanging down and always in the same olive cardigan with white golf shirt, old man crisscross leather slippers, and long, long black toenails.

He smiles at me. He knows I'm watching. Licks his hand and slicks back his hair. Licks his lips slow and gives me an eyebrow jerk. I run down the spiral cement stairs to the bathroom and throw up popcorn and bits of the wrinkly overcooked hot dog into the toilet.

My father and Uncle Ed enjoy the movie so much that they don't bother to get me until the movie ends. Uncle Ed tells me, "Ho, you lightweight. Lightweight, eh, your daughter, Hubert? Ho, you wen' miss out on *Kon-Tiki* and that papayraz boat."

I stand there and nod at Uncle Ed, the tacky dry taste of vomit still in my mouth.

"I like *High Plains Drifter* better."

My father nods.

All in all, I'd rather see Alexander Fu Sheng movies. My father and Uncle Ed say that all kung fu movies are phony. Uncle Ed says, "Sheez, so fake the way they make. The sound of them kicking, that stupid wind sound, no even match the kick. So fricken phony, I tell you. I hate for go kung fu movies."

"Me too, Lovey," says my father. "So damn junk. We no like go. I ain't paying money for that." Yet they pay money to see the Kulani prisoners wrestle in the Civic Auditorium. Now that's fake. And they watch Roller Derby. More fake.

But Alexander Fu Sheng. *Fu Sheng. Alexander.* The way they say it, it sounds like *Bond. James Bond,* but the Chinese version. And so handsome. To me, Fu Sheng is way handsomer than Bruce Lee. Even before Bruce Lee died, I said Alexander Fu Sheng kicks Bruce Lee's ass any day.

Now tell the truth about Bruce Lee. He wears makeup, eye liner and lip liner, and he's five foot three, and I swear he cannot speak a word of English, but Fu Sheng, he knows English like "Okay, cowboy. Wanna rumble?" And I saw him say "Cigarette?" which matched with the dubbing. Not "Ciga-lette," like most Chinese who cannot say the *r*, but "Cigarette." Now that's talking English.

But nobody will go with me, not my father, not Uncle Ed, not even Jerry, who does practically everything I want except this. He says the dubbing is bad enough, but Alexander Fu Sheng movies, they don't tell you when they have dubbing or subtitles. Subtitles make you miss all the action, and if you watch only the movie, you don't know the real plot.

So I force Nancy Miyamoto to come with me, but even she makes me pay the ticket, buy the soda and Big Dip, and buy her a present before we get to the Palace Theatre. She sets me back two allowances sometimes and Daddy's forced to give me burning-wire money or money from the family pot 'cause I lie and tell him I need money for PE shoes. One time, I had to go to Ben Franklin and buy her a Kona jacket, or one time, two yards of double-knit shirt material from Kress. But I figure, anything for Fu Sheng, right?

And I gotta be the one to walk up to the air-conditioned ticket booth and look at the theater owner, who I swear looks like Miss Mims from *Thoroughly Modern Millie*. The witchy-looking hotel owner who says *shu-sho, shu-sho* with her red lips and heavy eye liner and hair all rolled up in a huge bun with two chopsticks.

And the theater lady has the knobbiest, wrinkliest fingers with long red fingernails that slide the change and the tickets into the metal scoop under the glass.

More worse is when her and her son smoke in the booth and the white smoke slips in and out of the silver grill and Miss Mims and her son under the fluorescent light look greenish white like *The Revenge of the Screaming Dead*. She says to me things like "Oh, sho you li-kee Alax-unda Foo Shang, no you? I aww time see you. You li-kee come Foo Shang moo-wees, no you? You fat, thass why, mo' betta you be kong foo too, no? Nex time I gi-bee you dis-countu, no?"

But next time comes and we get no discount, only more of

the same stupid talk and spooky laughing from her and her son in the booth. Nancy looks at me and acts like she's ready to run, but I hold the movie present package. This time it's eye makeup and a choker from Kress, and I say, "Two twelve and under, please."

That tunta, skebe son of hers says, "Yeah, right. How many years you two been twelve and under? Yeah, right, two things like you cannot be twelve and under. Ma, they not, Ma. They mo' older than that. Shit, pay adult price."

The shu-sho lady tells her son, "Neva mine, you boy-san. Ho, dis one he for glum-bo, glum-bo, glum-bo. Go, go helpu Gladys in concession. Go quick, quick, *shu-sho, shu-sho*." Just kidding about the shu-sho part.

We hate when he takes the tickets too, 'cause one time he takes my ticket and fingers my palm. Then he does the same to Nancy and she almost cries, she feels so sick, and we go down the spiral stairs to the bathroom and scrub our hands. All through the time, we can hear his sick laugh.

This is how far I have to go to see Alexander Fu Sheng movies. I also have to do all kinds of other favors for Nancy in return, like last Saturday, Nancy wanted to go out to the movies with her new boyfriend, Craig Kunishige, but I had to be the choching because her parents didn't know that Nancy had a boyfriend, so we get dropped off at the Palace Theatre to watch guess what. *Sasquatch: The Legend of Bigfoot.* Because a Japanese movie was playing at the Mamo Theatre.

And there's Miss Mims and Miss Mims, Jr., and the smell of mildewy, damp velvet curtains and wet carpet that comes out onto the street as we walk to the ticket booth. Me, the choching, walking ten paces behind Nancy and Craig. And Nancy, when Craig's around, she likes to make me look stupid. Like she says, "See, Lovey, *Enter the Dragon* coming," and she points to the glass case with spiderwebs and papery-thin insect shells all stuck in the corners. "Ask your boyfriend over there to take you. Maybe his mother give you discountu."

And I mean I kick Nancy's ass too if I wasn't so scared to go to the movies by myself, sit in the third row, and see Fu Sheng up close and real. And not feel scared to stay in the theater alone when Nancy goes to the bathroom. I cannot skip one minute, that's why.

Not feel as though a man in an olive cardigan and with a flashlight with red plastic cover might sit behind me and smell like Old Spice and stick the flashlight between the seats and say something like "You sure you twelve? I tell my madda you thirteen. Same with my niece Tammy Okazaki. You no lie, small girl. You thirteen." And he rubs the flashlight on me.

I get so scared, I don't even move, don't look back, so he kicks my chair. And when I don't respond, he hits the flashlight on the chair behind me and laughs.

❨

Once there was a man named Alexander Fu Sheng. He comes to the Palace with me. Me. Nancy and Craig are there and Fu Sheng high-kicks the dirty glass case with a Bruce Lee poster inside and chops Bruce Lee's face.

Then he kicks open the glass case with his poster inside and autographs the poster of himself for me. All of this while Nancy and Craig look on.

When the theater lady's son takes our tickets, Alexander cuts his knees. When he falls, he takes the hand that takes the tickets and breaks each finger for rubbing my palm. The sound effect is of old rubbery carrots slowly breaking in half, one by one.

We sit in the third row, but Fu Sheng doesn't eat popcorn or drink soda, because kung fu masters eat raw turnip. He munches his turnip, and when he turns to me and offers me a bite, I don't even care that his mouth smells like fut when I say, "Thanks, Alexander," and he says, "Call me Alex," without a Chinese accent.

And all the while I'm thinking that Alexander Fu Sheng kicks Bruce Lee's ass, Sonny Chiba and Toshiro Mifune too. When we walk out of the theater, there's nobody there to give you a rough time 'cause that's how it is when you got somebody with you who can kick ass.

My father always says it's a man-to-man world. Doggy-dog. Toe the line. *High Plains Drifter.* Survival of the fittest. Nobody to go to the movies with. A man who rubs little kids. His purple-gums-and-rotten-teeth laugh. Nancy always makes me pay. But I gotta go. I love Alexander Fu Sheng. Even before Kwai Chang Cain. And "Grasshoppa, take this stone from my hand." Somebody who pays back with punches, a man with slick hair and long, black toenails. Doggy-dog. Ra Expeditions. No room for twelve-and-under girls like me except if you got a boyfriend who can kick ass.

NO NINJAS, FARMERS, OR WANNABES IN THIS FAMILY

Everybody here, every Japanee says they're from samurai family back in Japan.

"Samurai, my ass," says my father. "All a bunch of rice farmers who went straight from the stinken paddies to the damn plantation for dolla-a-day, break-your-ass work. Owe your whole life to the plantation general store. No more money. Gotta charge, charge, charge all the meats even, and we talking Vienna sausage and can corn beef. And everybody there is damn rice farmers, so the haole owner, he treat you like one dog, I promise, even his own dog eat and sleep better than us.

"But our family," he says, "we from samurai line, for real. This the story that Uncle Tora wen' trace all the way back to Russia. We Russian, you know, but not the white kine." And my father tells this story to me every time we take a long drive to the countryside.

C

"Long time ago, there was an uprising against the Shogun planned by the Lord Taira. Lord Taira, he was very shrewd and

165

smart, so he convince our family to rise up with him.

"Our clan, samurai of course, we follow the Lord Taira and get wiped out. Everybody in the Taira clan has to commit seppuku. Our clan gotta live on a very small island off of Yanai City called Heigun. On the island, they get incest 'cause only family lives there. Incest, all except for Grandma, who escape the island of Heigun and come to Hawai'i."

"Yeah, right, samurai. Easy escape, how come? Sure, Daddy, sure."

"You watch your lip, girl. 'Cause you talking to a man whose ancestors rose up against the Shogun. No, we ain't no ninja family like your KIKU-TV shows, no Sonny Chibas or Makos or Yagyuu Juubeis in this family, like on your low-class ninja shows. And we ain't no rice farmers either with their cha-cha rice and daikon for dinna.

"Samurai, I tell you. Samurai. Miyamoto Musashi and Zato-ichi all the way. Our mon on the palace walls at one castle in Himeji. I seen our family crest with my own two eyes when I went Japan. Grandma too with her own two eyes, before she die she seen her mother's own family crest right there in stone. Samurai, kid. And don't you eva forget it."

C

Then my father says this to me when he's fed up. When I get something expensive. When I don't take care of even small things:

"We no had car. No TV. No nothing.

"I walked two miles, no, five miles, no, ten miles to school. In the rain. Barefooted.

"We all sleep in the same room. Rice parchment pillow. Rice bag sheets.

"I wore all my brothers' shirts. Passed down to me.

"No candy. No ice cream. Never."

"Yeah, kid, you wanna be this, you wanna be that. I send you piano lessons, you just quit. You tink come cheap? I send you to one nada teacher, you quit. Lose money, I tell you. Then I send you City and County summer fun, you call um *summer junk* jus 'cause was free. Sewing class, you quit. I was picking flowas double time for that class and helping Jeffrey burn electrical wire on weekends, gunfunnit. You wanna be something, then you better learn how for stick to it.

"Me, I was one young boy growing up in the Rice Camp. I wanna job. I ten years old. You know what job I get? I digging up the gobo on the side of the mill. Some for my madda feed the family. Fifteen kids, no fancy foods. Most I sell um. I dig that gobo all day. I ten years old and I hurry up all the time.

"One time, I tell you, I had the sickest thing happen to me. My madda tell me go store for her buy bread with the gobo money. I stay thinking, maybe I buy one Hershey's bar with the gobo money *I wen' make, so* I take the bread to the counter and the Hershey's too. The store owner, he add um up, and I no more nuff. My hands too shame take the candy back to the shelf.

"I sitting outside on the bench wishing for one orange soda. Then the TipTop Bakery man come for delivery and that damn asshole, he throw the day-old pastries at the store owner's Weimarana hunting dogs. My mouth neva did taste one pastry like that till after I left that damn camp.

"Before, I wanna be one veterinarian. And I smart. Even though I no talk too much in school days, I know I smart. But the plantation owners, they make us think we so dumb. No can do nuttin' but stay on the plantation. Me, I write to my big sista in Milwaukee. I beg her send me out of the plantation. Please. Please. But when I get there, I work in one factory 'cause even if I know I smart, I think I dumb. You know what I saying?

"Then my haole friend, he wanna be one biologist. He tell me take one night class with him. Me, I smart but I think I dumb, but I figga what the heck. I came out more smart than him. More better grades. No can talk good as him in class but eh, when the test came back, who get the higher grade? And that's how I came one college student.

"And you, you wanna be this, you wanna be that, you better learn how for talk like one haole like me. 'Yes, sir, I would really appreciate this job. What a spell of nice weather we're having here. Oh yes, sir, I am a hardworking individual. Yes, I do believe I am quite qualified for this vocation. Yes, sir, uh-huh, I am quite capable of speaking the haole vernacular.' You know what I said? You know what I mean? I said you damn right I can talk straight English.

" 'Cause, kiddo, it ain't easy out there. It's a man's world. And a haole man's world more worse. So you better shape up. Stick to it. Stick to *something. Anything.* I tell you, you better practice starting from now. Throw the bull. Play the game.

"You smart but they think you dumb. Then you be like me. You go along, go along, go along, then when you get um by the balls, and that bugga ready to throw the pastries to the dogs, little girl, you twist um hard."

DEAD ANIMALS SPOIL
THE SCENERY

Don't talk dead animals around me.
I can't take it.

Father on his green La-Z-Boy. No shirt on, only his paint-stained khaki Bermudas, and Bob Sevey on the six o'clock news.

Father holds his chopstick with a sewing needle duct-taped to it. When a gecko crosses the screen, its underbelly throbbing with Tic Tac-sized eggs, he slinks up toward the screen slowly like one of his moves in aikido class at the old Cow Palace.

He's close enough to see the gecko's little toes clinging to the screen, his big black eyes, and the veins in his translucent body.

Jabs the gecko, who flies off the screen and into the dark yard. One after another. And my father laughs. On a good night, he double-jabs and two geckos fly off the screen at the same time.

Don't talk dead things around me.
Really, I mean it.

Mother has her own chopsticks in the vegetable garden. A Folgers can with Clorox inside and into the garden. She pulls slugs off of her pakalana vine. The eggplant bush. Across the driveway, swift into the can. The string beans, of course, at least three slugs there. And the chiso. The chives too. All over the ly-chee tree.

And how they writhe together in the bleach, a big brown slimy ball of slug bodies. The next day, it smells like bleached, rotten fishes. Sometimes she pours salt over them. Morton's or rock salt.

Dead animals stain your clothes.

At the Lei Stand, I sell Snickers bars to state workers on break, a bag of Lay's potato chips and orange Fanta to the life-guard. Then *snap*—another mouse bent in two.

Jenks's mother owns the stand and she tells Jenks or his brother Dwayne to take the mouse off, but not before they show me how the trap smashes it. And like in the cartoons, the eyes look like X's.

Jenks wants me to see. He always says, "Shit bricks," 'cause at the moment of the final snap, dead animals, they let it all out. Most of the time, there's no blood, but once in a while, it comes out of the ass.

There's a dark brown spot on my shorts. Jenks says if I have my rags and I say no. It smells funny.

Jenks tells Dwayne to ride his motorcycle back to my house in town and bring another shorts down to the Lei Stand. I change.

Mr. Martinson wants M&M's. I sell a pink shell lei with matching earrings to a lady with blue hair. The spot comes back. This time, Jenks puts his nose to it.

"You get yours, Lovey," he says.

"No, no way," I tell him. And now Jenks has the same spot in almost the same place. "You must have yours too," I tell him.

Then we both see the mouse smashed in the cabinet right under the counter of the Lei Stand, X's for eyes and bleeding from its mouth and ears.

Dead cats. Dead dogs.
They run in front of the car, better them than you.

Father's philosophy is: Don't swerve. Hit um. One more dead cat, so what? Better him than you. My mother hit a cow on the highway on her way back from Volcano Village one night. She didn't swerve and her car got busted up big time.

"Even one rare animal like one Kona nightingale," my father says to me, "I whack um wit' my car if the bugga dumb enough to cross without looking." If a Kona nightingale donkey crossed the street while *I* was driving, *I* don't think I would hit it. I've never seen one in my whole life and don't think I'd want it to die this way.

Father and me go to the Cow Palace every Tuesday and Thursday for aikido class. He takes the back roads through the house lots. Father sees the wiry orange cat. I know what he's going to do. It sounds like someone's head hitting a hollow dry wall and arms and limbs all over.

I turn back and see the cat's legs flailing, back arching. "Watch carefully, little girl, and learn," Father says to me. "Better it than us, that's my philosophy. Get it in your head. Humans more impotant than animals. So don't you cry now."

Dead animals are full of liquid.

Jenks is half Hawaiian, half Japanese. His mother, Aunty Shige, and his father, Uncle Melvin, play Friday night poker at our house. Jenks treats Jerry and me good when we fill in as cashiers at the Lei Stand. He likes us, but once the boys come down, he's the biggest actor around.

Dwayne, Larry, and Ernest don't treat Jenks like shit.

Just me and Jerry.

*

It rains for three days straight. I look outside the kitchen window for the hollow oil drum. The window screen is dusty black and oily-looking.

I can't see the goat. "Where the hell is she?" I ask my father.

I don't really care about this goat. She came to us when she was already old. Kind of wild and not cute like some of the kids we had before.

Calhoon won't even give her a name. "Daddy," she says, "let's let her loose, then shoot her and stuff her," and Father tells her to shut up.

The air glassy and the ground still steaming, I go back toward the hollow oil drum and find her. "Dumb, stupid goat," I say to her. She's already bloated and smelling bad, real bad, the X's in her eyes. I scream and run back to the house.

My father calls Uncle Ed, who brings Ernest, Larry, Jerry, Dwayne, and Jenks over to help us get rid of the goat. They go down the hill in the back and Calhoon, Jerry, and me see only the tops of their heads, when all of a sudden, Jenks comes staggering up the hill. He's gagging and saliva, the thick kind, lots of it, falling out of his mouth. The other boys take their shirts off and wrap their nose and mouth.

But Jenks comes up to the back porch. "Oh God," he says. "The smell."

"I know, Jenks, I know," I tell him.

"No, you dunno, Lovey. I wen' pick up the back end of the goat like your fadda said, and when I wen' put my hands underneath, had all maggots already, and my fingers went right through the skin, and had goat hair all stuck on me. Then she busted open."

Dwayne, Larry, and Ernest each haul a garbage bag. Murky water drips from the bags. "They musta chop her up," says Jerry.

"Aw, shut up, Jerry, you wimp," says Calhoon.

The smell hangs thick as they pass and lots of swearing from Uncle Ed when they heave the garbage bags into the back of his Ford truck.

"Pussy," says Larry to Jenks. "Pussies and fags," he says to all of us. And nobody says nothing.

Dead animals spoil the scenery.

Mizuno Pond at the end of a sunny day. Brilliant sunlight, yet the sky dark black and gray. Nobody poking around in the tidal pools. Just walking rock over rock. Sea grass. And water dark blue but calm.

Sea mist in the brightest beam of light. You know it might

rain, real hard, and Jenks says if his mother leaves us behind after cleaning up the Lei Stand, then we can call Dwayne to come
get us after from the pay phone next to the pavilion.

When Jenks stands by me, I swear I can tell he washes his
clothes with Ivory Snow. Jenks and me on a payday, his mother
not nagging us to sweep up or count change or put the candies
away. Jenks and me. Payday. Mizuno Pond. And nobody
around.

We walk a little more and a whole cow, black and white,
bloated and pink-bellied, buoys in the rising tide right there in
front of us. The body, like a light balloon, hits the rocks.

Jenks says something stupid like "Look, Lovey. Wow. I wonder how it died and floated down to the pond. And whole like
that. Wow, man, a whole dead cow. Wait till Dwayne see this.
Come quick. Look."

The cow in salt water doesn't smell. When the high tide
comes in, the dead cow floats away like a black, white, and pink
balloon that doesn't smell, not at all.

When you pose dead animals for eternity, you better plan
it well with your taxidermist.

It starts with a cow skull from the pasture behind the school.
Father has a Chinese ring-necked pheasant frozen and wrapped
in newspaper in the outside freezer. The mouth, plugged with
frozen, bloody toilet paper like the taxidermist said.

And Calhoon's dead chukar from the last bird season next to
it, frozen too and marked CAL/CHUCKA on masking tape. Father
and Uncle Ed got a partridge last weekend, broke in a new

springer named Alex, and kept the partridge in the refridge.

The pose is pheasant in the middle of cow skull, wings out-spread, beak screaming open.

Chukar to right of pheasant, wings also open, one kind of broken and hanging. A little Cutex for blood on the cow's skull.

Partridge near flight on the other side.

Use the beat-up California quail as the dead bird at the feet of the pheasant. Lots of Cutex around it.

Mongoose with teeth showing at base of cow skull ready to kill.

> *Repeat the pose of dead birds, hire the same taxidermist,*
> *and shoot another round of the same game. For Uncle*
> *Ed's coffee table.*

Uncle Ed and Father, they got all the birds, and all they need now is a mongoose.

> *Drown an animal if you want it to pose.*

"I gotta catch this sucka. I gotta finish the mount. The mount I going put on the coffee table this Thanksgiving. Sheez, Ed. Cannot shoot um or what?"

"Shit, Hubert. Shoot um, shoot um. We go up the cane field and shoot one mongoose. Nah, betta be two. Freeze one for mine next."

They blow it to bits.

So they trap a mongoose, use smoke pig meat as bait, and it hisses and snares its teeth when my father holds the cage.

I don't know why I watch.

He fills the cement washtub outside with cold water, and even until the moment my father lowers the mongoose into the water, it hisses at us.

Swims. Like dog paddle.

Drowning and writhing and twisting. Brown body turning. Eyes taking one last look at us. Mouth gasping, open, close.

Then a bubbling, gurgling sound.

The smell of stagnant, greenish-brown swamp water.

Father pokes at it with a chopstick.

Dead and float to the top of the cage.

Shit bricks.

C

I sit at the taxidermist's table. "Fuck, Hubert," the taxidermist says. "Fuck this shit, man." The taxidermist walks away. The smell so pure and strong. The smell of the dead mongoose. And Father not covering his nose. "Hubert—you sure you wanna do this shit, man?"

Father nods and looks at me. He wants to see me flinch at the smell. He wants to see me turn away. Wants to see me swerve. *Pussies and fags.* But I don't. I want to die, I want to feel sorry, but I don't. Want to hold my head high, unwrinkle my eyebrows, swallow all that spit, watch the skinning of a stinking animal, breathe deep.

Breathe deep, eyes open, Father, and watch.

MY NANNY AND
BILLY THE KID

In the home movie, I stand by the shave-ice truck. I hold the strawberry cone to my lips. I watch the billies surround my Nanny in the large goat cage at the zoo. I watch me watching her, my Nanny, get circled and smelled. And press up to the side of the fence and look for me and bleat that way. And my father filming Calhoon and me, he didn't know what else to do. Calhoon still holding the soft centers of the ti leaf that we thought Nanny might want to eat in her new home.

The Onekahakaha Zoo.

Some zoo. A bunch of iguanas in one cage. A loose peacock or two. A coatimundi. Two gibbon monkeys, a fat one and a baby. A pueo. An 'io. And a stupid goat cage in the middle of the whole zoo.

Nanny didn't want to eat the ti leaf. Animals, they know when something is not right. And Nanny, I could feel her heart beating, I knew her so well. I knew she didn't want to live here. I knew she was scared. And I knew that she knew we were leaving her.

C

When she came to my house, there were two of them. Nanny with her umbilical cord still stuck to her, black, shriveled, and smelling like dry fish. And Billy the Kid, the bleating baby ram. Father found both of them alone. On the same day. Strange, very strange.

Father always comes home from hunting near dinnertime and smells like the mountains. Sweat and wind. He's always dirty in his camouflage clothes and his fluorescent-orange hunting hat pushed back on his red forehead except for the creases that didn't sunburn.

But this day, when Cal and me run out to greet him, he's smiling and doesn't say why he's smiling. "What, Daddy, what? What's so funny?" This is when we hear them crying in the back of the Land Rover.

And there they are. The baby goat and the baby ram. Nanny comes wagging over to us. Father put her on an old rag covered with flattened goat shit. And Billy the Kid, he's still crying in the corner of the Land Rover.

"Strangest thing, I tell you," my father says later on, "these two all alone like that crying up Mauna Kea, spooky, I tell you, see this kinda thing. Thass why was a sign to me. Sign saying, Hubert, take these two babies home and raise um like your own."

C

Home Movie Reel #6. "Kids with Nanny" written on masking tape:

She's still a baby. The camera shows her bedding in the garage and the sleeping bags that Calhoon and me sleep in next to her bed. Then the swept-up pile of goat shit.

She's nestled up in her bedding and then in my sleeping bag zipped up, me and her inside it. I'm pretending to be asleep for the camera. Cal is on the side, laughing, then she tries to take Nanny out by her gangly legs.

Billy the Kid's tied up to the garage post. He's bleating and carrying on loudly, of course. He's pulling and yanking on his rope till his hind legs fly in the air, but he keeps doing it. I'm feeding Nanny, and Calhoon gets Billy the Kid, who struggles against his rope.

They drink evaporated milk, half-and-half, from Gerber baby bottles like two babies and Nanny nuzzles up to my face and cries. Her mouth smells like fresh warm milk and I love her so much, I examine each hoof and kiss them right on camera.

We're fighting over who feeds Nanny, since Billy the Kid, all he does is cry and the milk's spilling out of his mouth. He's kicking and fighting and doesn't want to be hugged and Father says, "Thass the true way of the wild. You can't never tame a wild animal. From the minute they born, they know how fo' survive. Survival of the fittest. In the wild, you dunno how fo' survive, then mo' betta you die. Billy the Kid, now ass one *real* mouflon, I tell you."

So Father takes care of Billy now, and Calhoon and me, the camera's rolling, walking Nanny around the yard on a leash and she's so happy, she's prancing for the camera. Billy tied up in the background eating grass and looking grouchy. I'm scratching Nanny's little horn nubs and she likes it so much, I scratch it with my chin and kiss her on her goat lips.

C

It started with that damn Billy the Kid. He's a ram, so he grew fast, I mean real fast. Pretty soon, he had more than horn nubs on his head. Billy had mouflon horns, two big curls with ridges in them that could cut your finger off. And that same grouchy face all the time.

Billy the Kid belonged to Father, who tied a tire on to the lychee tree for Billy, who'd lower his head, lift up his front hoofs, and butt that tire. Plenty times, not just once or twice. Then he'd butt the cement blocks next to the anthurium patch.

And he'd get loose all the time with all that butting. Once, Cal and me were walking Nanny around the yard. We sat down in the garage with some young lychee leaves.

Nanny sat on my lap like she always did, even if she was already a teenager in goat years, then Billy came barreling around the corner. I swear I saw steam coming out of his nostrils. Cal started screaming and I told her, "Don't run, don't run. Open the car door slowly and shove Nanny's ass in there."

That goddamn Billy the Kid lifted up his front hoofs and lowered his head for me as I fell into the car, smashing Cal and Nanny; we slammed the door.

Calhoon still had the lychee leaves clutched in her hand. Nanny, who's still smashed under Cal and me, started eating it. Then that stupid ram of my father's started head-butting the car.

"Oh my God, Lovey. His ass is grass and Daddy the lawn mower. Wait till Daddy see the dents in this car." Wham. Wham. Wham. Over and over until the car rocked, and Nanny's bleating, and Cal screaming, "Daddy, Daddy, help, help." I spit on Billy's head every time he came close enough to the window near me.

Father came running out of the back of the yard and grabbed a guava log from under the tree next to the shed. Billy turned his angry, grouchy face on him. Nanny's bleating so loud that her tongue stuck halfway out of her mouth slobbering all over Father's dented car.

My father hit Billy once on the side of his head with the guava log. This made Billy more angry. He charged my father but Daddy stood there with the log and hit him again over the head. Stunned, Billy staggered and Father beat his body until Billy fell down. Then Father got the chain, tied it around Billy's neck, and dragged him to the laundry line post.

Father beat him with that log every day, thinking it would train him to back off when a person came near him. It was a hollow sound, wood hitting the body, and like stick-fighting in an empty forest, the wood hitting his horns. And Billy never made a sound all the while.

C

Home Movie Reel #17. "Bye-bye Billy the Kid/Hello Ed and Helen's" written on masking tape:

The camera shows Uncle Ed, Ernest, and Larry tying Billy's legs. Pan to the side, Jerry, Calhoon, me waving at the camera and Nanny rubbing her horn nubs on my legs hard so I bump Cal, who bumps Jerry, and we all start pushing and shoving each other for the camera.

Say bye-bye Billy, everybody, as Uncle Ed drives the white Ford truck down the long driveway.

C

There was a Filipino lady who grew delicious bittermelon on a trellis all along the fence line between hers and Uncle Ed's house. When the bittermelon grew on Uncle Ed's side, she would come over and pick the bittermelons and give some to Uncle Ed and Aunt Helen.

As the story goes, she was on Uncle Ed's side of the trellis, bent over, picking dead leaves off of the vines. She already had an apronful of bittermelons when here comes Billy the Kid, rope hanging from his halter, head low, hoofs in the air, and wham, right into Mrs. Dela Torre's ass. There went Mrs. Dela Torre, headfirst into the trellis, the whole trellis smashed to the ground as Mrs. Dela Torre screamed, scrambled around, falling and rolling over on the bittermelon trellis to get up. Billy trampled the whole vine and Mrs. Dela Torre started throwing bittermelons at him while running back toward her house.

Uncle Ed and Father paid her medical expenses for a few stitches on her face at the emergency room price. This did not make them the happiest hunters. They shrugged off her threats of "I going sue your asses, you wait." And from then on, nobody never got another vegetable from her.

C

"Bye-bye Billy the Kid," Part 2:

They shot him up the ass for many reasons. They wanted his front quarters for mounting. He was a handsome mouflon, after all. They wanted his hindquarters for smoke meat. And they made Jerry, Cal, me, and the older boys watch. Father said that there is a lesson in all things: The boys, except for Jerry—how to kill a ram and use all parts. The boys all cheered and gave each other high five. How to kill a ram: shoot him up the ass. For Jerry, Cal, and me, the lesson was not too clear.

They skinned Billy right there in Uncle Ed's garage on a huge piece of cardboard. And Father sliced off Billy's balls. "Here, Lovey, put this on the side. Daddy make one nice coin bag for you."

And he did. Father tanned it himself. Punched holes on the top edge. Wove a piece of leather through each hole. Pulled it tight. And everybody, including the boys, wanted to hold my Billy-balls coin bag, stroke Billy's varnished horns, touch his glassy yellow eyes, his stiff face. Somebody forgot to tell the taxidermist how angry he was.

C

She was eating all of the good plants.

There was too much goat shit in the yard.

She needed to be with her own kind.

"She not human, you know, and she ain't going live in this garage foreva. And I seen you two girls take her in the house the other day."

Too easy to say that we weren't goats either and couldn't live in the garage in sleeping bags for the rest of Nanny's life.

What I will miss the most is the goat smell on my clothes and on my skin and hair.

Father lowers the backseat of the Land Rover and we hoist

Nanny up and sit with her on her bedding. Calhoon holds a bag full of ti-leaf shoots. And we pet her head all the way down to the zoo.

Everyone is amazed when she struts into the zoo with us and little kids pet her as she nibble-lips the ti leaves that Cal brought.

Once she's in the cage, the billies surround her like a gang of wild thieves. They smell her ass, she tucks her tail in, and turns around looking for me. She runs over the rocks to the side of the cage where I stand while the billies all chase her. They prance-run after her until she's pressed against the fence, her face turned and bleating the most aching cry as one of the goats suddenly mounts her.

The people around us, the kids especially, start laughing at Nanny and the billy on top of her. Somebody screams, "Look, the two goats ooofing!" But I can't do a thing—stand there and watch.

C

Home Movie Reel #20. "Kids at Zoo" written on masking tape:

I'm standing by the shave-ice truck. I hold the strawberry cone to my lips but cannot eat. Calhoon leans against the front of the truck.

This is not on the home movie:

"When the camera rolling, you betta smile now, you hear me, Lovey? Daddy treat you to shave ice. C'mon. Hup, hup."

Not on the home movie:

"It ain't that bad, Lovey. You gotta learn how to say goodbye. You gotta be tough. Don't cry, you hear me?"

Standing by that fence, I want to pull her out by her gangly kid legs. Spit on the billy's head and hit him with a guava log. And everybody who laughs, look them all in the eye until they stop. Lead her by the leash into the car and home to the bedspread in the garage. Breathe deep, the smell of goat all over me—on my clothes, my skin, and hair.

THE CROSSING

Emerald-green feathers Father and me pluck off of the peacock from Puuwaawaa Ranch off the old Kona Road. The body cold but defrosting, smelling a little bad already. We pluck and sort so there's no double work, sort them into the rows and rows of fishing-hook trays. So many bird feathers in plastic trays like feather apartments, one on top of the other.

It's Father's new moneymaking idea, and though we've worked hard—taking those long drives to the countryside to get the dead birds or shooting them ourself, it's been good money.

And Daddy talks to me all the time, sometimes like I'm not even there. Just going on and on. And he drives real slow even when the speed limit is 60; Daddy goes the minimum, which is 35.

If we come home Volcano way, he gets a good start, puts the Land Rover in neutral, and rolls all the way down from Glenwood to Panaewa. My mother gets mad if she's in the car, so he does this only if I'm there. It takes us double the time to get places. Daddy and me.

We're going to Waiohinu. The sky gray, rain slanting sideways. Daddy soaking wet after fixing a flat outside of Kurtis-

187

town, he finishes, stops, and stares at the sky, the rain pouring on his glassy face.

When he gets in and we drive for a while, he says, "I tell you one story, Lovey. About the three of us—Tora, Uri, and me. This been bugging me for all these years. But Daddy like you know the one thing I rememba about my small kid time. This is it."

It's like this all the way to Waiohinu to pick up the three Chinese ring-necked pheasants. Daddy telling me things that he may never say again. Sometimes like I'm not even there.

"Tora, he nine years older than me. He was one good-looking bugga, dark his skin, and one good leader. My bradda, he was brash. And cocky. But everybody was scared him in Rice Camp 'cause he like for fight. You know, he used to lick this Filipino guy once a week for nothing. I think his name was Pablo. No, the guy's name was Pundo. He was Tora's classmate and was smarter than my bradda. The teachers, they all thought my bradda was dumb—but he wasn't. Just playful.

"Uri, he one year older than me. Ho, I tell you, Uri was the fastest runner in the camp and the best tree climber. And him, he follow Tora whereva he went. Every time, just the two of them going hea and there. Had other kids in our family and other kids in the camp but they was my big braddas right above me, Tora and Uri, but always only them two—and then there was me.

"I going tell you some things right now and what I tell you, you betta rememba, 'cause there was nothing to say about this before and now there is."

He pauses and looks at me. The landscape changes fast out on the drives to South Point side. Rain, then ohia forest, then lava field, Ka'u Desert, cane field, fog, hail, cow pasture within yards of each other, they change. And Mauna Loa to the right of us.

My father says, "I had one shirt. Was one blue one with white flowas. You know that shirt belong to four braddas before me. Had fifteen kids in our family and we no could have new stuffs. You know, by the time I got that shirt, couldn't tell if was blue before. I only knew was blue 'cause my braddas rememba it that way. But me, I neva really care back then. I was only six, what the heck. You know what I mean? Small kid time, you dunno the difference, right?

"My fav'rite thing for do was hang around with Tora and Uri when they let me small kine be with them. I tell you, I use to wait on the roadside sometimes one hour if I hear Tora and Uri talking about going fishing at breakfast time. I no like them leave me, eh? So I make sure I there, waiting. How many days like that I listen to them buggas talk, then try be where I can follow, so I can go with them all their secret places, you know what I mean? But had one time, I swear, I neva going forget.

"You know what I rememba about that morning? I rememba kicking some small stones in the open ditch. The water in that ditch, all greasy and dirty from the kitchens and furos in the camp. I rememba how dirty that water was—Rice Camp, us neva have sewer system.

"That morning I remember thinking how your grandma make our camp house look so nice. She plant the African daisies, carnations, and Easter lilies all in the front. And on the side of the house, she wen' grow won bok, spinach, beans, peas, and turnips.

"I seen Tora and Uri with their bamboo fishing poles and other fishing stuffs with them, but I neva say nothing when they wen' walk pass me. I go pretend like I looking something way down the pasture side. Then I follow few steps behind. Uri, the bugga, go whisper something to Tora. All of a sudden, Tora, he turn around and whip the pole upside down on the ground.

"He draw one line deep in the dirt. 'See that line?' he tell me. 'You see um, Hubert? You try cross um. I going lick you with this bamboo pole. You cannot come with us. You too slow, not like Uri. Try cross um,' he threaten me.

"I know that Tora and Uri was going up Turning Pond or Scharsh Pond, maybe even up the O'va. If the buggas went up Huleia River, they was going for mullet or papio. In the upper river, had o'opu. You dunno how I wish I could see the fish they was going catch while the bugga thrashing on the line, not all dead and ready for the frying pan like I always seen um when my braddas come home.

"I just stand there behind that line on the road. I watch my brothers until they small specks up the road. Then I push my foot through the line. I erase um. No mo' line now and I run forward fast as I can. Ho, in my mind I can see all the mountain apple, the guava and lilikoi. So I run faster, maybe I get to heaven before them. I can already see my braddas ahead of me. Then Tora turn around. 'Go home, Inky,' he yell. He draw another line. 'You try cross this line, Inky. You going get lickens when I get home, I tell you. Stay home.' My braddas, they call me Inky Dinky Bali Boo. Sometimes they sing um.

"Me, I stop behind the new line and pull my faded shirt. I look at the long line Tora wen' draw across the whole road. The bamboo grove on the side of the road creak and brush in the wind. I sit behind that line and draw in the dirt.

"Then I yell loud as I can, 'T-o-r-a. U-r-i.' I know they cannot hear me. But I wait behind the line, all day that day, that's what I rememba. Had plenty days after that I wen' wait behind one line in the dirt. I always waiting behind the line my bradda draw for me.

"And I was small boy that time waiting, waiting. Some days I feel so scared all by myself waiting till dark, I sing some songs the haole lady teach me at school. Then I whistle little bit but I call the obake lady from the trees 'cause I whistling and I one small boy all by myself. She laughing 'cause look like I no mo' madda and fadda. I feel so shame, one obake laughing at me like that, and I all by myself.

"Some days I waiting, I think I missing out on heaven, the way Tora and Uri make um, the places they seen while I was behind that goddamn line he drawn in the dirt. And I so damn sad I cannot see heaven with them with *my own eyes*. Gotta wait at home with all my sistas for the guava, lilikoi, mango, and oʻopu.

"Not the same, probably no even taste as good as when you got um straight from God."

c

By the time we get to the Mark Twain monkeypod tree, by the Nishimoto Motel in Waiohinu to meet the man with the birds, my father's story is over. He wraps the frozen birds in newspaper and puts them in the Igloo in the back of the Land Rover.

Daddy and me on our way home, we stop by Wood Valley up

the hills behind Pahala. Wait in the cane and see, Chinese ring-necked pheasant, red face and orange eyes watching the sky. And Daddy lets me shoot first, aim away from the white neck so blood won't stain the most pure feathers on this bird.

C

Jimmy Lee, who runs the chicken hatchery, says that his friend at the Alii Feather Company on Mamo Street, next to AnToinette's Beauty Shoppe and Hilo Camera and Comic, wants golden pheasant.

What a lei that would make. Like strings of gold, the feathers that fall in shiny strands. And the red breast feathers, fine like the ohia lehua blossoms. Daddy knows a breeder all the way up in Hawi and makes a deal for dead birds. Not a real good deal, but he says, "The return going be three times when I sell the feathers, you watch, Lovey. And you see a real businessman in action."

We leave the next morning way before sunrise so we can make it home early in the afternoon to pluck the feathers. All the way to the halfway mark, Tex Drive-in, my father tells me about ghosts 'cause Daddy got the ghost-eye.

"I can still smell the smell of that pillow, you know, stuff with pigeon peas, rice parchment, and beans, if I think real hard."

I learn that if I let him go, the stories get real good. Never stop and ask questions—he gets grouchy and stops talking for miles.

He says, "Uri's snoring next to me, and next to him, Tora tossing and turning. Five of us younger boys in that room.

"I turn my face to the wall. The rice-bag pillowcase always

feel rough, even when dirty. I pull the futon my madda made from leftover rags close to my chin. Ho, I had to piss but I thought the outhouse was haunted.

"My madda use to tell me for wake her up or one of my braddas if I gotta go bathroom nighttime. So I turn to Uri. But I neva wake him up. I was mo' scared for make him mad than go outside face the obake.

"I look at Tora. Everybody in Rice Camp call him Captain. He use to wear army hats. He had plenny army hats but nobody know where he got um from. Ho, the night wind shake the mango tree. And when the moonlight come inside the room, I seen Tora's hats all stuff under the corner of his pillow.

"I look outside by the outhouse. Had one spooky bamboo grove around um and the whole grove whistle and brush when the wind blow. Sound like squeaking and whistling, like one old Japanee song on one flute. And the worse part was wheneva one of us kids went out there for use the bathroom nighttime, the next morning that person tell the whole family about the ghost that he seen.

"I wen' stand up and already the wind crawl up my pants leg. Uri wake up, he tell, 'Where you going, Inky?'

" 'Come with me, please, Uri,' I tell, and he come with me. Nighttime get plenny light, you know, if get full moon. And the sounds real loud, every sound, even your feet walking in the gravel.

"And right by the bamboo grove, right when the flute music from the bamboo reeds wen' start for play, I seen her. The obake lady with long white hair, no mo' legs, with one red mouth. Me and Uri, right by the outhouse. And you know what, I wen' piss right in my pants and by the time I was pau, she was gone."

Then he pauses for a long time. I see Tex Drive-in ahead of us. Still dark but I smell the malasadas from miles away. And Daddy says, "Remember I said I going take you up Kipu Plantation? First get that long road with pine trees. Get plenny obake in those trees at night.

"Rememba the pictures of the pile of stones I shown you? That use to be my house when I was small. And all the rusty totan roofs, all corroded in the middle of the stones—that was our roof.

"Haupu Mountain. You going see um. Thass where Tora and Uri use to go. That get my goat, man. How come I neva went there? Even when I got mo' big, I neva went there, 'cause I wanted for see um with them.

"Get one statue of Mr. Rice that says, 'Erected in his memory by his Japanese friends.' My fadda built the foundation part of that statue, you believe that?

"And I show you in the pictures, over there was the outhouse. Over there was the garden. Over here was the kitchen. But I get hard time even see um in my head sometimes.

"One day, you and me going climb Haupu Mountain and look around, 'cause I imagine get plenny for see. What you think? You eva thought you might see heaven when your heart was still going and your lungs was still breathing, or what? You be my company when we go visit God."

Something tells me I don't want what comes next. I don't want the dead barn owls this haole man from Volcano Village says he has. He tells my father on the phone that field poison the sugar company uses to kill cane rats make the owls brain dead, dizzy, and dazed by the time they die.

He tells Daddy he has *four* of them. *Four* white speckled birds, rare feathers for a lei that I would *never* wear around *my* lauhala hat. And the haole man tells my father he has a pueo he'll throw in for the right price. Daddy doesn't even want to consider this bird. He's mad that the haole even said he had it. Even if it died naturally.

The morning slides cold through the car windows. Pink light behind the African tulips in the back as we leave the house for Volcano Village before my mother defrosts the lup cheong for breakfast.

And Daddy begins, "Mornings was always the same. The men from Rice Camp, few Filipino, plenny Japanee, and one Portagee left for work at five in the morning. They end at five in the afternoon. All of them had for wear straw hats. Hot, you know, working twelve hours a day. And had to wear linen shirts bumbye the cane leaf cut your arm. Cane leaf get fine hair on top, and when you sweat, the bugga cling on you and you get one mean rash.

"Some workers make better pay—they get leather gloves. The poor ones get cloth. Everybody get arm protectors. All us get tabi 'cause was cheap and had socks kine leggings so the centipedes no bite your feet.

"My madda them had for work too. All the ladies had big

hats with scarf around their neck and face. The wahines had linen ahina pants so the cane no scratch. When they had babies, they put um in cloth slings and hang um by their hips when they work the fields. All day.

"This plantation was fifteen hundred acres but was small compared to some others back then in the 1930s. We earn one dolla a day. One dolla, and we bus' our ass, laying train tracks—that's heavy steel we carrying all day till our back feel broken, and cutting cane, hoeing, dig and plant and cut, bend ova all day long—we work mo' hard than you eva will in your whole life, and dirty work, pilau, break your ass. Yeah, we had free house and water and free medical but big deal.

"That goddamn doctor—he okay, but the bugga had one bad habit of taking out your appendix for one stomachache, I tell you."

My father shows me a scar across his stomach. Shakes his head, and soon after this, past the field of white ginger near Mountain View, I'm not in the car, as far as Daddy is concerned. And I'm glad, because he tells about my grandpa that no one talks about.

"My fadda was born 1890. Came Hawai'i 1907 for be one laborer in the sugar fields. He the only one came from his family. My fadda, and this what get me even now—he neva seen Japan again.

"He work that plantation all his life. Set the train tracks in the just-harvest fields. That's hard labor, I tell you. Broke your heart, then your body. When the old man was forty something, he bus' his hips in one industrial accident. Afta that, he was kinda cripple, no can walk good no mo'.

"My fadda, he love for go fish for koi nighttime. But koi,

gotta fish nighttime, eh, so kinda spooky. But my fadda, he no let nobody go with him even if we ask plenny times. On his way home from fishing, he stop up the graveyard for pay respect to all his dead friends. This usually around midnight. Ho, I tell you, my fadda seen mo' ghosts than anybody in the camp. Thass where I get my ghost-eye from. And now Calhoon get um, that ghost-eye. Not everybody get um, you know. You no mo' the eye. See what I mean?

"You know, my fadda, he neva say nothing about going back Japan. Was pau, everything he had with Japan. Except for one small package he had. He brought um with him from Japan when he was seventeen years old.

"He neva tell nobody what was inside. But he told all fifteen of us and my madda that we could open um when he die. In 1952, you wasn't even in my dream yet—I was seventeen, my fadda, he die of one heart attack. He was dead right there off the plantation truck. And where I was? I was in Milwaukee with my big sista working in one brewery. I neva had nuff money for come home say goodbye to my old man. But Uri tell me what happen.

"When my madda open the package, was soil—from Japan. My old man, he wanna be buried in Japanee soil. He carry that package in his one bag in 1907 all the way from Japan and keep um under his bed all those years. That was his way of going home."

C

On our way home, my father makes me hold the barn owls on my lap. I feel them pulsing. I don't want to pluck the feathers with him. I don't. But I know I will, one by one on the floor of the garage, feel the cold come up the legs of my pants, see blood drip out of each owl pore.

The white owl feathers worth plenty of money. And my father imitates their cry, goes "Kuri-kuri-kuri-ko" over and over again, and tells me he learned this from a pair who flew past the porch of his plantation house on Kaua'i every night near six. Learned it enough to sing it.

C

At the Alii Feather Company, a smell like the taxidermist's shop comes out the door. The chemical they use to preserve the pelts all hanging on the far wall. Rows and rows of plastic hook trays and bags of feathers sealed airtight.

Daddy and me park in the unpaved lot next to Mamo Theatre. Walk slow with our Ziploc bags full of barn owl feathers. The golden pheasant feathers, brilliant reds and golden strands.

The money we make, thick in an envelope. Daddy feels rich, goes to the '76 station and says, "Fill 'er up." He calls my mother from a pay phone and says we're driving to Pahala. "The Japanese blue," he says, "we go get um up Wood Valley. You know I kept nuff feathers from every bird we had for one lei for me and one for you? You be far away from home one day, you see the golden pheasant in China, you going think about the time you and me went up Hawi. Put your lei on your hat in the streets of Shanghai and you be on Mamo Street with me again."

We get to Hirano Store and my father buys us two boiled eggs each, gravy burgers, One Ton chips, and two Japan apples for dinner. We each have our own chocolate milk and sit outside the store. He tells me, "Hamamoto Store in our camp had wooden floors all cover with oil. Old lady Mrs. Hamamoto use to tell me, 'Keep the dus' off mo' betta. Too much dus' planting time.' When I look up from the doorway, I could see Mr. Hamamoto in the office on the second floor.

"I rememba had one soda machine right by the door and the soda bottles all full of cool moisture beads, make my mouth wata, but I neva have the five cents I need for buy one. Only had nuff money for buy bread." Father looks around the store we're in as if seeing his store.

"I dunno why my madda send me. I one small kid, youngest boy, eh, and I get seven sistas too, but me, I always the one gotta go. That day, Mr. Sadanaga, one of the reg-la workers, he come up to me with the pencil he wear on his ear every day and he tell me, 'So what, Hubert, Mama forget orda the bread? You know where stay. Go get um.'

"I rush past him. I look inside the chill box where get all the meats for little while, then grab one loaf bread. Mr. Sadanaga, he helping somebody else, so that day, I wen' look long time at the glass case with all the pocketknife and watch. I neva know my face was so close until I seen all the steam in front my face.

" 'Your papa buy you one wen' you mo' big, Hubert.' Was Mr. Sadanaga talking to me. The bugga knew us had fifteen kids and I could neva have my own knife but the way he said um, I knew he wasn't being mean. He lead me to the front of the store. 'Hea, you one good boy,' he tell me, 'I give you one Hershey's.' My mouth like take the candy. My head tell me no take um—we poor but I no need take um.

"I put my eyes down, slide my hand across the counter, say thank you small kine, and run out real fast bumbye he see my eyes, eh, and how much I wanted um."

I don't look at him and he don't look at me. I climb into the Land Rover and make my body small. Don't want him to remember how I ask for lots of things bigger than a knife sometimes that I throw around or break. Sleep all the way to Pahala.

C

Our feather business ended after our last drive to Laupahoehoe together. It was a long drive because of the sugarcane harvest mud sludge on the roads, the rains, and the slow-moving cane trucks full of muddy arms of cane hanging from their chain belly.

When we get to the Portagee man's house, he takes us in the back of his garage, lifts the foggy mouth of the freezer full of icicles, and what I see, worse than anything I've ever seen before: frozen bodies, a freezer full of animals.

Some aren't even wrapped and their eyes frozen open, mouths with tongues hanging out—goats, sheep, pheasants, quail, all those animals. The Portagee takes out six bundles in newspaper and unwraps them. "Four pueo, and check this out, brah, check this out, I get two 'io."

"Sorry, man," my father says, "Thass native birds—and if I was you, brah, I defrost them and go put um back where you got um before they come get you. I ain't talking the feds, brah, I talking those birds."

Walking down the man's muddy driveway, my father mutters, "Stupid goddamn Portagee. Look what we all stooping to for a few fricken feathers. I pau, Lovey," my father says. "Game birds, thass one thing. But pueo and 'io—that Portagee's ass is rats and the pueo and 'io going hunt his stupid ass down. Let's get outta here."

Once in the car, I get Daddy to finish the story he started on the road. I ask questions about Uncle Tora and Uncle Uri, and when he starts to answer, I make myself not there fast. He's talking about home again.

"Let me tell you about Haupu Mountain," he starts slowly, "so that when we go there, you going know you died and went heaven with me. Thass what you call one pristine forest. They always talk about the pristine forest on TV. I know my mountain is *pristine*. Nice word, eh?

"Get ohia trees all over. Mokihana ready for pick. And staghorn growing all over. Get tall eucalyptus and plum trees with plenny lilikoi vines. That's how you going know we there. On the day we get there." Daddy stops for a long while and looks ahead, leans on the steering wheel.

"Last summa when Uri and Tora came home, us three, and only us three, no other braddas or sistas, no wifes or kids, went up that old road line with pine trees.

"I watch them two old buggas walk slow up the road. You know, I look at them and 1930 seem so far back. I dunno why, but I wen' pick up one long stick for tap on the road as I walk.

"Tora tell me, 'Hey, Hubert, not so fast. We've got all day.' The bugga talk kinda haole, he been away from home so long. Then my bradda, he lean on one old ohia log that somebody made into barb-wire-fence post long time ago. He look into the mountains like one old hermit man. Study the fog little bit. 'Hey, Hubert,' he tell me, 'you gotta remember, I'm older now. Slow down.'

"Then I wen' tell him, no ask me why, if he rememba this, and I wen' draw one line in the dirt road. This where you use to draw the line for me, rememba, I tell him. I couldn't cross the line for go fishing with you two guys.

"My bradda, he frown little while. Then he look at Uri. But Uri, he turn his face away, he rememba too how he use to whisper to Tora.

" 'Yeah,' he tell. 'I remember.' He no look at me afta that and all day. He no smile in the pictures I wen' take by that pile of stones that we use to call home. He act funny kine all day and I regret I wen' bring um up. I neva mean no harm."

From his wallet, Daddy pulls out a neatly folded piece of paper and makes me read the letter.

Dear Hubert,
When we last saw each other, you asked me if I remembered something from our childhood. Yes, I did, but I wasn't aware of its importance until I was about fifty years old.

William and I were always together—fishing at the lakes for Charley fish, for o'opu at Huleia Valley, picking guavas and mountain apples up in the mountains by Huleia School.

Whenever I felt the trip wasn't too hard, Hubert, I would let you come along. Being the oldest of the younger boys, I decided who could come and who should stay. If I didn't want to take you, yes, I would draw a line in the road and tell you not to cross it.

You were only six or so and I was fifteen, so you stayed

back. I didn't realize what I was doing to you. I only knew this when you told me last summer how you felt.

It was a cruel thing to do. You were six. I'm sure you just wanted to show William and me that you could do whatever we did.

I've spent many nights wondering how I could undo what I did to you some forty years ago. I should have never denied you the right to go anywhere with us. I promise you, if not in this life then in the next, I will take you past the lines I drew for you as a boy to the mountains where we played, even if I have to carry you.

Tora

Nobody says nothing. No questions so Daddy can go home. He's muttering again about all those animals in the Portagee's freezer, those birds, the pueo and the 'io, so many of them, mouths plugged with bloody toilet paper—they were shot and wrapped in newspaper for somebody to pluck and sell to the Alii Feather Company for an envelopeful of money. Daddy continues his story.

"Mountain apple bigger than my fist and so juicy the red drops going plop off your lips all red.

"And gingers, I no think you seen all the kind gingers one place like this—yellow, torch, kahili, white.

"And mokihana—sheez, this place get nuff for make ten strands easy.

"And maile—I told you about the maile? The leafs so sweet and big, and when you pull the vine off the stalk, the bark smell stay unda your fingas for one week, the smell of the maile.

"Staghorn over the whole floor and the ohia lehua, the rain hang from her red flowa.

"I imagine the plum trees and lilikoi all sweet, what you think? I neva did taste the one from Haupu till this day.

"And the guava, we pick um and Daddy make jelly, so much, gotta give all my braddas and sistas at the next reunion.

"See, me and you, next trip we go over there, we starting from that statue of Mr. Rice, and this time, I swear I holding my head high and we walking up past the old house and up Haupu Mountain and eat our lunch up there and look around the *pristine* forest.

"Maybe I grab me some soil off Haupu Mountain and put um in one package under my bed, 'cause when you and me see this place, that's the only time I wanna go there. And maybe you remba, when I die, you know what for do with that package. Just pour um on me and I be home."

☾

———

THREE

———

HILO COUNTY FAIR

The Lehua Jaycees sponsor the Hilo County Fair every spring. Lots of Jaycees building the food booths from pieces of dirty lumber with paper peeling off of their sides. E. K. Fernandez carnies lifting the huge iron shells of all our favorite rides. And truckload after truckload from Hilo Planing Mill dumping wood shavings on the ground the day before the fair opens.

Jerry and me go on the first night of the fair. It always rains and the tent canvas smells like mildew mixed with mud and wood shavings. Tonight Miss Aloha Hawai'i will walk down a ramp runway. She'll wear a white one-piece swimsuit and white heels, do her all-wrist Miss America wave at the crowd. Then a clown will juggle some balls.

All the high school couples roam around tonight. The girls with hot-pink bears and pink panthers, and the boys wearing the all-time biggest rattlesnakes around their necks. And of course holding hands or the girl with her head on the boy's shoulder.

Jerry doesn't know what to do first, when all of a sudden he says, "Let's ride the Ferris wheel, okay?"

"Okay, the Ferris wheel first. Cut short through the Beer Garden." Ride the Ferris wheel first. Sit behind the iron bar that an ugly man in a red carnival T-shirt slams shut. The same ugly carnival guy every year with the red bandanna, braided ponytail with leather straps, and missing front teeth. The guy who says, "Eh, try move yo' hand, girl," then slam, secures the bar.

Every year, Jerry and me at the top of the wheel rocking ourselves slowly with no hands and cool, cool air up there way above the carnival music.

But Jerry pulls my arm to a sharp stop. "The Freak Show," he says. "C'mon. I treat." I really don't want to go. I remember last year, the Siamese twins, how the skin between their bodies looked so pulled and how Jerry said it must be okay to be so close to someone like that. But they looked so sad, the two twins. And the fat midget ladies we saw last year with chocolate all over their faces and how I saw everybody, including my dentist, laugh and cheer.

Right in front of the Freak Show tent is a huge banner— "BURNT TO A CRISP! THE MAN YOU WOULD DIE TO SEE!" When the man walks out onto the stage, his head is all burned up with little strands of hair. Shiny skin with real burns and lots of pimple craters on the side. And he pulls off the mask and his saliva falls out of his mouth and he screams, not a mad scream but a sad, long scream, so the audience screams. Jerry screams the loudest, and I watch the man. See his long hands put the mask back on his face and wipe the saliva off his mouth with the back of his arm.

"Let's go," I tell Jerry. And this is when we see our classmates. The popular Japanee girls who have their own YMCA club called Rays of the Rising Dawn. Jodie's carrying a blue bear probably won by Troy. One of the club's Dreamboats. Traci has a cloth striped bear in a plastic bag. Gina sees Jerry and me first.

"What a *cute* couple," she says. "You *match*. Two ugly freaks just pau see the sideshow. What, Lovey, went see your aunty them, the fat midget ladies? Can still see the chocolate on your face. You was part of their act, or what?"

"No, that was last year, she wen' see them," says Jodie. "This year they went for see Jerome's burnt-out uncle."

"And what Jerome won for you?" says Traci.

"Nuttin'," says Gina. "The invisible snake. See um around her neck? Two losers, you guys deserve each other. Two ugly ITs out on the town."

"C'mere and say that to my face," says Jerry, "so I can shove this corn on the cob up your ass, Gina, you short, hairy Oki-nawan."

"Why—the hag cannot fight her own battles, so one fag gotta fight for one lez-lee?"

"Aw fuck off, Gina," I say, "you stink rotten little Okinawan. Go collect some pig slops with your uncle them from Uka side, then put um in your grandma's andagi."

"Yeah, wise off, Lovey. Wise off, you loser numba one. You eva wonder why you no mo' friends, hah, Lovey? You one queer fucka, your whole family, fuckin' ka-naka style everybody sleeping on your living-room floor, eh? No mo' nuff beds and blankets so gotta use army sleeping bags from the Surplus Store, eh?"

A crowd gathers and everyone hears Gina say this about my family.

"Eh, you pick on her, yeah, come here and pick on me. C'mon,

Lovey, we go fuckin' kick their asses, fuckin' ho-as, fuckin' Va-Gina," and Jerry throws the slippery corn stick, napkin, and all at them, and they laugh. I grab his arm.

"C'mon, Jerry, let's get outta here. Never mind. Too much people watching." They all three make middle finger to us as I yank Jerry away.

They're all so rich. They got gold chains with lots of gold charms on charm holders and plenty pairs of high-heel Famolare shoes. They don't buy their clothes from Wigwam. They live in places called Sunrise Ridge or the Heights. They look small and cute with straight hair and long bangs. Gina's mother even lets her wear blue eye shadow and lots of kissing potion lip gloss.

Jerry and me ride the Ferris wheel once and the whole world from the sky down looks clear. Then we ride the Tilt-a-Whirl three times. Next, the Scrambler. Jerry and me scream and scream, so when my mother picks us up, we talk in scratchy voices. But we start getting low on money. We each came with five dollars. We ride the Ferris wheel again anyway.

Jerry says we better kill time or we'll be waiting for my mother in front of the Civic Auditorium for two hours. I tell him we should have skipped the saimin and teri beef sticks especially.

Jerry says, "Let's go to the games section." He wants to win a crystal glass ashtray by throwing dimes into them. Ten dimes one at a time but all ten bounce out. I don't know why Jerry tries for this game. I mean we would look stupid carrying a green glass ashtray around the County Fair.

Then Jerry tries to win a giant Coca-Cola. I tell him, "No, Jerry. It costs ten cents a ring to throw on the Coke bottles." But

Jerry buys *ten* rings. Now we're really getting poor. He throws nine rings, and of course, he misses on all nine tries.

So to act like he doesn't care about all the money he lost when I told him not to spend the money on stupid games, he turns around and flips the last ring high into the air. "A winner," the carnival worker yells.

I don't know why I jump up and down with Jerry screaming and yelling after we win the Coke. I think it was hearing the guy say "A winner" that did it, because now Jerry and me have to carry the Coke bottle around like the two most uncool people at the carnival with no stuffed animals to speak of but a huge, stupid-looking, uncool Coke bottle.

Then we see Larry by the knock-down-the-milk-bottles-with-the-baseball game. Larry with eight balls that cost four dollars in scrip and cute Crystal Kawasaki holding all of his stuffed animals. A couple of trolls with fuzzy, out-of-control hair, a snake, a couple of pink bears, doggies in plastic bags, and a purple cat. Crystal's wearing Larry's huge ag jacket.

"Hi, Jerome!" she says. "Larry, Larry, Jerome's here."

"So. Beat it, Jerry. You breaking my concentration."

"Shut up, Larry," I say.

"And you, Fatso, Clinging Vine, scram, shazam. Like make like a banana and split." Larry shoves me.

"Laaa-rry. Don't do that," says cute Crystal in a too large ag jacket holding tons of animals. "What did Jerome win for you?" she asks me as though I'm in kindergarten.

"Nothing," I say in a kindergarten way. I don't know why but Crystal makes me feel small kid again.

"Not, Lovey. I won this Coke bottle. See, Crystal. Please let Lovey hold one of your stuff animals," says Jerry all of a sudden. "I give um back to Larry when I get home. Please."

"You fuckin' scrounger, Jerry. Get the hell away," yells Larry. "Go win your girlfriend some prizes on your own. C'mon, Crystal." He pulls at her arm.

"Wait, Larry," Crystal says sternly. "Here, Lovey," she says in her kindergarten way, "you may wear this snake around your neck."

"Wow, thanks." The snake is purple and green and long like a mink coat. And soft fur by my neck.

"And here, Jerome." She lets Jerry carry a huge pink bear. Larry says *fuck* softly. Jerry knows he's getting lickens from Larry when he gets home but he looks at me and I know he's chancing it.

We have no money and we have an hour and a half still. We take a spin past the merry-go-round. Jerry breaks into a run. I see his long body on the ground near the merry-go-round. He's trying to hook something underneath it. "Eh, boy," the ugly man who runs the merry-go-round yells, "eh, boy, get outta there. Whatchu doing, fucka? Yeah, you. Eh, you fuckin' punk, I talking to you."

"Oh shit, he's coming."

"I goin' haf to broke yo' ass."

"Jerome!" I scream. Jerry scrambles to his feet. He's got a five-dollar book of scrip in his hands.

"Run, Lovey, run!" I nearly lose Crystal's snake.

"Five dollars," says Jerry. We decide to eat corn on the cob and cotton candy. Then we share an orange Fanta. Four dollars left. Jerry says, "Let's ride the Ferris wheel. For the rest of the night."

We pay the man a long paper strand of faded red tickets. Jerry puts the pink bear and the bottle of Coke between us and I put the purple-and-green snake around both of our shoulders. There's Crystal and Larry. "Crystal! Crystal!" we yell. She waves at us and Larry grabs her hand, then puts his big arm around her neck. She turns and waves even with all of her animals.

Then we see Jodie, Traci, and Gina. They see us as we pass on the bottom of the Ferris wheel. They see our wonderful pink bear and purple-and-green snake. Then we rise to the top of the wheel. "Spit," I tell Jerry. "Spit on those assholes."

"Hey, fuckin' lez and homo on a romantic ride. Kiss, kiss. Two ITs make one baby IT."

Jerry picks up the Coke bottle. I think he's going to smash it over their heads but he shakes it with all of his might until it bursts open like a bottle of champagne in the movies and he pours it over the side, all over Gina, Traci, and Jodie.

"Christen them," he says, "christen them for their new YMCA club, Drops of the Falling Soda." Then he swigs the rest of the bottle, me too, and we laugh and laugh, kick our feet, rock the seat, the drops of soda falling like sticky honey, falling all over the carnival grounds.

BLAH BLAH BLAH

These are the worst members of the YMCA club Rays of the Rising Dawn:

Traci Kihara. Dots the two *i*'s in her name with little hearts.

Gina Oshiro. Wears corduroy bell-bottom hiphuggers in every color you can think of.

Laura Murayama. Talks like a big baby but all the boys like it.

Jodie Louie. Also dots the *i*'s in her name with little hearts.

Lori Shigemura. Smart, popular, but chocho lips and crooked fang teeth.

Rhonda Whang. Also a Sweetheart for the Rogues.

Kandi Mitsuda. Formerly of the Chantilly and Lace Emeralds.

Who wouldn't want to be a Ray of the Rising Dawn? They all have the same Japan pencils in Japan pencil cases. And the same bubble-gum-smelling erasers.

They all smell like Love's Baby Soft. Or like lemons. Sometimes they smell like rain. Love's Rain Scent. Or blueberries. And all the *same* scent on the *same* day.

They all have straight, long black hair with long bangs behind the ears.

And all kinds of clogs, not from Kinney's but from Robin's.

Seventy fingers in pale orange pearl. Seventy toes in pale orange pearl. They all make their toes point outward when they walk.

I hate their beautiful handwriting.

The tiny purses they carry and their pink plastic folders for each subject, pink being the official folder color of Rays of the Rising Dawn members.

I hate their glossy lips full of Kissing Smackers roll-on lipstick. And every one of them with lilac eye shadow.

I hate their mothers' convertible Cadillacs, Chargers, and Thunderbirds.

I hate the way they drink milk from the bendable straws they bring from home.

I hate them all and they hate me.

Especially Lori. Lori Shigemura. All nicely dressed in her home-sewn butterfly sleeves, gauzy shirts with lace—all ten of them. From a Simplicity pattern too. Her mother owns a Bernina, not a Singer, and sells gold chains on the side. Lori with her new homemade clothes. Looking rich with lots of gold charms on nice charm holders on thick S-chains.

Lori, who yells at me in social studies one day that the world does not revolve around me. All the other Rays of the Rising Dawn look on to back up Lori with their sassy Japanee faces.

I don't know exactly what to say until I go home and get ready to sleep that night. Then I think of my snappy comeback, which should have been: "No, the world doesn't revolve around me. It revolves around the sun, and you of all people, a *ray* of the rising sun, should know this."

All I say at the time is: "Oh yeah?"

I hate that. I hate when it all comes too late.

Like when Lori tells me, "You tell the *same* damn stories over and over." Lori Shigemura, the chocho lips Ray, stays with Jerry sometimes. "Every time get somebody new around, you start telling all your fuckin' stale stories *again,* like you tell, 'Jerry, 'member the time you and me wen' ride on Jenks's bradda's motorcycle and the bugs was going in our mouth?' Oh wow, Lovey, *big thrills.* Or you say, ''Member the time me, you, and Jenks blah blah blahed?' You always using Jenks's name. Wait till I tell him you acting like you get something going with him, you actor. And you always dragging in Jerry's name too like all you guys three good friends or something, but you know what, Lovey? I wen' hear your stories ten million times already and every time I hear um, you fuckin' addin' in something new."

Again I say, "Oh yeah?"

I hate that. I hate Lori.

And that Jerome, fuckin' stink-ass traitor, sometimes he doesn't even back me up, I can't believe it, 'cause Lori is a stinkin' prestee-jess, popular Ray of the Rising Dawn.

Then Lori says, "How come you get such one elephant memory? How you can remember every small-ass detail of how something happened? What for you gotta *eggzag* these details? Eggzag is lying, you know. Yo' madda neva tell you that? That even one white lie is one lie 'cause smell the same. So that make *you* one liar. One *big, fat* liar."

All I can say is: "Not even."

Sometimes I really think Jerry just wants to be an honorary Ray of the Rising Dawn. Lori *promises* him all the time that she'll nominate him as Dreamboat. But only Lori likes him. All the other club members think he's an IT. And just because she's a Ray, Jerry thinks he's hot shit and he got a chance to be a Ray.

"Yeah," I tell him, "Lori one ugly shit, you one stupid shit, and all the other club members treat you like a piece of Lori's shit. Go for it, Jerome, you big, stupid dummy."

"You just jealous, Lovey, 'cause I one boy and yet I get more chance than *you* for be one honorary Ray or one Dreamboat for the most popular club in this school, the Rays of the Rising Dawn. Why you no just get a grip on yourself and feel happy for me, Lovey? Or maybe you just jealous of me and Lori?"

So I say, "Okay, yeah—well let me tell you something about Lori. And this is the whole truth."

C

There was this new boy at school who was fat but handsome and already had a girlfriend, who was Nancy Miyamoto, my sometimes friend when Jerry stays with Lori. The new boy, Fenton, came from Kam School.

Lori didn't know the new boy was special ed before, so she tries hard to catch him by pulling her shorts up very high so that her stink-ass leftover cheeks hang out.

Then she takes a blueberry Life Saver lollipop out of her leather saddlebag and tears off the cellophane very slowly and animal-like.

Soon her tongue is moving all over the lollipop. In and out of the Life Saver hole. The special ed boy grabs his balls area, I swear it, I saw it. And he head-motions for Lori to come by him.

They sit on the curb waiting for the sampan bus. Then they get on the bus and sit in the back. As the old man drives the bus off, I see the special ed boy put his arm on the iron bar behind Lori. Lori is the special ed boy's girlfriend from the next day and the boy dumps Nancy.

Then two days later, Nancy writes a "whole truth and nothing but the truth" letter about her and her ex: what they did, where they did it, how they did it, and especially telling Lori that she doesn't give a rip that she stole her boyfriend. So what if Lori's going with the new boy from Kam, her ex, 'cause he use to be *special ed*. And special ed boy and high-section English, math, and social studies girl *match* perfect.

And guess what, Lori dumps Fenton right there on the spot. After school, Lori goes to Wigwam to buy new pink folders because she wrote all over her old ones: LORI LOVES FENTON.

Why shouldn't I hate her? I read every letter she wrote to Jerry and I know what she says about me. I know every time she called him and what they talked about: me. And I know why Lori hates me.

She wants to say, *"I love you, Jerry."* But she can't. This frightens her. Even in her letters she can only sign them *Alwayz - n- Foreva Frenz, Lori -n- Jerri and Jerri -n- Lori.* She spells his name like this so she can dot the *i*'s with hearts. I know all of this.

I ask Jerry what he sees in a *friend* like Lori. Her face so round like a plate, and her lips all Ubangi and chocho, I say. Big-ass fangs for wolfen teeth. Her words so fake. Snobbing me for nothing.

I can say, "I love you, Jerry," and mean it.

All of this without rhymes or cute stickers or nonsharpening pencils. I can mean it straight without lip gloss or hearts. I can say it without perfect teeth.

(

Lori makes me so mad. She goes and says that mine must be the kind of family that doesn't refill the Tang pitcher when it's almost empty. We must be the kind of family that leaves the toilet-paper roll with hardly any toilet paper instead of replacing it. And our mother doesn't wrap her Kotex in newspaper before throwing it away.

Lori says she heard that we buy all our vegetables from the Open Market at the bay-front parking lot because we can't afford the fresh produce in Sure Save. My father feeds us meat that he catches, we're so poor, and he sells flowers to the Lei Stand for extra cash. Ours is the kind of family who doesn't iron their clothes and doesn't give out candy at Halloween, which is the only time we pretend to be Jehovah's Witnesses.

Lori says, "And you guys so fuckin' *poor* that you and your sista share the same stink shoes. You wear the same stink pants two days in a row or at least in the same week, now that's what I call poor, and your father drives that f-uga-lee brown Land Rover with no back window. You got zip gold and your clothes faded to the max."

To all this, believe me, I know what to say. Say something about her mother, who works in the macadamia nut factory with the little white kerchief on her head and white gloves and waves to the tourists who watch her mother like a mouse through the glass window.

Say something about her father, who is the part-time custodian at Uncle Ed's school, who mops the kindergarten and vacuums the library carpet. The heir of a preserved-seed business.

Say something about home-sewn Simplicity clothes from cheap Kress fabric.

Say something.

Say something.

Say anything but "Oh yeah?"

LOVEY'S HOMEMADE SINGER SEWING CLASS PATCHWORK DENIM HIPHUGGERS

Grandma makes quilts. All grandmas do. Calhoon and me can spread our quilts out over the living-room floor and tell you whose dress or shirt is there right under us.

Aunty Bing's last year's May Day muumuu. Mother's shortie muumuu for Uncle Steven's New Year's mochi-pounding party. Grandma's favorite lavender aloha print church dress. Calhoon's and my matching County Fair clothes from three years ago with matching bikini bottoms.

And whenever we get a new grandma-made quilt, we lay it down on the floor to see who's there. The more we know, the more we fight for the blanket.

c

There is an old blanket on the floor of the garage. Paper boxes ripped apart and blood dripping from the carcass of an axis deer hanging by its antlers from a hook on the ceiling of the garage.

c

Before the gully, there is a field of grass, rolling hills, and ohia-log wire fences far off in the distance. I imagine "The Sound of Music" playing, Julie Andrews spinning in her peasant dress and apron, and what Austria might look like. When I hear the shots from the gully, I spread the blanket on the bed of the truck and get ready to go home.

"Cal grab one antler, Lovey grab the odda one, and heave, ho. Pull um up, hurry up befo' the blood drip on you guys' slippas." Under the lychee tree, everybody poses with the buck, purple tongue hanging out, eyes purple clear, the flies swarming fat and black.

"Careful how you skin the hide, Ed," says Father. "We gonna sew us hunting vests with all the scrap hide I get in the freeza. For the *real* huntas for wear under the army jacket. Betta than down vest, I tell you, and I going sew um myself."

C

Mother says Cal and me should go to sewing lessons down in the cool basement of the Singer store. Concrete floors and the whir-whirwhir of the machine wheels. Bobbins all over the floor of the sewing class, strips of pattern tissue. Tracing paper in all colors spread out over the cutting table and tracing wheels with red-and-green handles hanging on little nails.

"I making a skirt first," I tell Calhoon. "McCall's 1064 or Simplicity 2761."

Mother says, "No Vogue patterns—too expensive and Butter-ick don't fit the Japanee bodies right. Even Grandma says so 'cause the Japanee get long body and short daikon legs, thass why. The waist of the Butterick pattern is right under your chi-chi."

Teruko Nakamura, the sewing teacher, wears a green tape measure around her neck. Every girl except for Cal and me, who share a sewing kit, has all of the following:

A satin pastel pincushion.

Sewing pins with colorful heads.

A huge plastic, see-through sewing chest.

And a shiny, silver, official Singer's scissors from the locked showcase.

We got this:

Grandma's old wicker chest. The string that holds the cover to the basket ripped off on one side, so the cover hangs when you open the basket. Rusty hinges and a lock that doesn't pop open. We gotta pry the chest open.

A cheapo tomato pincushion.

Needles that don't have heads. The kind the kindergarten teacher used to pin notes to your dress at the end of the day.

And the greatest shame, the poultry shears for sewing scissors.

C

Cut the body open from jaw to belly. Slice the hide off the head. Gelatin eyes, skeleton teeth—black-and-green smiling teeth hidden behind all that skin.

The fat bubbles where my father slices and the sound of Saran Wrap stretched and cut as he separates the hide from the body, careful not to leave meat on the hide. So much salt for one body, throw the rock salt over the carcass as he works. The flies buzz around the pieces of meat sliced from the hide and flicked off the hand, stuck on the floor of the garage.

(

From Hilo town as we leave in the morning, I see the *purplemountainmajesty*—Mauna Kea. I know exactly what the song means every time I see the mountain in the middle of my island. There on the slopes of Mauna Kea, we find a place to hide. Stay low.

Hide. Daddy filming us stalking the mouflons nibbling the shoots off the mamane tree. Huge-horned rams, blonds and browns. Mixed-breed mouflons and native sheep with one and a half curls on the horns. Ewes and babies.

Lava fields and brush all around and no sign of purple this close to the summit. The wind and the whirwhirwhir of the 8-millimeter camera filming this huge flock of sheep as evidence when we tell Uncle Ed about the hunt he missed for golf. So close and so many to shoot, upwind, perfect—Daddy, Cal, and me.

Cal takes off her fluorescent-orange hunting hat, wipes her head, and all of a sudden, the flock scatters, heads straight for us, gunshots, duck your head, scramble for cover, hoofs on rock, and sheep crying in all directions. Gunshots and Daddy screaming, "Who the hell's firing?!"

The black ewe that's hit scrambles to her feet, pulling her hindquarters. Father straightens his glasses—twisted sideways on his face—shoves the camera to me, and shoots her in the head. Thick gelatin blood spurts and sticks to our faces and black blood pools on the lava as Father kicks her to make sure she's dead.

"No can even mount this sunnafabitch. Look too old for meat. Gunfunnit, you, Cal. Why you wen' wave your hat like that fo'? Sheezus Christmas. And who the hell fired their gun? Dammit, Lovey. You coulda kill somebody. Freak accidents happen when somebody shoot stupid, *Stupid*. Here, you skin this sheep." Father snaps the buck knife to the ground and its blade cuts into the dirt. "Take the hide and leave the rest. I ain't carrying back this heavy shit-for-nothing sheep. Pick the best part of the hide for the vest I going sew. And pick good."

c

Teruko helps me pick my brown skirt material. It's gauzy but stiff and she charges the material and pellon for the waistband to my mother's account.

I cut the pattern carefully right outside the black lines. I lay the pattern down and measure the nap. Cut with the poultry shears slowly so that I hear the scissors' crunch, crunch, crunch on the Formica tabletop. I read the instructions two times over before I even pin the fabric together. Sew stitch by stitch a perfect five-eighths and zigzag, not pink, the seams. Steam-press every seam.

So how come Teruko doesn't tell me to iron the hem when I'm done is unclear to me. Why my mother expected Teruko, who is from Japan, to tell me to iron the damn hem before I wear the damn skirt to school is also unclear to me.

So that when Gina Oshiro says, "Oh wow, Lovey. Homemade skirt? Can tell. You neva iron the hem, that's why." It doesn't make sense to me. And I swear, I pull and tug the hem all day and nothing does it like Mother's iron when I get home.

Why didn't they tell me?

I make a beige gauze hippy blouse with gathers in the front. I iron the hem and wear it with my hiphuggers. A huge leather belt with painted engraved butterflies and flowers and a tarnished bronze buckle. Gina says in Period One, real loud, "The hiphuggas from J. C. Penney's and the shirt from Lovey's Singer sewing class." She's right and I gotta wear the damn clothes for another five periods.

I hate sewing. I want to quit.

I try to see who else in school wears Singer sewing class clothes. I cannot tell. Maybe Lori Shigemura and Laura Murayama, but their clothes look like they could pass for store-made.

From then on, I make throw pillows in sewing class with pink and red corduroy. For my bed. For the living room. For Mother's bed. And throw pillows for Grandma out of printed terry cloth.

Calhoon in the meanwhile makes the nicest jacket with fake patchwork denim with waistband ribbing and a real jacket zipper from the expensive zipper section in Singer's. It looks so real and so good until I borrow it for school one day and everybody says, "Rip-off patchwork denim. Phony-ass, fake stuff. Looks Wigwam or worse yet. Homemade."

Goddammit, I quit sewing for good.

C

"And no quit. Only losers give up the ship," my father says. "One day you be the best hunter, no worry. But, eh, maybe you ain't made fo' be *just* one hunter. I mean, maybe you be the vest seamstress. You help Daddy and Uncle Ed make their vest, and with the scraps, I make *you* one, okay? Only the top game hunters wear the kine vest we going make."

My father starts tanning the hides for the two vests for him and Uncle Ed. He throws the defrosted hides one by one over the sawhorse and slices the meat off the hides. "Gotta make sure no mo' nothing on the hide bumbye the bugga rotten right on your body," he says and flings the meat at me but misses and it sticks to the side of the Land Rover. Father removes the fat gelatin skin layer from each of the hides.

"Salt and air dry this bugga. Go put um out for dry under the lychee tree. Gotta be in the shade, let the breeze dry um out."

My father pickle-bathes the hides in lots of rock salt and water in the totan by the bathhouse, then puts them in the tanning solution.

In a few days, me and him running each piece of hide through the breaker, rubbing it back and forth on the cane knife until the hides are soft, softer than suede.

And Daddy says, "For my vest, my spirit is the axis deer and the mouflon we wen' catch up Mauna Loa, so half my vest going be deer and the odda half sheep. Ed one is the odda half of the axis deer and the pig he wen' catch up by Moniz them pastureland up Uka side. And nobody, nobody but you, me, and Ed can name um, the place where these hides all from, and how we wen' catch um, you hear? And for mo' power, I tanning the deer balls for my pocket on the inside of my vest and the pig balls for Ed 'cause the bugga almost snatch his leg befo' he blass um in the head. And the minute you tell, all this fo' nothing."

And then I know what I have to do. Daddy makes me thread the long hooked needle with black nylon thread. I stab it into the top of his worktable. We trace the tissue paper from the Simplicity 8132 from Singer onto oaktag from the stationery store and cut out the hides with the X-acto knife.

Put right sides together like Teruko says and stitch. "Take your time and make um good. Like each stitch is for make this vest strong." Poke the hooked needle, the sound of leather being punctured, slow. We take all afternoon and that night in front of the TV.

"See, Hubert, lucky thing I sent Lovey sewing lessons, eh?" my mother says. "And there you was, grumble, grumble, grumble about the money. So you need help, let me know, even if those hides smell like ten dead goats in a barrel of oil."

When I'm done, no hems to press, raw edges without zigzag, balls for pockets, Daddy says, "We going catch one big one next time we go hunting, I tell you." And Daddy wears his vest to sleep.

C

I choose for my vest:

Bully hide for the cow we couldn't eat who cried like a man.

Goat hide though it's not my Nanny, I wear it to scare away billies and for goat smell on my skin.

Ewe hide for the black one from Mauna Kea who dragged herself with a bullet in the side—a bullet behind her eye in a pool of dark blood.

Rabbit hides for Clyde, Lani, and Hokulani on my shoulders, killed by dogs, but close to my face. To dominate.

And no one—no one can name them but me.

C

"Rip-off patchwork denim. Phony-ass, fake stuff. Looks Wigwam or worse yet. Homemade."

And then I know what I have to do.

Calhoon says she'll help me make the real patchwork denim hiphugger bell-bottoms from Simplicity 1013. I go back for another lesson. Only losers give up the ship.

Calhoon hunts for her old kindergarten sleeping bag. Grandma digs in her three giant trash bags full of quilt scraps for my pieces of denim and sends it air mail to me from Moloka'i. We whirwhirwhir the fabric together.

Father brings his old chambray work shirts from the Salvation Army boxes outside in the aluminum shed. Cal and me sew all the denim pieces together but it's not quite enough. When Mother donates her old Baptist camp Levi's, all faded but rugged and washed out, we can finish the fabric.

Calhoon and me lay the pattern down and pin the nap carefully. We cut with the poultry shears that work extra well with the thick patchwork denim. To make it look really store-bought, my mother tells us to sew the bell-bottom hiphuggers on Aunt Helen's Bernina so the topstitch looks like store-bought.

When I put it on with my unbleached-muslin wildflower-embroidered halter top, suck in my stomach, and show a little bit of belly button, the fabric rubs me right—the patchwork jeans with Dutch clogs and a leather-fringe shoulder bag.

Gina Oshiro in Period One can't say anything about home-sewn clothes that look so expensive and store-bought that she resorts to say, "Eh, Lovey, pull up your hiphuggas. Can see your ass cleavage."

I say, "Hey, man, I planned it that way."

Grandma, Mother, Calhoon, Father, and me at that moment in the patchwork denim bell-bottom hiphuggers whose scraps nobody in the room could name but me.

WATER BLACK AND BRIGHT

Hers is the face of a Japanese angel. A princess from the Japanese comics in Hatsuko's Barbershop. A perfect oval face. Pure smooth and white. Pink cheeks and red lips. And white, white teeth. All straight and not too tiny like Marcia Brady and not too much like Marie Osmond. Crystal. Crystal Kawasaki. Larry's girlfriend.

Crystal, who my mother hires to tutor us after school and walk us, Calhoon and me, to her house until my mother finishes work. Jerry comes along and waits at Crystal's house for his brother to get him.

Crystal fixes us guava jelly and peanut butter on graham crackers or S & S saimin, not the dried, cheap Top Ramen saimin, and always gives us Malolo strawberry syrup juice in Tupperware cups with two ice cubes each. Crystal is the most perfect girl I know.

Crystal has a rich house with a koi pond in front and fat, golden-orange, white-gold, black, and bright neon-yellow koi swimming in and out of the lily pads. I mean real lily pads, not the plastic kind, with purple-and-white flowers. And dragonflies, huge purple-green ones, that hum past the top of the water. There's moss growing on the lava-rock stones around the pond. A waterfall too. I imagine Crystal hearing the sound of falling water as she sleeps in her bedroom at night.

She opens the lid of a rusty soda cracker can full of koi food and scoops out a whole cup for Jerry, Calhoon, and me to feed to her koi. The pellets plop into the water like little stones. I like the sound of koi sucking and smacking the food into their whiskered mouths.

Crystal.

Jerry says I could look almost like Crystal when I go to high school if I lose about twenty pounds, pluck my eyebrows right, and never get any pimples. Then my face will be oval and smooth. Calhoon holds Crystal's hand all the time.

Larry comes to get Jerry every day. He doesn't even knock, just barges in the back door and pulls open the refridge, pops open a can of Coke, takes a long, long swig, and burps hard. He flies the soda tab at Jerry's head. "Loose change, brah," he always says.

"Law-rence," scolds Crystal.

Then Larry bear-hugs her around her neck and she laughs as he noogies her head down the hallway.

"You guys go play outside," Crystal says to us every day, "and stay out of the fishpond, okay? I'll be out in a few minutes." And her bedroom door clicks shut and locks.

Crystal is in there every day for half an hour.

"What they doing?" Cal asks every day. "Whatchu think they doing in there, Lovey? Huh, Jerry?"

"I dunno. Talking, I think," says Jerry. "Talking about school and stuff. Maybe kissing and talking. Yeah, kissing and talking."

"Then why they laughing like that if they talking about school," I say. "What so funny about school? And how you can kiss and laugh like that at the same time?"

It is on a Friday when Jerry, Calhoon, and me quietly put the rusty tin can full of koi food under Crystal's window after the door has clicked locked. Jerry pushes my ass up, up, until my nose presses on the dusty screen that smells mildewy.

"C'mon, Lovey," says Cal. "What they doing?"

I see Crystal's stuffed animals all over the pink carpet and Crystal, her beautiful long black hair strewn over the pillows. Crystal naked and kneeling on her bed, and Larry straddling her, pushing and pushing on her, his ass squeezed tight together. Like two dogs.

Crystal turns her face, her beautiful face to Larry, and screams, "Omigod, Larry. Larry, *the kids. Larry, oh no,*" and she shoves his naked body off of her. This is when I see Larry, long and wet, yanked out of Crystal.

"You fuckin' assholes, fuckin' assholes. Jerome, I going broke your ass." He pulls his pants on, and I jump off of the tin can, pull Calhoon, and run screaming to the road. Jerry stumbles after us and we run all the way home.

Jerry, Calhoon, and me hide in the shed behind the garage. "Larry gonna find us pretty soon," says Calhoon. "And we left all our school bags at Crystal's house. Omigod, Jerry. He said he gonna broke your ass."

"What you seen, Lovey?" asks Jerry as if to make his future pain more worth it.

But the words to tell them what I seen on that Friday, I don't have a way to say it. So I tell them, they were kissing. Larry and Crystal were kissing.

"Thass all, Lovey? You lie," says Jerry. "Liar. Get plenny more but she not telling. Otherwise, why Larry so mad with us? C'-mon, tell, tell. Liar, liar, liar," they both start saying.

"Thass all," I scream. "They was kissing. Thass all. I cannot believe. Like dogs. Like two naked dogs." And nobody says nothing.

C

"Crystal going Japan with her mother. Larry no talk too much anymore. He no even swear at me or hit me. You know what that means? Means Crystal is you-know-what. Means she gotta go Japan for fix her you-know-what. She quit with Larry, you know. I know 'cause I seen him all sad and depress. He stay on his side of the room and stare at the wall and tell me, 'What you lookin' at, asshole, dick-face spy?'"

C

"I made Crystal break it off with that rotten kid. Goddammit. Two goddamn kids. Shit. Can you believe it? Shit. No way will she get it done in this town. My wife says all the goddamn big ears and big eyes and big mouths in that hospital. The whole town going know. Shit. You know how it is, big mouth Mrs.

Nakasone telling her sista Harriet from the moment she admit you to the maternity ward. Now my wife gotta take my daughta to Japan. Shit."

ɔ

"No tell nobody, eh, you, Hubert. Yeah, you know. Larry's girl-friend. Hapai, you know. Ass why they gotta go Japan. Ai-ka shame, no? Gunfunnit, thass why, you get girls, you get the *prize*. Boys, they no take home the prize. Ai, pua ting her. She neva going forget this one in her whole life. Ass all she going have is regrets, regrets, regrets. And plenty shame, no, Hubert?"

ɔ

"So what that mean? What you seen? Like what else they was doing? Like dogs, you said, right? What else? C'mon, tell already. Tell."

ɔ

Father found a bathtub at the rubbish dump. "One man's trash, another man's treasure," is what he always says as he pulls through the piles and piles of rubbish for an old tool, a broken linoleum tabletop, a cabinet door, plant pots, or an old stool. He loads the bathtub into our Land Rover.

The smell of the rubbish dump is always sickeningly sweet like souring milk and flowers, paper and dirt, and the constant buzzing hum of flies fat as my baby finger. When we get home,

Father puts the big white bathtub under the lychee tree in the backyard.

"You two stay outta there," he says. "I gotta get some supplies. I going make you one fishpond after I clean this sucka and going be nice, mo' nice than Crystal them one, the koi pond you guys is always talking about. Big deal, so the Kawasakis get one nice koi pond, ours going be nicer, you watch. You watch, Daddy going make ours one mo' betta with mo' nice kine fish."

Father comes back with a round piece of redwood and a strip of a tire inner tube. A soft black piece that he whips against his legs in rhythm as he walks toward us.

"Go drag the water hose down there, Lovey. Daddy gotta shoot down the tub first. All pilau." And he presses his thumb to the nozzle and makes a strong jet stream to shoot down the inside of the tub.

My father places the redwood circle into the drain part of the tub and tightly pushes and fits the inner tube around it, shoving it hard into place with a screwdriver. "Watch," he says, "no need even caulk this sucka." And he fills the bathtub all the way to the top with crystal cool, swirling water.

"Ho, Daddy," screams Cal, "we go down the Hilo Pet Store right now buy some fish, c'mon," and she tries to pull his hand. "Ho, Lovey, Jerry gonna be so jealous of our pond, yeah, Lovey, yeah?"

"I dunno," I say.

"She dunno," says Father, " 'cause this one rubbish dump fishpond, not like the one the Kawasakis get, so thass why Lovey dunno, right, Lovey? Well, I tell you what, go get coupla mayonnaise jars from under the sink. We go catch our own fish. You coming, Lovey?" He says it more like a command.

"Whoo-ta!" yells Calhoon. "C'mon, Lovey." Cal climbs into the Land Rover with the mayonnaise jars and I follow behind her. Father comes with a bucket and three cheesecloth fishnets.

We go all the way to Honomu. Father takes us behind an old Japanee man's house. He got lots of chickens in coops in the back and lots and lots of canaries. We go down a steep hill behind the coops and into an offshoot river of Akaka Falls.

Father scoops and catches a big, fat swordtail. Long and red with a black tail. "Ka-ne," he says, and dumps it into Calhoon's jar. Scoop. A fat red female. "No tail," he says. "Wahine."

Cal and me start catching upstream. "Wow, Daddy. Fantail guppies. Look, Lovey, look at the nice mosquito fish I got." And by the time we climb up the steep hill into the old man's yard, we got two mayonnaise bottles full of frantic, tail-whipping mosquito fish and swordtails with lots of long brown fish shit swirling in the water.

Father picks up some wild water lilies with purple flowers in his bucket, just like Crystal's, with fat bulbs underneath the lily pads with long black roots like a Chinaman's beard.

When we put the fish in our pond, the rainbow tails of the mosquito fish on the white sides of the tub and the red, red bodies of the swordtails, they are nice, nicer than koi. And Father plops the water lilies on top to protect them in the place under the lychee tree that smells like a river.

I want a room near a pool of water.

I want an oval face.

I want a big koi pond.

I want pet store fish.

I want to be real rich.

I want to be beautiful with long black hair, light brown eyes, a gentle way.

A room, a bed with a pink ruffle bedspread, every stuffed animal.

I want perfect teeth.

I want a bedroom window near a pool of water.

I want to sleep to the sound of water falling.

Every night.

❦

Jerry, Cal, and me made Tupperware Icee pops with the Exchange Orange juice yesterday. Today we eat two each by the bathtub fishpond, the water swirling shiny black in the shade of the lychee tree. Calhoon takes the container of fish flakes out of her pocket and twists the top open. Tap, tap, tap, lift the water lilies and all of our well-trained river fish come thrashing to the top.

"See, Jerry, how nice our fish?" Jerry stuffs the plastic Tupperware stick into his pocket and peels a couple of lychee. He throws the poky shells into the anthurium patch.

"Us go catch some and bring um in the house for little while, Jerry," says Cal. "Put um in one mayonnaise jar and keep um in mine and Lovey's room." Jerry and Cal run off to get the nets and bottle.

I tap a couple more dashes of fish food into the water and watch it swirl as fish mouths snatch at it. And the sound of water splashing like that sounds nice.

So I don't see or hear Larry coming. He says, "Eh, asshole, you like for spy, eh, asshole? I just came from the airport and wen' talk to Crystal one last time befo' she went Japan and you like know what she said for do to fuckin' asshole spies like you, hah?" Larry shoves my shoulder. "Keep your face where your fuckin' face belongs, you hear me, hah?" Larry smacks me across my head hard. " 'Cause of you, you asshole, that Crystal called it with me. You cunt."

"But I thought . . . I heard that . . . My mother said that . . ." I begin to say.

"Shut up, you hear me, shut the fuck up." Larry grabs my neck in the back and shoves my face into the fishpond. Bubbles all around my face, blackness, and the murky, thick taste of a fish-stagnant river fills my mouth. A burning, burning nose and a voice screaming but only bubbles swirling around me.

I remember falling into a muddy area in front of the fishpond and Calhoon hitting Larry with the mayonnaise jar. "Yeah, and you too, you fuckin' cunt number two." And Calhoon gets whacked on the side of her head. Her body hits the bathtub and falls in the mud. "Fuck, I hate *you,*" he screams.

Jerry drops the nets and runs full force to the house. "You two fuckin' cunts like know what I going do to you next time you spy on me, then tell the whole world what you seen when was none of your goddamn business?" Larry scoops the net into our fishpond.

The fish jump wildly in the net. One by one, he grabs them

and squeezes them by the head till black slime comes out of their mouths and their eyeballs pop out all shiny.

"Thass for Crystal. Think she dunno who wen' tell? Think when she come home she not going kick your fuckin' ass?" He throws the fish at Cal and me as he kills them. "And you, shrimp," he says to Calhoon, his eyes glassy and bulging, "you neva see what Crystal and me do, eh? Crystal wen' tell me befo' she went Japan that when she come home, you can sit on the floor and watch." He rubs his slimy hands all over his crotch.

Cal, she can't believe what she's hearing and seeing, the dead fish stuck all over her skin, fish tails still twitching and hitting her, the water in the tank splashing side to side and lily pads all over the ground.

After Larry walks away, Cal raises the mayonnaise jar as if to throw it at him, but she lowers her arms and rinses the fish off into the tank.

"Cal, they dead," I tell her.

"I know," she says, "you no think I know? I get eyes. And I not stupid, you know, 'cause you get eyes and now he think we all saw. When we neva. I no even know." Cal stops.

She throws the bottle against the lychee tree. It breaks into a million pieces. The red swordtails on the top of the water swirl round and round in the black water, no eyes in their heads, their mouths open. Already the flies humming around us.

THE LAST DANCE IS
ALWAYS A SLOW DANCE

From the window, we can see Jenks by the bathroom. He can see us too. Lucky if we get a head jerk by the end of recess. One by the end of the year. One that we can count.

At school, it's always Jerry and me in the typing teacher's class 'cause he's our next period after lunch recess and has a phonograph he lets us use to play our Carly Simon records.

At school, Jenks stays with Levi Nalani, Kenneth Spencer, Thomas Lorenzo, and Baron Ahuna, who's still going with Ginger Geiger. They hang by the courts or by B-building bathroom.

On the weekends, Jenks and me still work down at the Lei Stand for his mother, Aunty Shige. When we have nothing better to do on our lunch breaks and Jerry comes down to the Lei Stand with his mother on Saturdays, we count.

The fishing boats out past the break. The haole tourists with matching clothes. All the shells on the leis from the Philippines. Sand crabs. The stones in the moss rock wall across the street.

Jerry and me got our own count going at school. We figure by the end of the year Jenks will top five times that he actually made like he knew us at school. Count the time he sat with us at the bus stop. Count the time he sat on the bench with us at recess. By the caf.

We know that Jenks and us are good friends on the weekends, even though at school all we get is a head jerk, "howzit," but never when Lori Shigemura and her friends are around us or Patti Paet, Kawehi Wells, Natalie Leialoha, or Marlene Spencer around the corner. So we can count about five of those times too by the end of the year.

I guess God knows what kind of friends we are. That's what counts. That Lori, Gina, Traci, and Jodie don't know doesn't matter. God counts the times we all sat on the beach and ended the day leaning on each other talking story.

We read aloud too. Old *Watchtower* magazines from Mrs. Gomes down the beach road. "Masturbation: Why It's Evil and Against God."

C

Jenks got all tall and handsome this year. Part Hawaiian and Japanese with some haole blood. And after that dope-stealing thing passed and Jenks said it wasn't his anyways, we started work together at the beach on the weekends.

Mostly if Larry and Dwayne aren't there, we play Hawaiian music cassettes and harmonize so nice in our booth that the tourists buy lots more from us. Make our own lunch and trade sandwiches. Sew the ugliest lei contest and then who can sell it before the day's up. Wear matching T-shirts from the gift shop in the hotel. Just like Jerry and me but better.

Jenks told me last Sunday, "With you and Jerry, I can be who

I like, 'cause you guys no care. With Baron and Thomas them, gotta ack, eh. But they the braddas, right?"

I should've said something right there about ignoring Jerry and me in school and how one or several love or friendship type moves from him would instantly make us popular. But I don't.

In our school, if part Hawaiian goes with pure Jap, that's the ultimate. Everybody wants a hapa girlfriend or boyfriend. Everybody wants a part Hawaiian person. The Cosmopolitan May Day Prince and Princess, to our school, that's the Most Handsome and Most Pretty in the Hoss Elections. And Jenks was Cosmopolitan Prince and Most Handsome this year. Plus Valentine's Court King and Nicest Smile.

Jerry says, "For sure Jenks going ask you for dance so plenny times at the Grad Dance. Just like he going ask you for *go with him*. The way he ack when you guys at the Lei Stand—" Jerry says this at least all the time nowadays.

"Then why he ignore us in school?" I ask him.

" 'Cause, okay, Lovey, I your best friend so I going be honest, okay? He popular, right? He all handsome since Aunty Shige took him dermatologist, right? I mean, he going be on the JV volleyball team next year and all the girls kinda nuts over him, right? But he like you. But you *unpopular.*

"But I promise, I know his tricks 'cause I one boy too. See, on the night of the Grad Dance, he going ask you for dance with him fast songs for warm-up, then plenny slow songs to get the courage for whisper in your ear, 'I like go with you.'

"Then after that, going be summer and you guys going go together and next year, you guys already going be going strong and then, Lovey, and then, you going go from unpopular to popular over the summer. Promise."

"How you know this, Jerome?" I ask him. Then Jerry shrugs his shoulders and makes like he has the biggest secret he cannot tell.

"Believe me, Lovey, I *know*. And what I know, I know for a fact. Plus, I seen you guys holding hands by the ponds last Saturday. He going ask you for dance so many times, you going melt. Count on it."

From the window of Mr. Otake's typing class, we can see Jenks by the bathroom. He can see us too. Lucky if we get a head jerk by the end of recess. One by the end of the year. One that we can count.

(

Grad Dance. Semiformal Attire. Cafeteria. 7:00 P.M. to 10:00 P.M. Featuring the Sounds of Pegasus DJs and Company. Theme: *Seasons in the Sun.*

All the teachers say, "Wear like Sunday best, no miniature high school prom. Nobody better wear gloves or gowns or you going straight home. And, boys, no three-piece suits or tux or we'll call your father from the cafeteria manager's phone and send you straight home too. No bouquets or corsage. No be silly or we'll cancel the Grad Dance, you wait. Damn kids act like this one prom and all the damn mothers calling the school asking why they gotta spend one hundred dollars for gown, hair appointment, flowers, heels, makeup, and limo too. Get a grip on yourselves. Please."

Jerry got himself on the Grad Dance Committee. He worked all year on getting kind of popular so that he could make me kind of popular and on committees too. All he could do for now was put me on the Grad Dance Cleanup Committee. Not Refreshments even or, best of all, the Decorations Committee.

Seasons in the Sun—cardboard letters covered first with tinfoil, then blue cellophane, blue being everybody's favorite color these days, and the members of the Grad Dance Committee get to take the letters home. Usually the initials of someone they like or their own initials to masking-tape to their bedroom wall. But no J's or L's, so big deal.

When Jenks dances with me, and I know he will, all the Rays of the Rising Dawn and Chantilly and Lace Emeralds will wonder why this tall, athletic, and part Hawaiian chose me. And all those girls who thought I was making all this Jenks stuff up will finally see for sure who was telling the truth. And all those suicide notes I wrote for all the times Gina, Laura, Traci, and Lori humiliated me, I can rip them all up, after Jenks asks me to dance.

Grad Dance Committee members have to start off the first dance, so Jerry says he'll dance with me. Take that long walk across the cafeteria concrete floor to dance with me, the shiny mirrored disco ball spinning lights all around us.

C

6:30. My mother acts like it's a prom. Takes Polaroids of Jerry and me by the front door. Me with the Yvonne Elliman lip mole eyebrow pencil job my mother put on my upper lip. False eye-lashes too and jade-colored Revlon eye shadow. Eyebrows plucked for the first time and penciled in with an arch. Mother painted my fingernails and toenails Peachy-Keen Cutex to match my dress and makes a fake Press-on with Scotch tape for the baby finger only, the nail I bit off to the meat in nervousness over the Grad Dance.

When Jerry's mother drops us off, we act cool and walk to-ward the main door of the cafeteria. It smells stink in there. All closed up to make it real dark, the smell of sour milk, dry yeast, bare feet on damp cement, and stale heat. It's hot inside and the disco lights spin red and yellow like the lights on City and County cars, the Pegasus DJs and Company high on the stage borrowed from Mr. Hokama, the band teacher.

Everybody's here.

Everybody who's anybody served on the Grad Dance Com-mittee and arrived an hour early.

Lori Shigemura dressed in black chiffon all the way to the floor. Baby's breath and red baby roses with leather fern in her bouffant hairdo. A matching wrist corsage that she probably or-dered for herself. Grad Dance Committee chairperson can dress formal attire and not be sent home, I guess.

Gina Oshiro. Tiara in hair and long white gloves.

Laura Murayama. Home-sewn, shiny quiana lavender, off-the-shoulder, with lots of gathers by the waist, to-the-floor gown, looking pretty prom-ish to me and two tons of baby's breath in her hair.

I don't see anybody being sent home.

And all the Rays of the Rising Dawn and Chantilly Lace and

Emeralds members taking pictures with their Instamatic cameras and throwing the used flashcubes behind the hibiscus hedge. While dorks like Jerry stand around waiting to be asked to be in a picture or two with the great and popular ones.

The cafeteria doors close like institution doors. Clink shut.

Jerry dances the first dance with me like he said he would and all the time looking around the dance floor for who he can dance with next and who's dancing with who.

I go back and sit with Nancy Miyamoto holding hands with Craig Kunishige on the folded cafeteria tables. And whenever they go up for a dance, Nancy says, "Watch my bag, eh." All night long, "Watch my bag, eh, Lovey. Hea, watch this for me." Shove the shiny sequins black clutch bag across the linoleum tabletop. Like what she got in there? Only her damn lip gloss and a brush. Big deal.

Every dance I go to makes me think of every other dance I've been to—sitting there on the side, watching all the boys, and waiting as every crowd of boys comes over to the girls' side of the caf, waiting for someone's eyes to meet mine, waiting for the head jerk to the dance floor as I point to my chest: Who me?

Anybody.

And as the crowd leaves for the dance floor and the leftovers sit on the cafeteria chairs, Jerry's in the back of the crowd waiting to see if I need someone to dance with and it's him and me. Jerry and me.

But tonight, he wants to dance with Lori Shigemura. He makes like I'm jealous and maybe I am jealous but maybe it's because I'm always left sitting on the side with Ruby Hagimura, who weighs two hundred pounds, chews her bubble gum like it's always in the juicy stage, has pimples on pimples and gums swelling over her silver braces. Maybe I'm jealous because he acts like I should be jealous, so I pretend to be. Jerry dances lots of dances with Lori Shigemura. Black chiffon gibbon chocho lips monkey.

I dance once with Dennis Kawano. Short. Japanee. Side comb. Oily, slicked-back hair. Dances like an elf. I watch everything that Jenks does with side eye and he sees me, looks at me for a long time like he's about ready to come over, but always turns away. When my mother and Jerry's mother ask if Jenks danced with me, what will I say? No, but he looked long and hard at me. It's so humiliating. Looks, turns away, and talks to Thomas Lorenzo and Baron Ahuna, who has his hands on Ginger Geiger's ass. All night so far.

Jenks dances every dance with a popular cosmopolitan girl. Tonight, he didn't even say hi to me and he was here early because Lori put him on the Decorations Committee though he didn't do nothing but put up the letters 'cause he's tall. Not one hi. Not outside. Not in the cookie-and-punch break. Not on the cafeteria dance floor. Not once.

So far, Jenks danced with Wilma Kahale, Pop Warner cheerleader for the Homestead Chargers with thick thighs and one line of hair for eyebrows.

Kawehi Wells. Rich with haole father, who sends her to tennis lessons at the hotel with a real pro and never the Parks and Recreation League with the rest of us.

Natalie Leialoha. May Day Queen, Valentine's Court attendant, small waist and big ass but who can tell in a gown, right?

Marlene Spencer. Younger sister of the co-captain of the Hilo

High School Viking boys varsity volleyball team and cousin of Kenneth and Melvin Spencer.

Patty Paet. Sworn Jap hater, spent the whole year smoking cigarettes and swearing in the B-building girls' bathroom with fresh purple hickeys all over her neck every day.

Slow-dance twice with Jamielyn Trevino surfer style with his face in her hair, hold her hand onto the floor, then off the floor. Jenks's ex, Jamielyn.

"Lovey, dance with me this slow one, please."

"Feeling sorry for me, Jerry? Fuck off."

"Fuck you too then. C'mon, Lori." And all the Rays laugh. Then they all get the let's-dance head jerk one by one and I watch all the bags again. Tell you the truth, if Dennis Kawano asked, I would dance with him. I mean even if I would be dancing with an elf, better than sitting here behind the huge pile of bags and lace shawls.

Shame, I tell you, sitting here by myself with only Ruby Hagimura and Melody Maldonado on the other end of the cafeteria table and they so shame, they don't even talk to each other and they're friends.

"I go ask Jenks for dance with you already, Lovey. At least one time, that fucka."

"Aw fuck him too. Why, Jerry? What I did wrong?"

"Maybe that *was his dope* we stole long time ago to buy all that Barbie stuff but he holding out the truth."

"I doubt it."

"Maybe," Jerry says and pulls me to the dance floor.

"Frankenstein." "Pick Up the Pieces." "Chinagrove."

But the last dance is always a slow dance.

Jerry walks me off the floor. We're dripping.

"Nightbird" by Kalapana.

"Oh God." The whole class sighs at once.

"I going dance with Lori," Jerry tells me as he runs to get her. Trying to make sure he's for real popular next year.

I sly-eye try to look for Jenks. Like I care already. I hate him too, the coward. Cannot even make like he knows us Japs. Well, I don't know him too. Not even one fast dance. My nostrils start flaring. So I don't even know who taps me on the shoulder.

Him. It's really him. It sounds made up but it's for real. Feet don't feel the ground. Put my arms around his neck. He's so tall. And handsome.

"Soar onto the night wind. Take a star to her for me."

See Lori and Jerry and wave like I was meant to be there. Lori staring. Dot the *i* with hearts Traci and Jodie too—a popular Hawaiian and a Jap.

Jenks pulling me close. He smells like everyone else's perfume and sweat. Breathing heavy. My face on his chest, his mouth by my ear. My hands in his hair. *Oh God.*

Flute solo at the end of the song.

I want the song to go on and on, of course. It doesn't. When the dance ends and the lights immediately go on, Jerry and me sit together on the cafeteria chairs. Jenks goes back to Thomas, Baron, and Levi, who hoot and tease him about dancing all out on the last dance with a dork.

The teachers yak at the door, the disco ball comes down, and Jerry and me and a few other dorks start sweeping. The Cleanup Committee of five.

"Lovey, your Yvonne Elliman lip mole. Stay gone. And one eyebrow too. Musta smeared off."

"You mean I danced the last dance with Jenks with one eyebrow and no lip mole?"

"He waiting outside for us 'cause his mother and father playing poker at your house tonight. Tonight poker night, remember? He told me he catching ride home with us."

"Oh shit."

Jerry leans on his broom and peeks out of the dusty cafeteria window. "Omigod, Lovey. Jenks get your eyebrow mark on his cheek, look. The lip mole too, on his neck, oh no."

"Omigod, Jerry, my Press-on Scotch tape fingernail gone too."

"Holy shit, Lovey, where you was touching. I seen you touching all over the place. Ho, when we get close, I go look fo' um. Maybe stay on his ass. Nah."

I grab a broom and start to sweep. Jerry and me laugh and laugh until my false eyelashes peel off. Jerry peels them off and sticks them to his balls, says, "Fuzz." Then sticks them to his knuckles, says, "Uncle Ed. Hairy knuckles."

He holds the dustpan for me and by the time the five of us on the Cleanup Committee finish, even the yellow bug lights outside the cafeteria go off.

In the dark, Jenks, Jerry, and me wait for our ride home and nobody says very much. So that when my mother pulls up in front of us in the Land Rover missing one headlight, it's kind of a relief.

Then I see Jenks up close with the eyebrow on his cheek and lip mole on his neck. Jerry's scanning Jenks's ass for the fingernail. And Jenks, he looks so serious like he just made the greatest sacrifice of his life, the hero of the story, the happy ending, so that when we get home and Aunty Shige asks in front of all the adults, "So, Jenks, did you dance with Lovey?" he can say, "Yes, Mommy."

Jenks opens the backseat door of the Land Rover for me, and then the *after-you* gesture for me to get in the car before him so we can sit close together in the back.

But when Jerry climbs in the backseat after me, instead of Jenks, puts his arm around my neck, and kisses me, the two of us punching each other's arms and singing "Nightbird" in harmony, we look long into each other's eyes, Jerry and me. I rest my head on his shoulders and laugh on our way home.

PIN THE FAN ON
THE HAND

I want a Shiseido Makeup Party for my birthday this May 27. I'd even take a Pola makeup girl so long as she comes to my house in a white doctor's lab coat with her white pancake face all sugary soft and smooth, her capped teeth white and straight, and red lips, with a see-through cosmetic bag full of cotton balls and silver shiny mirrors too. So long as she makes the sound of a lady looking for a certain cosmetic in a small bag, the sound of plastic hitting plastic and silver objects clinking in there.

After our birthday makeup job with peacock-blue eye shadow and heavy eye liner, she would tease our hair up into the highest beehive and put tiaras in the middle of the hive, then take pictures of us with champagne glasses in our hands.

"Who would you invite?" Calhoon asks.

And that is the problem. I have one friend who is a girl. Nancy Miyamoto. And half the time, I hate her guts, unless Jerry's hanging around the YMCA with Lori Shigemura, who still hates me, in which case I'm forced to hang around with Nancy.

Most of the time, Nancy has a boyfriend, so I become the

most convenient choching for her so her father, Banjo, doesn't ask ten million questions before Nancy leaves the house and Nancy doesn't mind being my friend again.

"I could invite Nancy."

"Big deal. One friend. Wow. No Shiseido or Pola girl in her right mind would come for two girls."

"And you."

"Oh wow. Three girls. Whoopee. Some party."

"Jerome."

"Wow, a boy. And what he going do? Play with the mascara? Suck thumb? Big thrills."

⟨

I want a Shiseido or Pola girl in a white doctor's lab coat. A cake from Robert's Bakery. The glass punch bowl with balls of orange sherbet bobbing in foamy bubbles on top of the punch, sliced orange swirls, ginger ale, and mint leaves. The real punch glasses.

I get zip.

Mother says I'm ridiculous. We'll have a homemade Betty Crocker Butter Recipe cake with whipped cream and sliced can peach frosting. She'll serve it on Friday's poker night. Uncle Ed, Aunt Helen, Aunty Shige, Uncle Melvin, and Jerry's mother and father will sing "Happy Birthday" to me.

"You not getting little bit old for this birthday jazz? And c'mon now, Lovey, you not little bit young for one Shiseido party? Who the heck in this town had one Shiseido party? Crystal Kawasaki? Well, that figures. The Kawasakis probably tipped the

Shiseido girl fifty bucks and then took all Crystal's girlfriends to the Kiawe Photo Studio for pictures."

How did my mother know? Only Calhoon and me saw the pictures on the Kawasakis' piano. Crystal and all her friends, Pamela Sumida, Claire Hamasaki, Donna Hamane, all five of the high school JV cheerleaders, and all of the members of White Lace and Candlelight Y Club with Shiseido faces and long white prom gloves and quiana gowns.

Mother says for my birthday we'll make a camp-out in the backyard. "Take out the army tent, make a real campfire, eat campfire cook food, tell ghost stories—go 'head. Invite two friends."

"Two friends?"

"The tent holds four. You and Cal make two."

"Cal?"

"Yes. She your only sista and blood run thicker than water."

I don't press it before I get the blood-runs-thicker-than-water lecture, which begins with "You know, Lovey," and ends in "So my sister Yumiko and me sold tofu and konyakku in Camp Fourteen, then split the profits and then I used to French-braid her hair for free and charge all the other girls in our camp 'cause *blood run thicker than water.*"

"Two friends. Jerry, of course. So that means you can invite one other person."

Oh wow. One more person to sleep in a tent that smells like ten years of mildew on a rag, mosquito-punk smoke in the tent all night, a staticky transistor radio on an AM radio station with old-fut music, so cold, old army sleeping bags and dew all over your face in the morning and lucky if the roosters don't start crowing at 3 a.m. when Father turns on the bathroom light.

I call Jerry and he invites Jenks.

Some Shiseido party.

Jerry says, "Don't worry. I make this the best party you ever had."

"Oh *really*?" I tell him.

"You watch," he says. "And I going plan all the games too."

Calhoon pitches the army tent way in the back of the lot near the stone wall so she can steal a few rocks to surround the camp-fire. She pounds the broom handles with nails on both ends into the soft ground. The yellow paint comes off on her sweaty hands.

We hoist the heavy army canvas tent, pull the sides tight, and pound the wooden pegs into the ground. "All set," she says, and then she makes a small fire for practice.

Cal shaves down some guava sticks for the cook-out, gets a bag of marshmallows and Redondos hot dogs, and puts kerosene in the Coleman lantern. She puts goza on the ground and lays all the army sleeping bags down. Cal even brings the camping pillows to air them out and fresh pillowcases too.

"So you and Jenks can pretend be Samantha and Darrin," she says, though I never told her about that daydream of mine. How I used to think Samantha felt so safe having someone next to her every night, Samantha, Darrin's wife, with her face on his chest after the show turned color and they traded in their twin beds like Lucy and Ricky and bought a queen. How safe she must've felt even if she's a witch with way more power than him.

It's Friday night. Poker night. My birthday night. Jerry made the cake. He even turns the cake over on a cookie sheet covered with tinfoil so it looks more like a Robert's Bakery cake. It's chocolate and covered with can frosting and party sprinkles. Jerry squeezed store-bought cake decorations in squiggly words that say "Happy B-day, Lovey!" Looks like flowers on the bottom surrounded with silver pebbles cake decorations.

Jerry's mother sticks toothpicks in the cake and covers it with Saran Wrap and Jerry's father punches my arm for happy birthday when he comes in the house. Uncle Ed, Aunt Helen, and Ernest give me a *Hawaii the Aloha State* history book, Aunty Shige and Uncle Melvin give me OP shorts from Fashion House, and my father takes out lots of smoke meat for pupus. Jenks hugs my face and pretends to be my boyfriend for a little while, for my birthday present, I guess.

Jerry starts his games.

Calhoon wins a calendar from Larry's Chevron for her drawing of the Eiffel Tower on the Etch-a-Sketch, which beat out my father's Peacock in Heat in the final round.

I win two Big Hunks for the steadiest hand in Operation, saving the wishbone for last.

Mother wins a pen from Island Insurance for doing a Hubert-Before-and-After on the Powder Pete—The Man of Many Faces magnet and lead shavings game. Hubert with hair. Hubert all bolohead like now. Everybody laughs except Daddy.

Then Jerry says, "So that the night not one total washout for

Lovey, we get this Shiseido calendar for our final prize for a game of Pin the Fan on the Hand."

Jerry tapes a picture of a Shiseido girl to the far wall. She's in a kimono and her dark, black hair is pulled back into a bun, her face perfect. The Shiseido girl tilts her hand as if holding an invisible plate in the air.

Jerry takes out an envelope full of handmade origami fans and puts tape in the back of each. "Like Pin the Tail on the Donkey," he says, "but the one whose fan comes closest to the hand wins. Get it? Pin the Fan on the Hand?"

Jenks wins and gives the calendar to me. "All prizes compliments of the following merchants," Jerry begins.

"Larry's Chevron. (Thank you, Jenks, for asking Larry yesterday.)

"Island Insurance. (Thank you, Dad, for the pens.)

"Hatsuko's Barbershop. (Thank you, Uncle Hubert, for asking the barbershop lady for a few black combs.)

"And thank you, Hilo Drugs, for the Shiseido calendar."

Jerry lights the candles on the cake, and before I blow them out, I look at the Shiseido girl on the wall with all the colorful origami fans covering her face, arm, and hand.

My father will take a Polaroid of me next to the Pin the Fan on the Hand game while I hold my Shiseido calendar. He will take a Polaroid of me blowing out my candles in the dark dining room. These two pictures he will put on our TV to slowly develop after the lights go on.

WRONG WORDS

I like the smell of gas stations and airplane exhaust. The wavy heat that rises, the smell right up your head, sore and sweet.

The gas station sign said STOP YOUR MOTOR. NO SMOKING. I thought it said STOP YOUR MOTHER. NO SMOKING. At the Chevron by Uncle Ed's house, someone erased the s from SMOKING and it read NO MOKING like no mokes could moke around the station.

I wondered how I was supposed to stop my mother from smoking being that she smoked from one butt end to the next and no one, not even Grandma, could stop her.

Mother was like that. If she wanted to eat chili, we ate chili for a month, every night, with kidney beans, then with garbanzo beans, fresh chili peppers, no chili peppers, dried tomatoes, Lawry's, Schilling's, A-1 Sauce, mild Portuguese sausage diced, chorizos, and grated carrots. She cooked all versions over the course of a month. And we ate chili every night.

Then it was corn chowder and hunting for old bottles. My mother was like that. If she was going to hit you, she hit you good, long, and in every way she could imagine. That was her way. But back to STOP YOUR MOTOR. I read the words STOP YOUR MOTHER and really, I didn't know how.

(

Somebody told this joke to me.

What's P-I? *Pee.*

What's P-E? *Pay.*

What's L-I? *Lee.*

What's N-E? *Nay.*

What's it spell? Pee-pay-lee-nay. No. Pipeline, stupid.

Same as what's M-A-C? *Mack.* H-I-N-E? *Hine.* What's it spell? Mack-hine. No, stupid. Machine.

(

Everybody in Hilo thought the name of the store on my street was Poi Kakugawa Store. Everybody called the old man, "Eh, Poi. Eh, Poi, where the Milk Nickels?" or "Eh, Poi, the Naalehu Dairy milk delivery came yet, or what?"

And Mrs. Kakugawa, she was always bossing her son Harold around and we all called him Poi Jr. Harold was nice enough for a guy who made a big deal every time you asked him for a small brown package for your candies. Like it really hurt him to give it up.

I think the reason everybody thought the store was called Poi Kakugawa Store even if the owners were Japanee was because there used to be two signs. One sign said FRESH POI and the other, KAKUGAWA STORE until the FRESH on the first sign got broken off.

I saw a picture of my mother and Aunt Helen from their small-kid days, ponytails and puka teeth, eating shave ice in front of the store. This was, of course, a long time ago and there in back of Ma and Aunt Helen are the two signs. Soon after this, the sign broke and the old man got to be Poi.

Same like MOMI'S KITCHEN, the Chinese place, downtown Hilo side. At night, the K in KITCHEN fizzles off and on, so the sign says MOMI'S ITCHEN and the joke in town, especially downtown side, is, yep, she itchin' all right.

Crystal used to walk with Calhoon, Jerry, and me to Poi Kakugawa Store and treat us to slush and Chee-tos after my mother paid her for tutoring us after school. Larry and Crystal holding each other and Jerry, Cal, and me walking ten paces behind them as Larry said all good chochings do.

Crystal, who'd turn around and say, "Anybody thirsty? C'- mon, slowpokes, hurry up." Then Larry, who'd say nothing anymore about ten paces but give us the bird and a hard backhand to the forehead if we got too close.

This was all before Crystal's trip to Japan. She didn't tutor us after school after that and I really didn't see her again except maybe once in a while in church. The evening service only.

My mother said that Aunt Helen said that Mrs. Kawasaki picked Crystal up every day from school but that Larry was always with her hiding behind the building so that Mrs. Kawasaki couldn't see.

Aunt Helen's the health nurse at the school. She tells my mother, "Ho, Verva, you should see those two kids. Like they in heat, I tell you. Like nothing happen. Business as usual. Like her madda and fadda neva spend thousands, I tell you thousands, Verva, for that girl's you-know-what. I hate to say this, but I seen this with my own two eyes, and your own eyes no can lie, right, Verva, those two damn kids rubbing each other and kissing like there's no tomorrow. I hate to say it but that girl's one ho-a, Verva. Rich, neva mind. Even the rich get their ho-as."

And Mother hisses at me, "Outta here, big ears. You repeat one word of this and you dead, kid. You hear me, Lovey? Big mouth and big ears, I tell you. Try wait, Helen. I no trust this kid. Sometimes I hear my very words coming outta her mouth but all wrong so my own madda get mad at me from what this kid tell her. Out, Lovey. Now."

I miss Crystal.

C

In the first grade, my teacher, Mrs. Bell, made up a way for us slow readers to read better. Fast Boat. Slow Boat. Two rows of chairs back to back and one chair facing out toward the door for the captain, who was the reader.

But there were so many of us first-graders that Mrs. Bell had to make three boats. She got the smart fifth-grade girls to help teach us stupider first-graders how to read.

That was when I first fell in love with Crystal.

The rules were simple: Read from the Red Primer. *Run, Jane, run. Run, Dick, run. Run, Spot, run. See Jane run. See Dick run. See Spot run.* And so on. If you read perfectly without one error, you got to go on the Fast Boat, where everybody was happy and smiling, and if you sat next to another girl, even if you normally hated her, you held hands.

If you made one little mistake, you were doomed to ride the Slow Boat full of all the stupid dummies. Mrs. Bell said, "Don't smile. Don't talk. Don't do anything but practice your reading on the Slow Boat because you MAY, if time permits, have another chance to read this period and maybe ride on the Fast Boat."

And if we talked at all: "All right, everyone on the SLOW BOAT, all three ships, open your mouths wide like hippopotami and catch flies." The whole class would be quiet. "See?" said Mrs. Bell. "Always the Slow Boat making all the noise. Same people all the time on the SLOW BOAT. Delveen Simeona, Thomas Lorenzo, Wilma Kahale, and you, Lovey Nari-yoshi. Thank you so much, FAST BOAT passengers, for always being so cooperative and making our reading cruise such a pleasant experience."

Mrs. Bell always says my Japanee name like it's not supposed to be there with the other names on the Slow Boat. Passenger on the Slow Boat, Lovey Nariyoshi.

But there would be Crystal holding the Red Primer in her long fingers. Crystal wearing the silly sailor's hat that Mrs. Bell made all the fifth-grade helpers wear. She would smile at me as if to say, "Don't give up. Holding your mouth open wide for so long hurts, but you'll be okay." All of this in Crystal's smile. I'd try to smile back.

"Lo-vey Nari-yoshi, you do not deserve to look upon our fifth-grade helpers. Close your eyes and leave your mouth open." And when Mrs. Bell said we could close our mouths, all dry and the jaw sore, I would want so bad to get off the Slow Boat full of

Delveens and Lorenzos and Wilmas. Be on the Fast Boat for once with all the Loris, Tracis, Lauras, Troys, and Jodies.

In the first grade, Crystal read me *A Pair of Red Clogs* and *Ping* stories every day after school. She made me read some parts like I really could read smooth sailing like the Fast Boat first-graders. I loved her. Did I tell you?

C

I didn't know I was singing wrong words, Calhoon and me, singing with the Wild Billy B. AM Saturday Night Radio Show. Me and Cal in our dark room with her new clock radio listening to all the dedications and trying to figure out who was dedicating to who and singing, of course, if we knew the song.

"Can I dedicate a song, 'I Honestly Love You,' to J.M. with all my heart?"

"You sure can, sweetheart. Wow, heavy song. Heavy, ba-by. Too heavy for even me, Wild Billy B. How long have you and J.M. been together? C'mon. C'mon. Now let's be honest. I honestly love you, right?"

"Oh, okay, we not really together. Nah, kinda two months. Oh and can I dedicate this song to Sandi and Mikol, Nancy and Wimpy, Janis and Allen, and all the A-building bathroom girls?"

"Okay, for all you honest-type girls and guys, and the honest types only, here's Olivia Newton-John with 'I Honestly Love You' on your radio station with me, Wild Billy B., on Hilo's 83 AM on the Dial."

"J.M., thass Jason Mercado and he going with Beverly Ballesteros," I tell Calhoon. "Beverly, the one with the lip mole like

Yvonne Elliman. Thass a real lip mole, you know, 'cause I saw um up close from side view. Get one lump, not flat like she made um with eyebrow pencil."

Cal's trying to call the station to dedicate a Paul McCartney song to ourselves and pretend it's from someone else.

"Yeah, hi. I like dedicate 'The Bitch Is Back' to Pum-kin, who just change schools back to ours one."

"*Q-kay. 'The Bitch Is Back.' Elton John, no? Hmmmm. 'The Bitch Is Back.' Song title, Hilo, song title. Well, you sound kinda mad at Pumpkin, sweetheart. What's going on that you can tell all of Hilo about? C'mon. Tell it. You know you want to tell it. Okay then, tell it to me, just me, ba-by, Wild Billy B. Who loves you, ba-by? C'mon. I got the record right here if you tell it like it really is right now.*"

"Nah, I no like tell um on the air. We on the air, eh?"

"*Well, can you tell us a little bit about it? A teensy-weensy little bit just so all of Hilo can know about this bitch, oops, song title, folks, song title, this bitch who is back named Pumpkin?*"

"Nah, we stay on the air."

"Bitch, bitch, bitch is back . . ."

"*Hi, 83 AM on the Dial. What can I do for you tonight?*"

"Oh, can I play a Paul McCartney song, I mean can you please play a Paul McCartney song for L.C.?"

"*For Elsie? Any song in particular, sweetheart?*"

"No, L.C."

"*That's what I said, honey, Elsie. How's about this one . . . ?*"

And Cal and me singing "Man on the Run, Man on the Run. And the jailer man and sailor Sam were searching everyone. For the Man on the Run. Man on the Run."

"That was 'Band on the Run' for Elsie."

"Band? I thought was Man?" And Cal and me laughing and falling off the bed.

"Well here's a coupla messages. Chaddy's burgas is the bes', Chaddy's burgas beat the res'. Cafe 100. Home of the first loco moco. AnToinette's Beauty Shoppe for the latest in hair. Hilo Music at the Hilo Shopping Center."

"Hey, Wild Billy? Can you play 'I Feel the Earth Move Under My Feet' for Maile Pacheco, 'cause, brah, when she walk, I feel the earth move."

"Hi, 83 AM on the Dial."

"Yeah, can you play 'Stone in Love with You' by the Stylistics for Crystal 'cause I stay stone and I in love with her."

"So, the song has great meaning to you then?"

"Yeah, Wild Billy, yeah."

"And what's your name so I can tell Crystal who this special dedication comes from wherever she is tonight."

"Nah, she know. I can say something to her? Crystal, I love you, babe, and even though we apart right now and things looking bad, we going be together forever, you wait, 'cause I stone in love with you."

"Wow, Hilo. You heard it right here on the Wild Billy B. Show. So romantic, no? What you all think? Oh wow. 'I'm Stone in Love with You,' Crystal, from you know who."

I always sing this song wrong. I sing the part that goes, "If I could, I'd like to be the first house on the moon. Filipino neighbors and no population boom." That never made sense to me about having Filipino neighbors and no population boom. But I didn't sing tonight.

"That was Larry," I tell Calhoon.

"I know, I know. Call Jerome, quick."

"Hilo's 83 AM on the Dial. What can I do for you tonight?"

"Yeah, can you play 'Mista Big Stuff Who Do You Think You Are?' for Murz."

"Sure can, sweetheart. How come? Murz think he's big stuff, huh? Japanese with middle comb and mustache? Drives a rust-colored Celica with rims and cassette deck? And flicking cigarettes at Isles like he's Charles Bronson?"

"Yeah, Billy. How you know? Ai . . . you know this guy?"

"Wild Billy was taking a wild guess 'cause Hilo, you know Murz, we all know Murz. The Japanese boy, five foot three with Tojo complex. Tora, tora, tora, right?"

"Nah, okay then, Wild Billy, play 'Mista Big Stuff' for all the boys 'cause you like know what? Who do they think they are?"

"Profound thought. Yes, Hilo. Who do you think you are? Me, Wild Billy B., I'm a lover, not a fighter, but for all you boys out there hanging out by the Dairy Queen parking lot, 'Mister Big Stuff' . . ."

"See, Cal, that was Larry. Jerry said so. And they dunno where he is but Jerry said he might be someplace with Dwayne and his father went to get Uncle Ed for help him find Larry."

"Not. For real?"

"Hi. 83 AM on the Dial."

We do this every Saturday night, Cal and me.

"83 AM on the Dial."

"Can you play 'Seasons in the Sun' for Crystal?"

"Gee, popular girl, this Crystal."

"Nah, she nice, thass why."

"And who does this dedication come from?"

"From L. C."

"For you, Crystal. From Elsie."

C

Mother drives us to church every Sunday, but only to Poi Kaku-gawa Store because when she used to drop us off in the church parking lot, Reverend Smith would say hi and ask her when's she coming back to church. Mother hates that, so we get dropped off at the store. We used to ride our bikes to church until Mrs. Nishibayashi, this fat, old church lady, made a big issue about how unholy it was for us to ride our bikes with our Bibles under our armpits.

When Mother drops us off at the store, I notice a nice orange Pinto like the one Sabrina Duncan drives on *Charlie's Angels* in the parking lot. It has a license plate that says OTOOLE and I start sounding it out. O-to-lay. O-to-lay. I thought only our family called okole o-to-lay. Like I'd say that Maile Pacheco had a big, fat o-to-lay, to hide what I really meant, which was that Maile had a fat ass. Like our own secret family code. And here it was on this orange Pinto.

"Look, O-to-lay, Cal." And Cal looks once, twice.

"Stupid, Lovey," she says. "Now I know you really dumber than me, huh, Lovey? Says O'Toole. Like Peter O'Toole, the man from La-muncha," and I really feel dumb all the way to church.

C

It's Spring Revival for the next two weeks, which is a big deal in our church. Someone in our stupid Sunday School class nominated me to represent the Youth Class in the choral reading for the evening service on the last Sunday of the revival.

I already did more than my Christian share for this year's revival—I volunteered for the Saturday preschool cleanup. Me and Cal went door to door for loose change to fill four of the plastic bread loaves to feed the hungry someplace. I washed communion glasses, wiped pews with Pledge, and volunteered to bring palm leaves for Palm Sunday.

And now this. This stupid choral reading. Someone reads for the Adult Sunday School Class—probably Mr. Suehiro, the offering collector; the Young Adult Class—probably Adele Ige home from college since early May; the High School Class—probably Pearly Smith, the Reverend's daughter; and this year, for the Youth Class, me.

It's very unfair. Just because my sister puts her feet on the Bible as a footrest and says "I pass" when it's her turn to pray for the pastor's mother-in-law, who is on our prayer list this week, the Kimura twins are introverts, and Bradley Kinoshita, Jerry, Jenks, and Ginger Geiger don't come to evening service does not mean that I automatically have to represent the Youth Class.

I just can't do it. "Yes, you can," says Mrs. Ikeda, intermediate school typing teacher turned Sunday School teacher. "Let us all bow our heads and ask God to give Lovey the strength and courage to represent our Youth Class. Calhoon, let's begin with you. Ask the Holy Spirit to fill your sister Lovey with the needed strength. . . ."

"I pass."

I knew she'd do that. Shit.

The prayer should be more like "Let's bow our heads and pray for Lovey to drastically increase her reading ability and find the extra cash for a crash Evelyn Wood Speed Reading class before she humiliates herself in front of a *churchful* of critical *people*."

Worse yet, it's a candlelight ceremony. It's all dark in the church, solemn and still, all deep thinking and everybody dead serious 'cause they're so full of the Holy Spirit from two weeks of revival. Last year, some ladies started crying as soon as the first candle was lit, then one from another and more sobbing as the Scriptures were read by all the Sunday School representatives.

My mother says it's an honor to be chosen and that she and my father will probably come to the evening service that night. And she even calls Grandma, who's proud of me, I don't know why, when I got this by default.

C

The song leader with the harelip wrote the script and we get it for the first time that night. "I hope you don't need too much of a we-hearsal," he says. "Don't wor-wee. Twust the Lowrd. Gosh, you look so nervous, Lovey. Evewybody weady? We're on," he says and hands everyone a long white altar candle. We don't even have the time to practice a little bit.

And I'm so nervous and it's dark and my mother, father, and sister walk in and they smile at me like I'm important. I feel ill.

I see Crystal walk in from the corner of my eye and she sits right behind me with her mother and father on both sides of her. She keeps her head down even when I try to meet her eyes.

The song leader with the harelip lights Pearly Smith's long white candle in its silver holder and white ribbons flowing. And she's acting all pure and full of the Holy Spirit, all emotional and good actress. I quickly scan for all the parts marked Youth and count just three parts. Not too long. Then the lights dim even darker until only the pulpit's dull shine glows in the dark church.

The night is muggy and the voices when they sing sound muffled by the thick air, pretty but ghostly. And Reverend Smith prays a real heart-wrencher, this being the last night of the Spring Revival. I already hear ladies sniffling.

Then Pearly Smith lights Mr. Suehiro's candle. I realize then that it's so dark, I can barely see where Mr. Suehiro is and his words get muffled in my panic. *Jesus, Lord and King* . . .

I see a little more now as my eyes adjust, but still want to read past his part to get to mine. In the panic and rush of words and feelings and crying of ladies in the dark pews behind me, Adele Ige's candle gets lit and Lord, I know I'm next, and I see the words that I have to say for the first time now, but before I even finish the second line, Adele's leaning her candle toward mine and the church is so quiet, I hear the wick light. Then, my voice.

"And our Lord Jesus," I can barely see the words with the candle flickering, "He raised His hand and made the crowd still. For in that crowd was a woman misjudged by all, but a righteous woman in God's eyes. A woman that hemet . . ." (hemet?).

Try that again, I think to myself. "For in that crowd was a woman misjudged by all, but a righteous woman in God's eyes. A woman that hemet in the road to . . . hemet?" People start to laugh. Reverend Smith lowers his great hands into the pockets of his robe. "Hemet? A woman that hemet. Helmet?" and I stop.

The dark, still and heavy, so quiet that I hear laughing, and I can't read good, I knew it before they forced me to do this, this choral reading. And I knew that I broke the moment of ladies crying and lines of people walking down the aisle during the benediction to rededicate their lives to Christ, blew it. "Hemet a woman," I try again. Not fair, not fair. Head down and Adele pokes my arm hard. "Oh Goddammit," she whispers, "c'mon and finish. Hurry up."

I turn and see my father shaking his head and my mother rolling her eyes. My sister laughing so hard and so silently that the tears practically fly out of her eyes.

Someone's hands take the candle from mine and the script that the harelipped song leader mistyped and she reads, "For in that crowd was a woman that *he met* on the road to town, a woman who was scorned by man but whose heart loved the Lord Jesus, a woman whose faith in Him was unshakable and true."

I don't even lift my head.

Crystal read the rest of the script that night and when the lights go on, people are still laughing. Reverend Smith ruffles my hair even if only two people walked down the aisle on the last night of the Spring Revival. He grunts something in his slow Southern drawl.

My father *tsk-tsks* and shakes his head while walking out of the church without even waiting for me.

And Crystal leaves before I can say anything to her. She leaves the candle on the pew next to the script.

I never got to say a word to her.

☾

I like the smell of baby powder, old corduroy pillow shams, newborn-puppy mouth, fresh-struck match, and ripped lemon-tree leaf. I like the sound of water falling. I would like it at night, right outside my bedroom window.

Crystal hung herself from the pneumatic arm of her back door. Naked and dripping with water, long wet hair. The last thing she saw was probably Mauna Kea or maybe the sky. The door was open and the view spectacular.

C

Ernest told Uncle Ed and Aunt Helen. Aunt Helen told Aunty Shige. Dwayne already told Jenks. Jenks told Jerry and Jerry told me:

"Was at Pamela Sumida's party. You know their YMCA social club always having pool party at Pamela's house and gotta be their YM social club invite your YM social club and only the pop-ala guys can go, right?

"Jenks wen' tell me that Larry and Dwayne was there with their social club, the Dukes of Hazzard, and Pamela wen' make um so that the guys who *going* could use the downstairs bedrooms, get two down there, for whatevas they like. So Larry and Crystal was in one room.

"I guess was in there that Crystal wen' tell Larry that she skip her rags two months already and that she probly two months pregnant. So first Larry wen' make like 'Oh shet, no can be, 'cause you just went Japan for abortion the odda baby and we in fuckin' deep shet now,' but eh, he wen' look

Crystal's face and he thought maybe he betta back her up.

"So Larry, he start for say that good she pregnant 'cause by the time May Day next year, she can bring the baby to school like all the Portagee girls do for all the friends carry um around.

"But I guess Crystal neva like, so this the part Dwayne actually seen. Crystal come out the bedroom all crying and every time somebody try touch her, she yank away from them, you know what I mean, eh? And Larry too, he go by the boys and guzzle the Buds and take couple hits off the crutch that Dwayne had.

"Then Crystal, and this the part I no get, she walk to the pool and all the girls follow her telling her what the fuck she doing. She walking in the water, slow kine, up to her knees, her waist, her neck, she keep walking till her hair floating all around her and she sink to the bottom. Pamela had to dive in and pull Crystal up.

"Meantime, Larry stay in the house, he see all this from the big window all stone and drunk and the mento ass he wen' stick his fingas in the fan on table and the blood wen' fly all over the room and his fingas was hanging by the meat before the towels came out. All blood on the walls and Crystal coughing and gagging by the side of the pool."

ℭ

Through the stained-glass windows of our church, you see the sun. The slow turning of the ceiling fans.

The Kawasakis hold the wake at our church for Crystal. The

coffin covered with strands of maile, pikake, baby's breath, and pink roses. Pictures of Crystal's YMCA club, White Lace and Candlelight, at Kiawe Photo Studio, sunglasses and Coppertone Dark Tanning Oil, car keys, a gold chain with lots of charms on a charm holder, a rabbit-fur bag, and Cecelio and Kapono 8-track tapes. Candles and champagne glasses with ribbons from last year's Winter Ball when Crystal was Junior Class Attendant.

But when I look into the coffin to see Crystal, the rope burns, purple and raised, red like a huge welt—I can't swallow. Why didn't the mortician cover it up better? Why didn't Mrs. Kawasaki buy Crystal a special holoku like the May Day princesses with high-laced necks?

I hold my breath. Pull eyes away from the scar across her neck. Look at all the gifts on the coffin. I have nothing for Crystal—not a gift like her YMCA friends Pamela, Donna, and Claire. Not the courage to lift the veil of her coffin to kiss her cold face goodbye, not a thank-you or see-you-in-heaven like Mrs. Ikeda explained to our Youth Class after Crystal hung herself.

The Kimura twins crying, Jerry with his face in his hands. Calhoon's lips quivering. And me. Mrs. Ikeda said, "Let's all pull ourselves together for the Kawasakis, because you know, children, we'll all see Crystal again. Don't worry. She's with Jesus and we'll all meet in heaven one day."

I stare at the rope burns, the sad closed eyes. Ma nudges me from behind. Last look at Crystal's face without a goodbye.

Crystal. The sound of water falling. White Lace and Candlelight. A huge purple-and-green snake she gave me from the County Fair. *Ping* stories. Ho-a. Guava jelly on crackers and Malolo strawberry juice. Crystal in the sailor hat. Crystal.

And down the pew of family: A big brother, Elden. Older sister, Clarice. Grandma and Grandpa Kawasaki and Grandma Oshita. Mr. and Mrs. Kawasaki. I have no words. I have nothing to say.

The lady in front of me is really good. "So sorry, nei." Next person: "So young, nei." Then: "Take care, nei. So sorry, so sorry, so sorry, nei."

No words to explain anything, the line moving forward and my mother gently nudging from behind. Elden. Clarice. Grandma and Grandpa Kawasaki. Grandma Oshita. Mr. Kawasaki, he says to me come by and feed the koi. Mrs. Kawasaki. I've never seen eyes like hers, pulls me to her and I say in her ear, "She's home with Jesus." Holding on to me so tight and rocking—Mr. Kawasaki and my mother have to pry me out of her arms.

The sun through the stained-glass window. Pearly Smith on the piano with "Just As I Am." Mother with her head bowed pulls me close.

So when it happens, it's as if I've known the Holy Spirit forever. It happens at the moment the congregation sings, "O lamb of God, I come."

See golden arms reaching through the stained-glass window, lead me down the long aisle, lift the veil, and see the face of an angel. "I'll see you again." The words warm and kiss Crystal goodbye.

THE BURNING

In the night, the smell comes through the window when the curtains breathe in and out, suck to the screen, and let go. On the first night without a moon, Katy prepares the incinerator for burning.

Burn the black rubber tubing off of the scrap electrical wire that Jeffrey brings home in the Big Island Electrical van. The copper wire hidden inside coils of electrical wire in the back of their lot, the rubber burns off, leaving mounds of copper-gold. For four more nights, the burning, crackling sound.

I lift my face to the window, Katy's black shape against the thick black of the smoke, the smell of rubber burning. Rubber and plastic, a sweet smell that makes my head feel light and I sleep like I'm floating.

Katy lets me help her get the copper wire on the sixth day. She tells me that Jeffrey said she could burn the scrap electrical wire to make money for Charlie Bubbles's first-birthday luau.

"Going cost so much," Katy says. "I had for go to all of Jeffrey's job sites, even other electrical companies, and ask if I can have the scraps. Sheez, so shame."

Katy and me poking around the incinerator with bamboo fishing poles for all of the scraps that cooled off overnight.

"The luau, I like um at Seven Seas Luau House, I like Hilo Gomay cater the food, and I like hire one kachi-kachi band, the one Richie Toledo and his fadda Freddie Sr. wen' put together, Sweet Inspirations, so all the old folks can dance too, and of course, I like get Gerald the Portagee Clown come make balloon animals for the kids."

"How much all that going cost you, Katy?" I ask her.

"I figga I get about two hundred fifty guests, all the relatives and friends—a thousand dollars, but right here, after we sift through all this ashes, eh, Lovey, we get about four hundred dollars. And you help me today, I pay you five bucks and I invite your whole family, of course."

"Four hundred dollars?! Right here in all this ashes?"

Katy and me scooping the trash and poking around for the copper wire, Charlie Bubbles all covered with soot, on his hands that make handprints on the side of the warm incinerator. I ask Katy, "How come you burn nighttime?"

" 'Cause the cops catch you burning big time like this, and you cabbage. You can see me hauled down to the Hilo police station and Jeffrey gotta come bail me out? Lovey, I be the next night's kalua pig and cabbage. I do um little by little so the smoke go away mo' fast, but still so thick, I gotta wave my hands in the air while the bugga burning."

There's so much heavy copper wire, pretty soon, the sun climbing high over the African tulip trees in the back of their lot, I climb into the incinerator for any we missed.

Katy brings the wheelbarrow with Charlie in it and together

we heave-ho to push all that heavy wire across the muddy back-yard, hose it all down, and lift it into Katy's VW hatchback.

Katy, Charlie, and me chugging down to Lorenzo's Hilo Junkyard. And when Mr. Lorenzo pays Katy $432.25, mostly in twenties, Katy pays me my five and lets me hold the wad. In my whole life, I never held so much money in my hands. My face, my shirt, my hands, and my feet covered with gray ash.

And Katy feels so rich, she takes me and Charlie to Itsu's Fishing Supply and orders us deluxe strawberry ice shave with azuki beans and vanilla ice cream, which we eat on the wooden bench outside the store. State workers in their official cars eating hot dogs nearby. Watch the fishermen driving home from Hilo Bay. The county road team pouring hot tar in the potholes. 83 AM on the Dial from somebody's transistor playing Charlie Rich songs. Katy, Charlie Bubbles, and me.

C

Lori Shigemura brings this cassette tape to school. All the top hits to play in the Homeroom Dance that the smart math class planned for the last day of school. They invited our dumb math class 'cause only got dorks in their class and all the mokes in our class. The mokes in our class like to slow-dance and boogie-oogie-oogie till they just can't boogie no more.

And Lori brags, "My brother Kendrick taped all of his forty-fives for me on his reel-to-reel Sony, then transferred onto the Kenwood cassette deck player." All of us are impressed already. "Thass why the sound so clear. One side is all fast and one side is all slow. You lucky in our homeroom meeting Jerry *moved* and I *seconded* that we should invite you guys' stupid, I mean you guys' math class to our Homeroom Dance," Lori says all parliamentary procedural-ish.

Lori lets Jerry hold the tape. Figure he'll probably start the dancing with her and ask her song after song—that way, all the boys think she's popular from seeing her on the dance floor so much and she gets asked by everyone else. She thinks I'm dumb, but I get it. That's what happened at the Valentine's Dance and the Grad Dance.

We take the tape to the typing teacher's class during lunch recess, and boy, what a tape. "I Shot the Sheriff," "Everybody Was Kung Fu Fighting," "Cut the Cake," "Tell Me Something Good," and "That's the Way (uh-huh, uh-huh) I Like It." Hit after hit after hit. Anyone sitting down will really feel jealous.

And the slow side, "Let the Side Show Begin," "Wishing You Were Here," "Betcha by Golly, Wow," and all the best Kalapana songs, "You Make It Hard" and "Nightbird" and the last dance, Cecelio and Kapono's "About You."

Jerry says, "You think you and me can make a tape like this or what? Ho, Lovey, we can make all the songs we like play at our funeral on one side and the other side all the songs that make us cry, like 'Haven't Got Time for the Pain' and 'Precious and Few,' what you think?"

"But I no mo' one tape recorder," I tell him. "And no even think about using Larry's. He kinda been nice to us now that he got Donna Hamane and all those hickeys on his neck, but I promise, Jerry, no even touch um."

The bell rings and the typing teacher, Mr. Allen Otake, starts class. He's nice enough to Jerry and me, letting us hang out every day this year in his class during lunch recess, use his tape recorder or phonograph, and write on the chalkboard so long as we erase all our nonsense, as he says, before class starts.

Today, he says while pulling on his goatee, "Eh, Nariyoshi, let me use that tape you and your boyfriend Jerome were playing." Everybody laughs. "Nah, just kidding. Ho, no need get mad, Lovey. Let me borrow."

I wonder what he plans to do with the tape. He pops it into his cassette player and the whole second-semester typing class tak-taks the keys in time to "Everybody Was Kung Fu Fighting," Mr. Otake acting out all the kung fu moves, yelling, "F . . . F . . . F . . . F . . . the . . . the . . . the . . . the . . . Q . . . Q . . . Q . . . Q," and laughing the whole time.

Jerry and me want to steal Lori's tape so bad, my fingers curl on the keys, type "take . . . it . . . home . . ."

C

The Family Money Pot never got filled enough to buy that Magnavox console stereo TV we wanted. Daddy went to Kino's Second Hand Furniture Store and bought us a kind of new thirteen-inch mustard-color TV. He put tinfoil on the antennas and all four of us sitting close to the TV 'cause you can't see it from far.

My father built a homemade stereo before Cal and me were born. It only plays on 33⅓ and Daddy plays his Harry Belafonte and Atta Issacs albums on it. Trouble is that it takes so long to warm up.

It needs to wind up first. Take "Let the Side Show Begin" by the Stylistics. It starts with that carnival music, "Hurry, hurry, step right on in." On my father's stereo, it sounds like the merry-go-round is winding down, like somebody better crank up the horses.

So that when I ask him to buy a Kenwood cassette deck to connect to his homemade system, I figure he might agree. I also figure that I'd let the stereo warm up for forty-five minutes, then I could make tapes off of albums I borrow.

My father says, "Who you think me? Henry Kaiser? Rockefella? I no can afford one cassette deck. You think I wouldn't have buy one already with the Family Money Pot? Us needed one new color TV. And I dunno what you putting in your two cents for, Lovey—you was the one *lying down* picking macadamia nuts like was the hardest thing you eva did in your whole life."

I knew somebody was waiting to shove that in my face.

"What you like with one tape recorder anyway?"

I tell him as nice as I can, "Daddy, I like make my own tapes like Lori Shigemura so we can play the tapes at recess time."

"There you go again," he says. "Lori Shigemura, that's Henry's daughta? Sheez, Henry the Yick Lung preserved-seeds distributor for this *whole island,* you neva know? From his pa-ke mother's side. He no even need be part-time janitor at Uncle Ed's school no more. And I dunno why you need tapes for recess when the school year almost pau anyway."

No wonder Lori had all those cracked seed and li hing mui that she was tempting Jerry with at lunch recess.

My father's such a cheapo. Mother says when he's being a tightwad, "Even the birds are saying it." I want a tape recorder real bad.

Calhoon and me decide to sell YMCA butter toffee peanuts for our own fund-raiser. Box after box, can after can to Reverend Smith, Aunt Helen, Aunty Shige, Mrs. Ikeda—Sunday School teacher—Mrs. Geiger—Youth Choir director, Jerry's mother and father, and Mr. Otake, who takes five cans and says, "When you done making those tapes, let me use um in typing and I take three more cans."

"*Eight cans.* That would finish off this whole box."

Jerry says, "See, Lovey, I told you Mr. Otake was our best teacher."

"Yeah, right," Mr. Otake says, "no act, just make the tapes good so everybody type good, okay?"

That night, after pork hash and steamed nigagori, the bitter-melon taste still in my mouth, I tell my father, "I got fifteen bucks here, Daddy. Cal and me want two allowances in advance, and if you give it to us, we clean the chicken coops for the next month for you and mulch with the rabbit shit if you like too."

He can't refuse this. Cal and me *never* volunteer to clean the chicken and rabbit cages. "Okay. You sure you want this, Calhoon?"

She nods, "Yup, Daddy. Lovey and me."

"Give me the money," he says. "I going buy this cassette deck 'cause I the stereo expert. I made that stereo myself, you know, before you guys was born."

And we listen to the whole story, like the blood-runs-thicker-than-water story that our mother tells, the way he put all the scrap items together, who gave what, what wire went where, how many hours of blood and sweat he spent, and *voilà*, a stereo was born from his own two hands.

Daddy went to Maurice's Pawnshop for the tape recorder. A little rectangular Sanyo with the silver peeling off of the amplifier part and the plastic over the cassette tape broken off. "I got one good discount on this one. Here, I even get change for you. Thass what you get when you the world's best bargain hunter."

Five dollars and thirty-seven cents left. Cal, Jerry, and me catch the sampan bus from Poi Kakugawa Store and go to Hilo Music, and it's real close to closing, so we decide that we better get 45s so that the money stretches far.

"Seasons in the Sun" in memory of Crystal, "Band on the Run" for Calhoon, "Precious and Few" for Jerry, and two K.C. and the Sunshine Band records for me. We buy a Maxell blank tape too.

By the time we get home, it's dinner, and Jerry stays to have chicken long rice with us. Besides the records we already bought, Jerry brought over his whole album collection, mostly of his favorite self-picked funeral songs and the Doobie Brothers, the Edgar Winter Band, War, the Jackson 5, and plenty other albums and 45s that he "borrowed" from his neighbor and his cousin Ingrid.

It's so late already after we clear the table, wash the dishes, warm up the stereo so it plays on the right speed, set up the phonograph for the 45s since Daddy's stereo only plays on 33⅓, then get the extension cord to put our little Sanyo way in the middle of the floor between the two huge homemade speakers.

Fast side first, it's getting late, Jerry has to sleep over. "On a Sunday night? You two get school tomorrow," says his mother over the phone. I can hear her clearly. "Let me talk to Verva."

"Why you gotta do this tonight?" asks my mother.

" 'Cause we promised Mr. Otake that we would make the tape this weekend and let him use um in typing class tomorrow," I say. "Plus he bought eight cans of butter toffee peanuts from us so that we could have the money."

"Eight cans? Verva, he nuts or what?" says Jerry's mother over the phone. "I tell you, I see one mo' can butter toffee and I going huli over."

"And he said if me and Lovey do this, we get big points, and for the end-of-the-year grade, he going give us A," Jerry lies.

"Let the two knuckleheads go. I take Jerome school tomorrow," my mother says. "But bring him one new bee-ba-dees and school clothes before you go work tomorrow," my mother tells Jerry's mother. "I make him bathe after they pau and turn his bee-ba-dees inside out for go sleep tonight."

As soon as they hang up, we continue. Fast side going halfway. My father burps, then farts loud, on purpose. He laughs and turns on all the lights outside to fan out his pants away from us.

"Ho, Lovey, why your father gotta do that? Now we gotta rewind and find the exact place. I getting tired. What time? Ho, ten o'clock already."

"We still neva do the slow side. Okay, Cal, you ready? Put on one album next, 'Dancin' Machine,' Jackson 5 . . . okay, ready, put the needle down . . . nobody talk . . . okay, go . . . shhh."

And by the time we finish, with all the stops and goes, Father yelling, "Go sleep, goddammit," rewind, do over that song. "Make um soft, sheez, you damn kids," fart, burp, laugh. Rewind, do over that song. It's 1 a.m.

C

In the morning, Jerry runs the tape over to Mr. Otake and asks about the extra credit he lied about. Mr. Otake says, "Sure, anything for you and your girlfriend, Nariyoshi. Thanks, eh. I'll play it during your typing class."

"For nobody but us, okay, Mr. Otake?" Jerry tells him. "Don't play it for the seventh-graders or even for Period Four, okay? Promise?"

"Ho, tight, eh you, Jerome? Okay, okay, since you guys so *special*. Better be good."

The day passes so slowly.

"You think the tape came out good or what, Lovey?" Jerry asks. "I mean, we worked on um all night, but we neva preview um."

"Of course we made um good. We worked hard on um all night, right?"

When the Period Five tardy bell rings, I poise my fingers on the keys. Jerry's trying to look humble as Mr. Otake says, "Class, my *best* class this year, a-hem, last week, we had a real nice treat when Jerome and Lovey brought in that good tape for us to type in time to . . . and today, they made another tape of all you guys' favorite songs for us to enjoy again."

The whole class claps and cheers for Jerry and me.

We're not used to them all liking us so much.

Gina Oshiro, Jodie Louie, Kawehi Wells, and even Jenks for once act like they like us. Smile. Pat Jerome on his back. Jenks even moves his chair and sits at the typewriter next to me.

"Okay, everybody ready, let's start with THE . . . THE . . .

THE . . ." The tape clicks on. There's a long scratchy sound and soft shhhh. Probably me. But the guitar part of "Frankenstein" starts and everybody gets into typing and Mr. Otake's acting like a Frankenstein with stiff legs and ugly face, yelling in his Monster Mash voice, "With . . . with . . . with . . . J . . . J . . . J . . . J . . ."

Near the middle of the fast side in "Dancin' Machine," Mr. Otake doing the robot like Michael—a chicken crows over the song. The whole class stutter-stops and Gina says, "Eh, get one chicken in their album."

And dogs start barking in the background, chickens crowing, a door slamming. Jerry looks at me. "Your father, after he made fut and turn on all the outside lights. Thass why the chickens crowing and thass Katy them's dogs 'cause he went outside. Shit. So shame."

Jenks moves away from me.

The whole class laughs. And I feel so small. And shame. Gina yells, "Fuckin' dogs too!"

"Lovey, you loser, so *good* your tapes."

"You guys go work for Motown already."

"C'mon, Otake, do the funky chicken for match their tape."

Mr. Otake breaks in. "Enough. Class dismissed." Even if the bell didn't ring. "Out, get out, you guys."

After the whole class leaves, Mr. Otake puts the tape in my hand and says, "That's why you go college. So you can buy a Technics stereo system like me." He writes passes for us to stay with him for the last period. We don't have to go out of the door where Gina and Kawehi and Jodie wait. By the time the tardy bell rings, Lori Shigemura stands out there with the rest of them laughing loud on purpose.

Jerry and me correct papers for Mr. Otake until three o'clock. We walk home after the last school bus leaves and the campus clears.

(

In the night, the burning feels warm.

Calhoon saying, "Why, Lovey? Don't do it. Daddy going see this and kill you, Lovey. No, thass half my money too, you know. I sold some butter toffee peanuts too. Why you doing this, Lovey?"

First, the tape, burn, sizzle, the smell of plastic. "I hate anything homemade. Shut up, Calhoon. You just like Daddy—even the birds saying shit about you."

Then the Sanyo tape recorder from Maurice's Pawnshop. "I hate secondhand shit. Like this fuckin' cheap tape recorder. Like Daddy's stupid stereo. And our ripped-up La-Z-Boy and tinfoil TV."

"Stop it, Lovey, stop it. Shut up. Daddy going hear you saying all this about him."

"You shut up. Next Daddy going tell us eat dirt for dinner 'cause good for our body and you going believe him. He take us to the dump and tell us thass treasures and you believe. Not me. I ain't being dumb no mo'." I watch until the sides melt, feel the flames on my face till it stings. "And I ain't one fag or pussy either." Inhale the plastic fumes till it burns deep inside.

Cal looking over the incinerator, bends low, says, "Whoa, I no can see nothing but smoke. Where the tape recorder? Where stay melting? Yeah, right, Lovey. I no see nothing melting."

And from deep in the incinerator, a blue flame. Bluer than the gas oven bursting on, I turn to see my sister's hair on fire. And she doesn't know it at first until she hears the crackling like noodles frying right by her ears and the smell of burnt hair.

"Your hair, your hair!" I remember the fine crackling sound and watching, unable to move. My sister's head on fire and Daddy comes running from nowhere, throws her to the ground, slaps her hair, and rolls her around. Dirt and stones get stuck on the oily red part of her forehead that burned. She has no bangs anymore. Burnt eyebrows and half eyelashes.

And Daddy says to me, "You fuckin' rotten kid. You rotten to the core. You see what you done, hah? Look what you done."

My father never hit me, not once in my life. He never swore at me but this one time.

"You look, Daddy. You the one. Thass your fault. Even the birds saying it about you. That cheapo tape recorder. I no can even go to school. I hate you, Daddy. You—"

"Fuck you, Lovey. Good-for-nothin' nobody. You always make like we something we not, I tell you. When you going open your eyes and learn, hah? You ain't rich, you ain't haole, and you ain't strong inside. You just one little girl.

"Take a good, long look at your stupid self, kid. You cannot take it, you cannot take nothing. Thass why I wanted boys. Look what I get. You weak inside like every other goddamn wahine I ever met. You ain't shit to me." He picks up a handful of dirt and stones and throws it at my face.

"You see what you did to your sister?" My father grabs Calhoon by the neck and puts her red-oily face in mine. "Your own goddamn sister, hah, Lovey? Shape up before I kick your ass to

kingdom come." He shoves me to the ground. "C'mon, you."
Calhoon gets dragged into the house.

I sit on the cement steps to the incinerator. Close my eyes
tight. Replay my father's words again and again in my head.
Push my back into the warm bricks. It feels like somebody hug-
ging me. There are crickets somewhere. The smell of smoke, I
taste it in my mouth. Dogs howling.

I go to sleep in the backseat of the Land Rover that night. But
in the morning, I find: my body covered with the old goat blanket.

C

Daddy stayed out late drinking beer every night that week.

Then planned a three-day hunting trip with Gabriel Moniz
for the Kamehameha Day long weekend.

He never looked at me or said my name.

But I saw my daddy by my bedroom door every night. Looking in, a shadow, then gone.

That weekend, Daddy got his eyes blown out hunting for
goats down at the Kalapana side of the Chain of Craters Road.
Two bandages over his bruised eyes, swollen. Greasy film like
Vaseline all over his face. It was the day after Katy's big baby
luau for Charlie Bubbles at the Seven Seas Luau House.

This is the story he tells my mother, Cal, and me from his
hospital bed:

"Was the biggest eruption of Mauna Ulu I ever seen and the
flow was coming over Holei Pali. Gabriel and me heard that the
place the goats stay was getting all wipe out, so the goats was
running all in one place 'cause they had nowhere else for go.

"There we was, Gabriel and me, all hung over from too much Crown Royal at the baby luau, but what the hell, had to refill the freeza with smoke goat meat 'cause I gave um all to Katy for the pupus.

"Ho, when Gabriel and me came to the lava flow, the steam from the hot lava was unreal. I seen one herd of goats trying for escape from the heat of the lava. So we wen' space ourself out by about hundred yards and tried for get close to the goats.

"Then I wen' fall down on the side of the lava flow, I was kinda hang over and was dark still yet. Lucky thing I neva fall inside the flow. Thass how I got all these cuts on my hands from the fine kine lava threads all over the ground. The barrel of my .243 wen' hit in the loose cinders. But eh, I get up and dust myself off. So long as Gabriel neva see.

"Neva have no cover, so the goats seen us, but they was trap between us and the hot lava flow. I signal Gabriel 'cause we get one easy catch, eh?

"Then, the leader of the goats, he wen' snort goat style and got his herd ready for make one dash. Me and Gabriel was ready too 'cause we know they going funnel pass us. But when the leader of the goats wen' snort again, and they wen' run, and Gabriel was firing already, the goats, those stupid goats was running over the hot lava.

"The flow was so wide, was at least one mile, they got hundred yards, I swear I neva seen anything like this and I neva going, I swear to God, they all got stuck in the lava, billies and nannies and kids, all of um.

"I took one dime out of my pocket to mark the spot, but the dime wen' turn to dark metal. Then I put my hunting boot on the lava and smelled the burning rubber. My whole rubber sole wen' melt off.

"Then I thought about you, Lovey, and how you wouldn't like see one kid or one nanny die this way, all that goat hair burning and the smell, but what I neva going forget is how they was crying.

"Was so loud and pitiful, the way they all was crying till their last breath and their face sink in the lava and they still bleating, I tell you. So I took my gun, aimed um, and shot at the kid close by me. I was going shoot um all to put um out of their misery.

"I heard Gabriel yelling at me, I know that much, something about 'What the hell you doing, Hubert?' and then, I dunno how come I wen' see nothing next. Gabriel was still yelling and dragging me from the lava, was coming close. I figga was when I wen' fall down, the barrel came jam so the bullet wen' backfire, but the whole gun wen' recoil and felt like my whole face wen' broke.

"I sorry, Verva," my father says all of a sudden. Like he could still see. See her face all broken too.

My mother and sister crying softly now.

My daddy said my name. I feel numb.

"You know what I mean, how they cry like that, eh, Lovey? Me, I cannot stand when they suffering like that. Like your Nanny. Their faces burning like that, the tongue all hanging out. All the babies burning and melting away."

❨

That is when my father's eyes got blown out and he burned his face and cut up his hands. The first few nights when we visited

Father, all of his friends would drop by to talk story and cheer him up.

Uncle Ed: "You know, Hubert, I eva told you about my nephew, Neal? Stupid bugga, my sista Hazel's son from Pearl City. Real townie, eh them. I take him and Ernest bird hunting couple seasons ago, and my stupid nephew, he load the wrong bullets, gotta be real dumb for do this. I dunno, was freaky, man, the way that gun wen' backfire, but the kid was like you, no can see. Eh, but today, he okay, just kinda floating eye on one side."

Gabriel Moniz and his wife, Lurline: "Brah, you rememba the time I told you I like try out my grandfather's old gun, eh? The time me and Eugene went up the cane fields pass Wood Valley? Eh, that bugga wen' misfire with one funny kine sound, man. I swear, wen' kick back so hard, I thought my shoulda was knock out of place and I had to force Eugene drive me down the valley, and what, Lurline, he was only eleven that time, no? All the way down Wood Valley I made that kid drive in first gear. Me, I neva play with old guns no mo'. No worry, Hubert, freaky things happen every day."

Jeffrey, Katy, and Charlie Bubbles: "One time when I was small, my brother Kyle and me was playing at my uncle's anthurium farm up Kaumana. We was firing Nelson Caraeg's twenty gauge getting ready for bird season—we was all out for chucka for couple three years, me and my brother them. So anyway, Glenn Campos's cousin Snake-Eye, the one from Wainaku, was his turn, but the bullet was one dud, you heard of this, eh, Mr. Nariyoshi? That bugga wen' jam the gun and the way Snake-Eye was rolling on the ground and holding his face was just like you, Mr. Nariyoshi. The bugga had bandage all over this face, but was pau in few weeks. Snake, he reg-la guy today except for his kinda rotten eye—we no tease his eye now, us call him Snake now. No worry, Mr. Nariyoshi, yours going be pau too pretty soon, you watch."

c

One week later, Uncle Tora comes from Guam to help my daddy. Uncle Tora's my favorite uncle. He tells me, "Don't need to go to school today. Let's you and me go stay with your dad all day at the hospital. You be my navigator as I drive to the hospital, okay?" Uncle got a real nice haole accent.

"I'll treat you to some lunch in the hospital cafeteria." I don't respond right away because today is the last day of school and I actually want to be there for the Homeroom Dance that Jerry's math class planned.

"Okay," Uncle Tora says, "and you got five bucks coming your way too. And look what I got for your daddy. It's an eye patch made of real leather from the Philippines. I figured while he recovers he might look real swollen for a while, so why not look rough and tough with a high-quality eye patch when he goes downtown, huh, Lovey?"

Uncle pulls it out of a brown paper package. "Wow, Uncle, just like the one that Yagyuu Juubei wears on *The Yagyuu Conspiracy*. And Miyamoto Musashi. Daddy going like this." Uncle Tora doesn't know about the Japanese shows that we watch on TV.

Daddy reads one subtitle and I read the next. Daddy reads his real good like a real samurai, just like Sonny Chiba: "We must go to Edo and intercept the magistrate. Let us go now before the daimyo arrive at the castle."

It makes me sad for a moment, Daddy not able to read those subtitles like he does, till Uncle says, "Five bucks, lunch in the cafeteria, and I'll let you wear the eye patch all the way to the hospital."

I figured I'd be sitting on the side of the fake dance floor in Jerry's math class anyway. Somebody would probably wise off and crow like a chicken and howl like a dog when "Dancin' Machine" came on. "Okay, Uncle, let's go."

All the way there, Uncle talks. "Never you mind if you're limited because you're a girl—reach for the stars, the future is yours." He talks about Aunty Erma, his wife, and his small-kid days in Kipu, Kaua'i.

When we get to the hospital and see my father, his eyes look greasy and purple. The bandages soaked with yellow pus and some blood. He doesn't smile even when he hears Uncle's voice. So Uncle tells him, "Hubert, look who's here with me." Daddy gets mad. He thinks it's a sick joke, "Look who's here."

"I ain't got eyes. Who stay with you, Tora?"

"Lovey came with me today."

"Eh, kid, you get school, eh? What the heck you doing here?"

"Today the last day, Daddy, and only half day."

"You lucky your uncle stay, or else I send you packing. You heard what this kid did, Tora?"

"Well, Verva kind of filled me in, but let's talk about that later, huh? How you doing, Hubert?"

"What you tink, brah?"

"What does your doctor say about your eyesight, Hubert?"

"Damn haole ain't saying shit. But my hunting friends been by and from what they tell me, get plenny freak accidents like mine. Get plenny stories like mine, so I not, I not. I not real—" Uncle places his hand on the back of my father's neck and his whole body exhales.

"Hubert, I got lots of stories too and I tell you, a friend of mine back in Guam had the same thing happen to him that happened to you and he's just fine today."

Uncle Tora and Father in the hospital room that first day and every day after that—sometimes just Uncle and me, sometimes Calhoon. Mother comes every night after work, stays with Father to keep him company.

They talk about the old days at night.

"You remember that old Philco radio we had, Hubert? The one the old schoolteacher, Mr. Sheets, sold to Father when he left the plantation school? I thought that was pretty nice of him to do that at the time. I mean, he taught ten of us by the time he left Kaua'i."

Father says nothing for a while, but Uncle doesn't feel uncomfortable like sometimes you do when you talk and then the other guy doesn't talk for a long time.

Then Father says, "I rememba that old Philco. I rememba you, me, and Uri listening to the radio. I no even rememba what we was listening, maybe *The Whistler,* but had one thunderstorm that night, and you rememba, Tora, the lightning wen' hit the pole outside and had one loud crackling and sizzling, then the blue flash. And you wen' tell me, 'No sked um, Inky, thass nothing.' Then the radio wen' explode. You tell me, 'Come, Inky, come look the tubes in back the radio. All black and smoking.' And you let me stay by you that night, rememba?"

I watch them carefully. Daddy says all these things and cannot see Uncle Tora's face. Uncle Tora sometimes forces himself to look out the window when Father tells him stories and doesn't look back for a long time.

"Then you remember the huge Norfolk pine tree that got hit by lightning while we were walking to school the next day, right, Hubert? Boy, that must've been a hundred-fifty-foot tree."

"Ho, musta been something for see the lightning hit the tree but I rememba the smoke—halfway to the bottom, the tree was all right, but the top half was all black and smoky. Yeah, I rememba that, Tora."

It's late at night when we all leave. Daddy turns his face away from us. Turns off the light. Uncle Tora pats his shoulder. Takes one last look, says, "We did all right, Inky. Hardly had a cent to our name, but we did okay. G' night, Inky."

☾

Today, my father's bandages come off. Uncle Tora gives him the eye patch and Father says, "Tanks, Tora." He feels the leather, the stitching all around the eye patch, and says, "Just like Yagyuu Juubei."

The nurse carefully removes the gauze. When it comes off, my father's face is badly bruised and red with cuts like a boxer on his swollen eyelids, his eyes so bloodshot that I can't see the eyeballs, and the smell of pus and medicine from the gauze—I start to gag. My head feels light and the salty spit that comes before vomiting fills my mouth. I swallow it all down.

And Father starts to cry, says, "Tora, I can't see nothing. Tora? There the window. There the door. I can't see. Gimme one mirror, I like see my face." Father starts to get up and the nurses and Uncle Tora hold him down. "Lemme go. I gotta see my face. Tora, I no can see."

"Dr. Knight should be here any minute now, Mr. Nariyoshi. You just relax."

Daddy sitting on his bed, holding his eye patch, says to Uncle Tora, "Maybe I need two."

"You can see, Hubert. You just have to give it a try. Can you see Haupu Mountain, Hubert?"

"What you talking about, Tora, you crazy old man?"

"I said, you can see, Hubert. Lay back now and relax. The doctor will be here any minute now. The mountain, Hubert. It's there, right in front of us."

"I no can see nothing."

"C'mon, Inky, you can do it. I know you're smaller than Uri and me, and we left you behind many times before, but you can do it. Here, let me hold your hand."

Uncle takes my father's hand in his and holds it tight. "There, pick that mountain apple. No, not that one, the one right above it, the biggest, most reddest one.

"See the gingers? There, the yellow ginger. And over there, the torch red and pink. And the kahili? There's a whole field of white ginger. Can you smell it, Inky?

"Wow, there's so much mokihana here. We can make ten

strands easy. And the maile, well, Inky, the leaves are so huge in the growth right past that plum tree. I'll pull it off the stalk for you. Here, smell this."

My daddy breathes deep into Uncle's cupped hands.

"Could you smell that, Inky?"

Daddy nods yes, slowly.

"Come with me. Let's pick some lilikoi for our mother from this vine. This one's real tangy. And there, let's get the guava off of that tree so she can make us some jelly. Don't pick too many now, or we'll have a hard time getting down the mountain, you're so small.

"See our house down there? There's our mother. Wave at her. Watch the staghorn, there might be a huge hole underfoot. Look around, Inky. All around. Mark the spot, clearly, 'cause when your eyes get better, we'll go to Kipu, okay?"

Dr. Knight finally comes in and tells my father, "Mr. Nariyoshi, it may take a couple of days for your eyesight to even *begin* coming back. Please, let's not overreact." Dr. Knight's looking at Uncle and me now. "Take it easy on your eyes, don't strain them, and we'll take this one step at a time."

"Tora, I going be blind. The doctor don't wanna tell me." Daddy's crying now. Never seen him like this before, so sad and pitiful, thinking the worst. And I got my head bowed so low, deeper than I ever did even at church. *Rotten kid, rotten to the core. Good-for-nothin' nobody.*

Nothing matters. Secondhand eyes to see Haupu Mountain.

Homemade sight. He can't build it.

He wants to look deep into the valley.

Treasures he can't see.

I want to leave the room.

Watch Uncle cover my father when he turns his back to us. Lead me out the room and to the elevator. From the parking lot, see the light go out in Father's room.

Run out of the car to Katy's yard. Uncle yelling, "Lovey, Lovey!" Hide by the incinerator. Kipu. Secondhand eyes. I've never seen Haupu Mountain but in pictures. I grab a handful of dirt and stones. Watch the way the dirt bleeds lines into my sweaty palms. It's at this moment that I know what I have to do. My father told it to me, what to do, what matters between him and me.

Go by Charlie Bubbles's nursery window and call Katy. "Lovey, thass you? Shhhh, the baby going sleep. Come by the back steps."

I tell Katy everything that happened. "You mean, he might be blind, Lovey? Nah, maybe his eyes just jam up for coupla days, eh, Lovey?"

"Maybe. But I wanna burn some of the electrical wire for fifty bucks, Katy. I pay you back, I promise. I can go the YM and sell butter toffee all summer to pay you back, please, Katy. I need some money for my daddy now."

"I dunno what you going do with fifty bucks, but whatevas, Lovey. Yeah, go burn the wire. I tell Jeffrey tomorrow."

Katy's garage feels cold. I load the wheelbarrow with scrap wire. Push the heavy load to the incinerator. I need fifty dollars, one good load. Push through the thick muddy lawn, hoist the copper wire into the incinerator, run to the house for old newspaper and matches, watch the flame, hear the crackle and sizzle.

The thick black smoke, fan with my arms like Katy does until I taste the smoke in my mouth, feel it burn in my nose. My head goes light.

When I wake up in the morning, hear the roosters crow, brush the dew off my arms and face, I climb into the incinerator and lift the copper wire, gleaming like gold, into the wheelbarrow and push the whole load through the back of Katy's lot and into the way back of our own yard. Hose down the wire and wash myself with the cold, cold water.

Uncle's in the kitchen drinking coffee. He's just like my father—up at five. I walk into the house wet and cold, so he runs down the hall to get a towel. "Uncle, I went all over town with you the last two weeks," I tell him. "Now I need a ride from you."

"Where to?" he asks.

"Just down to the Hilo Junkyard. Katy, my next-door neighbor, lets me burn the scrap electrical wire for her for extra money," I lie, "and now I gotta trade it in for cash."

"Is that where you ran off to last night? Not that I'm complaining, but why can't she drive you down there if that's her money?"

"I always do it for Katy on Thursday nights and I forgot to do it since we were at the hospital," I lie some more. "And she cannot go down there because she has a little baby and her husband went to work."

"Well, let's load um up. You get changed and I'll drive you down there. Then we can go to the hospital and visit your dad. Dr. Knight's going to be there to tell us your dad's prognosis, so we'd better hurry."

Mr. Lorenzo at the Hilo Junkyard gives me a hard time. "Eh, girl. Where you wen' get this wire from? You the one came with Jeffrey's wife the odda time, eh? Where she stay? Eh talk, small girl."

"Listen here, you," my uncle says. "My niece does this as a favor to the people you're talking about, so refrain from any further accusations or I will be in touch with the Better Business Bureau."

Mr. Lorenzo looks confused. "Sheez, no need get all huffy. Who da guy, small girl—your law-ya? No get uptight coun-sa-la. Here. $52.35. And no ask fo' mo'."

I tell my Uncle Tora that I don't want to go to the hospital today. That I gotta see Jerry before he goes to his Aunty Gertrude's house for his Disneyland trip. I tell my Uncle that some of the money is for Jerry to buy me some Disneyland T-shirts.

Once I get home, I put all my father's pictures of Kipu in a backpack in a couple of Ziploc bags. I ask Katy to give me a ride to the airport and she says no first but I tell her, "Please, Katy. You dunno what I gotta do, but I have to do it. And I be back today, I promise, but no tell nobody, Katy, please."

And that's why Katy's a big sister to me always. She says, "Okay, get in the VW. But if Verva gets nuts, I ain't lying to her, you hear me, Lovey?"

The plane fare's thirty-nine dollars round trip from Hilo to Kaua'i. I'm not real good at talking even to ask for a plane ticket. I can't even order a hamburger at Cafe 100 without feeling shame of the way I sound, but I force myself.

On the plane ride over, I arrange the pictures of Kipu the way Daddy told it to me. The statue of Mr. Rice at the head of the road. The long row of pine trees on the road to Kipu. The Rice house. Old plantation homes. The stable. A rubble of rocks that was their house—see the grove of bamboo beside it as a marker. I've been there so many times in pictures, I know I can find it. There, on the hill next to the graveyard forest, is the place we'll sit and have lunch, he always tells me, there on the hill above our camp.

The plane lands smoothly.

I follow all the other passengers to the Baggage Claim area. I watch the haole tourists ask a Japanese man with a yellow shirt with the words TAXI DISPATCHER stenciled on it for a taxi and the man waves one over.

So I do the same. The driver says, "Where to?"

I tell him, "Take me to Kipu, please."

"Kipu? Whatevas, man." He drives out of the Lihue airport to the outskirts of town, turns left on the cane road to the Rice Plantation. Winds down through cane fields and pastureland. Over the bridge and down the road of pines, full of ghosts like Daddy said.

I study the pictures, and as I pass the bridge, I put that picture away. The statue, put the picture away. I hold a few more in my hands: I know I'm almost there.

A cowboy stops us along the road of pines and says, "Whass your business?"

The taxi driver points to me in the backseat.

"I . . . I . . . my father told me . . . he used to live here. His name is Hubert Nariyoshi."

"Hubert? They call him Inky?"

"That's my father."

"What you doing here all by yourself?"

"I came to finish some business for him. I want to see his

house and the hill above his house. Can I do that? My daddy told me that the foreman here is the nephew of my Aunty Agnes's husband, Elton."

"Yeah, the foreman's the guy, Reggie Pavao, but he stay Kipu Kai today. But if you like go inside, I telling you now, Mrs. Rice not letting nobody up into the old camp, so bes' you turn around, go home."

"But I came all the way from Hilo and I got to do something for my father."

"I go ask Mrs. Rice, but I no can promise nothing."

I look at the last two pictures. I see the rubble of rocks ahead, just beyond the bend in the road, the grove of bamboo behind it. I see the patch of dirt on the hill beyond the pasture. So close to heaven.

The cowboy rides back, looks into the window of the taxi, and says, "Sorry, man, but no can. Mrs. Rice said no, only immediate family members of past plantation workers, and thass that when she say no, so you best be turning around. Sorry."

Nobody keep my daddy from seeing heaven.

I get out of the opposite door of the taxi and run to the side of the road. I grab two handfuls of dirt and fill a Ziploc bag from my backpack with the dirt and stones from the side of the pine tree road to Kipu.

The cowboy's so stunned and confused that he shakes his head, pushes back his paniolo's hat, and says stern but not mean, "Mrs. Rice said get off the property."

In the distance, I see the patch of dirt beyond the water tank where my father spent his days looking down at the camp and daydreaming. Right before my eyes.

Drive back to the airport, slow and silent.

Pay the cabdriver $24.50.

Wait for the last flight home.

C

Mother, Calhoon, and Uncle Tora come to get me at the airport.

"Stupid Lovey. Ma thought you was murdered."

"Gunfunnit you, Lovey." I get slapped across the head twice. "You see what I mean, Tora? This kid get a mind of her own and sometimes she got her head so far up her ass, she do things like this—you know that we call the cops for a missing person report, Lovey? You grounded for the whole summer—no, for the whole summer and two quarters next year. And I cannot even tell you what your father thinking right now, poor thing, all by himself in that stupid hospital thinking about his stupid, lost, runaway daughta. Where you was?"

"Let's calm down, Verva. Lovey, you want to tell us where you been? Does this have something to do with that wire we sold? You know that your mother and father and me and Calhoon have been so worried and crazy over where you ran away to."

"Thass another thing. Don't you eva speak to Katy again. I so shame of you, Lovey, for asking Katy for money, like they get so much. You gonna pay her back every red cent. You see what I mean about this kid, Tora? This more worse than running in your pajamas to the launderette and the cops picking you and Jerome up. You rememba *that*, Lovey?"

"Hold on, now, Verva. We'll let Lovey explain the whole incident to her father once we get to the hospital tonight." Uncle thinks this will scare me. "Stop by the house first, Verva, I need to pick up those Violets breath mints and dental floss I promised Hubert."

Once home, I quietly walk to the anthurium patch near the incinerator and dig fast, a handful of dirt, bagasse, and stones, into the other Ziploc bag. Heaven out back, my daddy knows this, the hours we spent picking the seeds off the nose of the anthuriums for planting, self-pollinating and cross-breeding the obakes. All our rabbits and chickens out back, the ducks before, Nanny and Bully, the fish from Wailuku River in the bathtub fishpond, all out back.

"Get in the car, NOW," yells my mother, and the drive to the hospital takes twice as long in all the silence. When we get there, I look up toward my father's room. A hazy blue light comes through the window, probably from the TV.

Walk down the hallway, my mother still complaining about me. Take my sister's hand and lead her into the hospital room. Looking at her burnt bangs and half eyelashes, I feel so sorry for what I done to her. Calhoon sits on a small chair in the corner to watch the TV. I sit next to my father's bed.

"Well . . ." starts Mother.

I pull the two bags of dirt from my backpack and put the first one in my father's hands. "What's this?" he asks.

"Remember, Daddy? Like your daddy. You said you gonna see heaven on earth, remember? And be home again. You going know you home."

My father opens the bag and takes a deep breath. Puts his hands inside and runs the dirt and stones through his fingers. "Then this gotta be dirt from Kipu if I gonna be in heaven." He runs his fingers through the dirt. "Yep, this feels like Kipu," he says.

Daddy breathes in deep. "So thass where you went. You went Kaua'i. I neva woulda thought you know what for do or how for get there or what."

I'll never tell him in my whole life that I got this from the side of the road lined with pine trees and ghosts. I give him the other bag.

"This one smell like bagasse. So this one must be from our anthurium patch out back. Bagasse, I smell um a mile away. I guess this is our dirt, what you guys figga? So what you suppose to do from here, Lovey, you get um all straight so far?"

Mother and Uncle Tora sit down. Cal turns off the TV and sits with Mother. "I put the dirt in a brown paper wrapping and tie it with twine. I going mix the two bags together so you can be in two places at the same time. Then I put it under your bed and unwrap it when you die. Then, Daddy, you be home."

"And thass where it's all at, right, Lovey?"

The answer is small. I don't even have to say it.

Uncle Tora walks over to the bed. "She's already there, right, Hubert?" Daddy takes two stones, one from each bag, and places them on the nightstand next to the bed.

When we leave, I look up from the dark parking lot, see the light in my father's room, his shadow moving toward the window. See my daddy wave a small goodbye to me from the light warm all around him. He tells me across the night, "I be home."

MY DEEPEST THANKS TO THE FOLLOWING PEOPLE:

To Carla Beth, Mona Lei, and Kathy Rei for the long-distance phone calls, for the letters, and for seeing time in a room clear and remarkable.

To my grandma, Yoshiko Narikiyo, who in this life showed me God.

To Cathy Song and Juliet S. Kono; through the highs and lows of our lives, we continued to write our stories and poems.

To the Bamboo Ridge Study Group for the longest, most patient mile. To Darrell H. Y. Lum for calling these *stories* and for saving their endings time and time again. To Wing Tek Lum for answers and advice.

To Melvin E. Spencer III for spirit-filled reading, Shari Nakamura for knowing that a bath *sometimes* makes me feel better, and Nancy Hoshida for ordering music to fit the moments.

To my friends in the Central District Office, thank you for your selfless generosity. Thanks also to Charlotte Nagoshi for understanding and support.

To the National Endowment for the Arts for their generous assistance.

To Lynn Chang, Joanne Parrish, Faye Jones, Crisana Naomi Cook, Josie Woll, Dora Jean Ota, Denise Webb, Liz Watanabe, Grandma Maria, Dr. Maggie Koven, Mari Ann Arveson, Janice Simon, Pam Sakai, Kristi Lucas, Joy Sakai, and Pauline Kokubun—my son's spirit whole in your unconditional love.

To R. Zamora Linmark and Morgan Blair forever.

To Susan Bergholz for vision.

To my editor, John Glusman, for faith in my first language.

To John Maurice and JohnJohn Torao Sebastian, "I love you," the first words you say out of silence, and you say it to me and me to you, a hundred times a day.